HOLD FAST

HOLD FAST

A Novel

MARSHALL HIGHET
AND BIRD STASZ JONES

Globe
Pequot

Guilford, Connecticut

Globe Pequot

An imprint of The Rowman & Littlefield Publishing Group, Inc.
4501 Forbes Blvd., Ste. 200
Lanham, MD 20706
www.rowman.com

Distributed by NATIONAL BOOK NETWORK

British Library Cataloguing in Publication Information available

Library of Congress Cataloging-in-Publication Data available

Names: Highet, Marshall, author. | Jones, Bird Stasz, author.
Title: Hold fast : a novel / Marshall Highet and Bird Stasz Jones.
Description: Guilford, Connecticut : Globe Pequot, [2019] | Summary: In 1761 Italian cousins Joseph Carlo Mauran, thirteen, and Suchet Mauran, twelve, are impressed into the English navy on the man-o-war Deptford and face countless threats while traveling the seas.
Identifiers: LCCN 2018047851 (print) | LCCN 2018052906 (ebook) | ISBN 9781493039449 (ebook) | ISBN 9781493039432 (pbk.)
Subjects: | CYAC: Seafaring life—Fiction. | Impressment—Fiction. | Cousins—Fiction. | Great Britain. Royal Navy—Fiction. | Great Britain—History—George III, 1760–1820—Fiction.
Classification: LCC PZ7.1.H5465 (ebook) | LCC PZ7.1.H5465 Hol 2019 (print) | DDC [Fic]—dc23
LC record available at https://lccn.loc.gov/2018047851

♾️™ The paper used in this publication meets the minimum requirements of American National Standard for Information Sciences—Permanence of Paper for Printed Library Materials, ANSI/NISO Z39.48-1992

Printed in the United States of America

For Dyer, with love and thanks. —BSJ

For Kian and Brylea, my inspirations. —MMH

Chapter One

1761 Italy

WHEN THE KNOCK ON HIS DOOR CAME IN THE DARKEST HOUR OF the night, Joseph Carlo was waiting.

"*Siete pronti?*" his cousin hissed through the thick wood. "Are you ready?"

Joseph Carlo swung open the door to let Suchet slide in, a lit shuttered lantern in one hand, held well away from his thigh. A book with a crumbly spine was clutched so tightly in the boy's other hand that it looked as if it might disintegrate from the pressure.

Suchet tiptoed over to Joseph Carlo's window, put the lantern by his feet, and pushed open the leaded panes of the window with considerable effort. The rust on the old mechanism creaked and groaned. Joseph Carlo raised his eyebrows at his cousin and pulled on another layer against the night air.

"For our return," Suchet said, picking up the lantern again. The large fig tree outside the window rustled in the breeze like a sigh. The smell of damp earth wafted through the window.

"Right, ghosts. Street of shadows. You don't really believe we're going to see ghosts, do you, *cugino*? You can't believe everything you read." Joseph Carlo knew it was futile to try and dissuade his cousin for another few hours of sleep; Suchet's heart was set on this grand adventure.

"You promised! I did your rotten chores for a week," Suchet whispered hoarsely. "Your catechism too!" The boy was well aware that waking the rest of the household would mean the certain termination of his quest. "You know how much I hate that miserable rooster!"

"All right, all right," Joseph Carlo resigned himself.

Suchet was right. To ensure his cousin's cooperation, Suchet had taken over the chicken coop chores for the week, where Stronzo (as their Uncle Tomas called him out of his sister Madalena's earshot) reigned supreme. To fetch the eggs each morning was an act of uncertain survival as the old rooster considered it a breach of his territory and attacked with a ferocity matched only by the Turks of old. The only reason Stronzo wasn't a stew was that Madalena considered him too stringy to cook. When the coop-cleaning task fell to Joseph Carlo, he would bear the rooster's abuses by imagining Stronzo's ineffective flapping as he was catapulted off the closest cliff, which in their harbor town dropped a hundred feet to rocky shores and deep waters. Their plucky *paisan* wouldn't stand a chance.

Suchet, satisfied that his older cousin was coming with him, turned towards the dark hallway. Joseph Carlo shook his head. If he knew anything about Suchet, it was that there was as much of a chance that he would give up his search for the ancient spirits of bloody, murderous Turks in the Street of Shadows as he would voluntarily spend time with Stronzo. A book and a ghost hunt would get this boy up and running day or night. Joseph Carlo's interests didn't grab him in the same fervent fashion. His gaze lingered on his bed one last time. But he'd promised and Joseph Carlo always kept his promises. He was a Mauran.

The boys wouldn't open the lantern's shutter until they were well away from the house. Besides Madalena's fitful sleeping habits, there were a dozen other household members and staff whose job, literally, was to keep their eyes on these two boys, the newest roots of family Mauran. They would be *very* interested in the duo's early morning excursion, not to mention what would happen if their uncle Honore caught wind of it. The whole thing was just daring enough to make it worth doing in Joseph Carlo's book. Just his style.

Suchet paused before stepping into the silent hallway, listening with such intensity that his lithe body trembled like a sapling in a spring squall. After a moment, he beckoned to Joseph Carlo with the hand still clutching the book and melted into the darkness. One of the charms of Casa Maurano was its intimacy. In her more claustrophobic moments, Madalena called the deceptively large house the *conigliera*: the rabbit warren. Tonight it felt like one more than ever before. In the darkness all he could do was feel his way through the well-known passage, hoping he wouldn't run into a piece of furniture. His knuckles brushed the rough wall as he trailed the shadow that he assumed was his cousin. They followed the hall as it led them around an inner courtyard, windows opened to let in the night breeze. The astringent smell of lemon blossoms floated in with the muted moonlight filtering through the tree's oily leaves and gnarled branches. The boys wound their way down the wooden stairs, almost as familiar to them as each other's faces.

The foyer of limestone tiles led to a large chestnut door, usually a burnished yellow in the sunlight but a monochromatic gray tonight. It had a coin the size of one of Joseph Carlo's eyes embedded in the center, the metal oxidized to a light filmy blue by sea air and time. Impossible to see in this light, nonetheless he knew what was etched on it and had since his earliest memories. It was the Mauran family crest: a bloody severed Moor's head. It'd been placed there so none of them would forget who they were when they left the narrow walls and low ceilings of the Casa for the outside world. Mauran: the word, the idea, the name, was as embedded in Joseph Carlo as it was in this door.

Joseph Carlo stood just behind Suchet in the night-cool foyer as the younger boy pushed the door open a crack. The hinges issued a muted shriek and they both hunched their shoulders, waiting for a sleep-bleary call from one of the rooms overhead. There was only silence.

Suchet pushed the door all the way open, allowing a cool breeze to waft through, and then they were out in the night. A feeling of jubilation swept through Joseph Carlo as the door settled back with a thunk. They stood staring at one another outside the Casa, maniacal grins unfolding on their faces. Joseph Carlo could almost believe that when they reached the Street of Shadows, they'd find the ghost of a Turk, the blood of his enemies dripping off his scimitar's curved blade. Another fragrant breeze whipped around the corner, propelling the boys away from the Casa and into the night like small sailboats before a storm.

Chapter Two

Villa Franca was nestled amid the steep peaks of the *cornici*, land chiseled out of ancient rock running to the harbor. In certain lights and in certain seasons, the harbor shone like a sapphire amongst the pinks and ochres of the buildings, pulsing like a precious jewel. Indeed, the harbor gave the town its life, as it was one of the most valuable ports on the Mediterranean. This accessibility had brought violence to the town too. A harbor such as Villa Franca's was a prize worth dying for, as many an Italian had in the face of the marauding Turks. But the Italians, Maurans included, had held the line and repulsed the Turks.

Joseph Carlo and Suchet walked through the dark streets with the assurance of natives. Candlelight peeked through shuttered second-story windows; a dog barked and was silenced by a gruff command; a baby's bawling echoed, a crooning lullaby accompanying it. The blanket of night sky with its splash of dazzling stars seemed closer than the wrought-iron balconies hanging heavy with geraniums.

Each breath of wind brought the harbor's tang, reminding him of its presence, and Joseph Carlo's blood pulsed through his veins. He glanced at his cousin trotting beside him with his precious book clutched to his heart. He felt such a fierce love for Suchet. They'd always been closer than other cousins in the kaleidoscope underfoot at the Casa. Their bond puzzled the family as they were so different, but it was undeniable. The Maurans were a family who blended the physical and the metaphysical. They were Knights of Malta: their mental acuity was balanced by the nobility of their hearts and the strength of their sword arms.

In a way the combination of these two cousins, Brainy and Brawny as they were teasingly called out of Madalena's earshot, was an apt illustration of the family ideal. Joseph Carlo's coppery skin and golden curls, unruly at best, had long ago earned him the affectionate name of *Brunito* around the Casa. In the same way, Suchet's large eyes, a dark green often mistaken for black, had Madalena calling him *Gufo* since early babyhood. The family teased Suchet that the deepness of his eyes rivaled that of the Canyon of Villa Franca, the enormous trench in their harbor that made it so desirable to the ships passing by in the Mediterranean.

Joseph Carlo had been more than just surprised when Suchet had come to him a week and a bit ago; he'd been flabbergasted. He'd been splicing a line at his uncle's bequest in the courtyard. The rope was old and tough, cracked and worn by use, and Joseph Carlo's hands ached as he untangled the stubborn strands. A shadow had fallen across him as he worked and he'd looked up to see Suchet blocking out the sun.

"I need a favor, *une favore*," the small dark boy had said.

Joseph Carlo had been so surprised at Suchet's request to help him sneak out at night that at first he'd laughed, as if it were a joke, and then, noting his cousin's stony expression, asked Suchet to repeat himself.

"I want you to come with me on an adventure," Suchet had repeated, setting them on this unlikely path.

Winding their way through the familiar streets, Joseph Carlo almost wanted to thank Suchet for being himself, so odd, so intense. They wouldn't be here without Suchet's impressively weird mind. *Dios* knew Giorgio, another cousin, would never have concocted such a madcap scheme. Ghosts? Ancient books? Turks? Not a chance. That boy's idea of a good time was collecting hermit crabs to set against one another in a crustaceous wrestling match.

Suchet moved with quick confidence down the dark maze of streets, eager to reach their destination. He stumbled over a cobblestone, Joseph Carlo reached out to steady him, and Suchet threw his cousin a look of thanks. After a few minutes they stood on the brink of the Rue Obscure, Street of Shadows. Shallow steps led down into a dark tunnel that burrowed parallel to the harbor.

In ancient times this tunnel was used as a conduit for the militaries that had fought for control of the harbor. In the relative peace of recent times it had fallen into disuse or, more correctly, disrepute. Its subterranean locale made it perfect for all manner of shady activities as well as being an enclosure for animals and storage for other goods. The tang of goat urine hung in the air.

Suchet fumbled the metal shutter of the lantern open, and a focused beam of light pierced the darkness in front of them. Somewhere ahead an animal shrieked, like a woman in pain. Joseph Carlo felt a violent shudder run through the boy next to him. As they stepped down into the Rue Obscure, orange-tinted walls wavered in the uncertain light. Joseph Carlo felt the temperature change each step he took, as if he was submerging himself into a subterranean pool inch by inch.

They reached the bottom and stopped. The beam from their lantern stretched for ten feet and then was swallowed by darkness. Vague sounds of movement reached them, some sharp and raspy, others slow and wet, like giant slugs oozing through the tunnels. Again an animal shrieked from somewhere ahead of them, too human for comfort. In this moment, all Suchet's wild talk of haunted tunnels filled with the mutilated bodies of doomed Turks didn't seem quite so unbelievable anymore.

Joseph Carlo's eyes bulged, straining to make out a flickering movement beyond the reach of the bulls-eye's beam. *What was that? A cat? Or something else?* He tried to keep panic's jaws from closing around his neck. Suchet squared his shoulders, holding the book in front of his heart like a shield, and stepped forward.

Joseph Carlo, for perhaps the first time in all of his thirteen years, falteringly followed his twelve-year-old cousin instead of the other way around.

The sharp and ammoniac smell of the tunnel enveloped them as they shuffled forward and the reassuring view of the street fell away behind a dark corner. Joseph Carlo thought he detected the metallic smell of blood lingering behind the more powerful odors of piss and vomit. The next otherworldly shriek was muffled by the thick rock of tunnel now standing between them and the outside world. All at once Joseph Carlo felt that this quest seemed like a very bad idea.

A rustling came from ahead, freezing both boys, something not very big but big enough to be threatening. Skittery noises and underlying that, a whispery sound, heavy and soft, as if something long and leathery was being dragged. The lantern's single beam served less to illuminate the darkness and more to bring the boys' attention to the complete darkness outside its small circle of light.

The boys stood frozen, clutching one another's forearms and straining with every cell in their bodies to hear as an errant breeze funneled through the tunnel, slicing the lantern's wavering beam in half. Suchet uttered a breathless shriek, twisting the lantern to get it out of the wind. After what seemed like many minutes but was only seconds, the flame recovered, the beam stretching like glowing taffy. Both boys breathed sighs of relief. But now there seemed to be many dragging leathery sounds, definitely coming from behind them. And closer. Much, much closer.

With one another's arms in death grips, the boys shuffled forward down the tunnel as a four-legged, two-headed creature. Suchet trembled, shaking the lantern so it created weird shuddering shapes on the wall in front of them.

Joseph Carlo's blood beat in his ears, making it difficult to follow the scratchy sounds. Were the sounds catching up? Getting farther away? At some point in the stinking tunnel, Joseph Carlo kicked something hard. It rolled out of the way and bumped up against the wall, just inside their aperture of light. Joseph Carlo disengaged himself from his cousin's grip and leaned down, groping along the slimy cobblestones with one hand as Suchet tugged on the other.

"What are you doing?" whined Suchet. The tremor had also invaded his voice.

"Arming us." Joseph Carlo picked up the broken pipe. It was about as long as his arm and twice as thick. But it was hollow, thus not quite as strong as, say, a club. He wrapped both hands around the haft of the damp clay pipe. Everything down here was damp, even the boys. Joseph Carlo imagined mold growing over his clothes. Every breeze carried the putrid smell of offal and rotting detritus strong enough to cause tears. His eyes bulged out of their sockets in an attempt to make out movement in the soupy darkness. The tendons of his arms were wire taut, his legs shaking with anticipation of flight, to where he had no idea. He was slightly concerned he might piss himself, but this seemed like the least of his worries.

"Great idea, *cugino*," Joseph Carlo half-snarled, half-whimpered. "Let's go look for ghosts, he said. It'll be an adventure, he said. *Che palle!*" He spat into the darkness. Regret for his gruff words washed over him the instant they left his mouth. More than anything (and he would never be able to admit this, not to Suchet, not even to himself) where he wanted to be was at home, close to Madalena, watching her take up her mending, or sitting in absolute safety on her lap, something he hadn't done in about nine years.

"You always wanted me to be more adventurous?" It sounded like a question. They stumbled forward, the unspoken agreement being that it was better to be heading *away* from the spooky dragging sounds than towards them. Also, they knew that this tunnel would eventually spit them out at the church.

If we ever get out of here that is. Being adventurous is one thing; having a death wish is entirely different, Joseph Carlo thought as he shifted his slick grip on the pipe, holding it aloft. *Just keep going forward. No sweat.*

They shuffled another couple of feet, this time Joseph Carlo in front and Suchet stuck like a limpet to his shoulder, holding out the lantern and shaking so badly it was as if he had a palsy.

This time when the scratchy, dragging sound came from behind them, it was much *much* closer. They both whirled around so quickly that the flame in the lantern guttered again, their circle of vision narrowing to only a couple of feet. Suchet's nails dug into Joseph Carlo's skin like Stronzo's beak. Whatever was making the scratchy sound did not seem to care about the agitation it caused as it closed in with its dragging gait. Joseph Carlo's brain screamed for him to run but his feet weren't listening.

Movement flickered just outside the lantern's circle of light. Whatever it was, it crept along the edges, not wanting to leave them alone, but not wanting to be fully exposed either. Squinting, Joseph Carlo could tell it was the size of a large cat. This should have been a relief but wasn't, not in the least. Nor was the realization of what the thing was. Sometimes identifying the threat did nothing to relieve one's terror, especially when that thing was a rat. And not just any rat, a Rue Obscure Rat. These rats ruled the underground tunnels with iron claws. They were large, fearless, and rarely travelled alone.

"*Ratto rabbioso,*" moaned Suchet.

The rat's matted brown fur and intelligent, malevolent eyes shone as it scrabbled along the proximity of the lit area. It stopped, testing the air, oily droplets dripping from its whiskers. In this light, those droplets looked like blood. To the boys, there was no doubt that they were. The rat froze, arrowhead-shaped head cocked in their direction, and then, with surprising speed, scurried directly at their ankles. Both boys yelped and stepped back, Joseph Carlo onto another rat. It shrieked in pain, and Joseph Carlo hollered and swung at the shadows with his pipe like a housewife swatting at a dusty rug.

The darkness was now a teeming tapestry of rats. One twisted around Joseph Carlo's ankle in an almost friendly manner. He screamed again as he felt the scabrous claws on his bare ankle and, without thinking, swung the pipe, connecting with his own shinbone. Pain exploded up his leg and he yelped, hopping on one foot. At the same moment a rat dropped directly onto Suchet's head and neck from one of the many hollows made in the Rue's ceiling by missing masonry. Suchet's shriek bounced off the rounded tunnel walls. The boy was at his limit, no adventure left in him, only terror. He broke and ran, the bobbing lantern punctuating his panicked progress.

"*Attesa!*" Joseph Carlo watched as his cousin and the only source of light disappeared into the darkness, leaving him with all the rats. *All the rats!* his brain squeaked. He careened after his cousin, booting a rat out of his way as he ran.

It felt like Joseph Carlo ran for half the night. The wet cobblestones had terrible traction and he slipped on their mossy surface. It felt like for every step he took, he slid back two. Although Suchet was never the strongest runner in their pack of cousins, tonight he would've won every race. Panic had made him as fleet of foot as Hermes. Joseph Carlo tried to keep the bobbing lantern in view but it winked out around the tunnel's long curved length, leaving him in complete darkness. He bounced off the wall and fell to his knees, ripping his pants, and scrambled to his feet.

After what seemed like hours, he rounded a corner and found Suchet, hands on his knees, lantern at his feet throwing sick shadows onto his face, puking his guts out onto the already slimy cobblestones.

"Su . . ." Joseph Carlo began.

A voice interrupted him from the darkness beyond. "That's not going to improve the smell in here at all, I'm afraid."

Chapter Three

AN APPARITION FOLLOWED THIS DECLARATION INTO THE LIGHT.
Joseph Carlo rubbed the sweat out of his eyes in case he was
imagining the man standing in front of Suchet offering a handkerchief. Suchet took it and wiped his mouth without a word.

What Joseph Carlo noticed first was the newcomer's attire.
His stunned gaze took in the polished Spanish leather of the
man's boots, and then ran over the light *calza* which were tied just
below the knee with satin ribbons. The voluminous breeches were
stained but made of fine material. The lantern light winked off a
dirk's silver sheath from the wide leather belt at his waist. Above
the waterfall of lace frothing from the stranger's neck was a face
at the same time beautiful and foreboding, the expression in the
eyes sly and curious. The straight nose lent him an air of nobility
while his crooked grin made him look like a jester waiting for
everyone else to get the punchline.

The stranger was young, as young as Madalena, with swarthy
features. Joseph Carlo could imagine Imogen, Lena's best friend
who fell in love with anyone who came within six feet of her longer than a heartbeat, fanning herself under this stranger's insistent
gaze. Joseph Carlo was unable to look away from those sky-blue
eyes, or were they sea-green? It was hard to tell in the lantern
light. Around the man's neck was a white fur stole, unbelievably
pristine and clean compared to the rest of his clothes. Although

his outfit looked as though it had cost *some*one a pretty penny and was obviously cared for, it still bore the wear and tear of a life hard-lived in the shadows. The stole, however, was spotless.

The outstretched hand was adorned with rings on every finger and a set of timpani, small cymbals threaded onto the tip of his pointer finger and the tip of his thumb. His gaze switched from one cousin to the other as he clinked the timpani, the bell-like chime hypnotizing. The stranger's ears were multiply pierced with heavy hoops, and when he cocked his head to study the boys, the hoops glinted in the flickering light.

"You better grab your night light, children, or it'll go out. Nothing worse than the Rue Obscure in the middle of the night unless it's the Rue Obscure in the middle of the night without a light," the stranger said, chiming his timpani at the end like a period at the close of a written sentence.

Suchet snapped his mouth shut and reached a hand down to right the lantern without tearing his gaze from the stranger. "Thank you," he said, straightening and holding out the handkerchief. "This is yours. Thank you for that too."

"*Prego*," The man said. He whisked it under his long coat, a dark, heavy antithesis to his other clothes. It was so dirty it looked as if it may at one point have been a different color. It was like a puddle of oil on a sunny day, the colors swirled in the weak lighting. Joseph Carlo wondered which one represented their new acquaintance more aptly: the dandy's clothes or the beggar's cape. *Perhaps both. Remember that*, he told himself.

The stole swirled around the man's neck like fog. Joseph Carlo's mouth dropped open as the stole sat up and turned towards the boys. Before his mind could grasp what he was seeing, the stole jumped down to the cobblestones and trotted towards Suchet, who shrieked, sending an eerie echo down the tunnel. Joseph Carlo brandished his pipe-weapon at what he was sure was an albino rat.

"*Pace!*" The man held his heavily ringed hand out in an admonition. "It is only Gingilla. She will not harm you, she is as curious as I am."

Joseph Carlo's nose wrinkled in disgust. *He's got a rat for a pet?* Then he saw that the Gingilla the man was referring to was a cat who now meowed beseechingly at Suchet's feet. With a tremulous grin, Suchet leaned down and scooped her up, folding her into his arms and stroking the fur along her jawline. Gingilla was almost pure white except for a reddish-brown blotch on her back that looked like a coffee stain. When she ceased bumping Suchet's chin with her forehead, she turned to look at Joseph Carlo with deep yellow eyes like sunflowers backlit by the rising sun, and winked.

This broke the enchantment. Joseph Carlo took a step towards Suchet. "*Quis iste est?*" he asked clearly in Latin, figuring the man wouldn't understand it.

The man grinned, revealing a set of straight white teeth, eyes snapping. The smile transformed his face into one of a courtier, but a scheming one since it didn't quite reach his eyes.

"*Viator et temporis et spati sum,*" the man answered Joseph Carlo in perfect Latin. Joseph Carlo looked at Suchet in astonishment and Gingilla once again dropped him a wink.

Joseph Carlo tried again, this time in French. "*Pensez-vous qu'il est dangereux?*" Translation: do you think he's dangerous? This was the real nut of the question: should they run or should they stay?

"*Seulement pour les dames.*" The man chimed his timpani and bowed with a flourish. "*Et alors seulement si j'ai de la chance.*" Despite his unease and wildly beating heart, Joseph Carlo couldn't help himself, he laughed. Suchet laughed as well, sounding as surprised at the sound as he was when the man's stole had turned into a cat.

"You . . . you speak French," Suchet paused. "*And* Latin?"

Gingilla looked up at her newfound friend and meowed in affirmation.

"Patently obvious, *caro*, but I appreciate the recognition of my gifts all the same."

The stranger's speech was oddly intonated; its cadence went up and down like a child's rhyme, as if Italian was not his first language. Distrust curdled in the pit of Joseph Carlo's stomach. He narrowed his eyes, studying the situation for a way to, one—snap Suchet out of whatever trance this man and his familiar had cast on him, and two—get out of here as quickly as they could. The man now dancing a jig on the underground cobblestones didn't *look* dangerous, but Joseph Carlo's instinct about people was rarely wrong. He'd learned early on to trust his gut; it almost never led him astray.

"Who . . . who are you?" Suchet asked, staring at the cat.

Joseph Carlo rolled his eyes; Suchet's question sounded wary, but he could hear wonder lurking just beneath caution's surface.

"Who am I? I am Gyorgy the Gorgeous, the Gumptious, the Gregarious." The man did another two-step on the wet cobblestones, his bootheels making a muffled clip-clopping sound. "I am a stroller of life, a *passeggino*, me and Gingilla both." Once again the cat meowed as if on cue. "I come from the East, from the Land of Morning Light. And you are?"

"I'm Suchet." The boy spoke with an eagerness that made all of Joseph Carlo's alarms go off. "And this is my cousin, Joseph Carlo."

"Suchet. Rhymes with *touché? Incantato.*" Each of Gyorgy's intricate dance steps brought him closer to them. Suchet didn't notice, utterly entranced as he was, but Joseph Carlo's gut did. He stepped nearer to Suchet and the cat recoiled, hissing.

"What do you want with us?" Joseph Carlo asked, the strident tone of his voice overly loud in the damp close corridor.

Gyorgy was unfazed. He chimed his timpani as if signaling the start of another dance number. "It was hard *not* to notice you two with all the clatter." His feet did the jig: a one and a two. "And I am a student of all life." Timpani chime. "You piqued Gingilla's curiosity. She wanted to meet you." A twirl and a flourish.

Joseph Carlo's nose wrinkled. Did this man think dancing would distract him from his words? Fat chance. "That cat told you to talk to us?" Joseph Carlo's arms were threaded over his chest, hiding the rabbit-crazy bumping of his heart. "*Burgiado.*"

That had an effect: the man stopped his odd dance maneuvers and turned a lighthouse-like gaze on Joseph Carlo, causing the boy's heart to stop for a few beats and then start again in triple speed. "I'm not a liar, *tasca*, Gingilla is an excellent judge of character. She's been at the helm for a long, *long* time."

"What do you want from us?" Joseph Carlo repeated. His gruff voice belied his squirming belly.

"I want to *give* you two something." The fancy footwork resumed. "Your fortunes." Another twirl, a timpani chime, a bow. "Unless you're too scared."

Joseph Carlo scoffed. If this stranger thought that the charming act was going to work on him, he had another thing coming. The dancing bit was good and the cat was an excellent touch, but Gyorgy didn't know he was dealing with *Brunito*, handsomest lad in all of Villa Franca, according to Madalena and agreed upon by Imogen. And Joseph Carlo was no Imogen; fancy boots and an impish grin wouldn't butter his *pane.*

"*Dai, cugino.* Let's get out of here." Joseph Carlo tugged on Suchet's sleeve. The cat stared at him, growling so low in her throat that it might've been a purr.

"But 'Seppe, aren't you curious? Adventure, remember?"

Usually Joseph Carlo did all the urging, like Suchet was an over-laden cart being pushed up a muddy hill. Not this time. This time Suchet had sought *him* out. He worried that if he refused Suchet his adventure, there would never be an encore. So Joseph Carlo did something that he hadn't done in recent memory: he went against his gut.

He smiled. Suchet whooped and Gingilla leapt from his arms. Gyorgy was watching this exchange as a seasoned chess player will watch not just *where* his opponent moves but *how* his opponent moves. "Okay Gufo. We'll get our fortunes read." Suchet whooped again. Joseph Carlo turned back to the gypsy. "What do you want in return?"

Gingilla now sat on her master's shoulder, licking one paw.

"Why would I want anything?" Gyorgy spread his palms out before them, rings winking in the lamplight. "Perhaps I only want to see what lies ahead for such an intrepid pair?"

"'Seppe, he isn't going to . . ."

Joseph Carlo silenced his cousin with a raised hand. He cocked an eyebrow at the stranger. They were a frozen tableau of three figures except for the cat grooming herself as she watched.

Joseph Carlo's heart slowed considerably; he was exceptionally good at negotiation. He'd laid his cards out; now it was Gyorgy's turn.

Gyorgy was frozen in his surprised stance of supplication. He looked more like a jester than ever, with the leather tip of his boot pointing out, hands spread before him, and oily cloak hanging heavily to his knees. Just when Joseph Carlo was going to grab Suchet's shoulder and propel him down the rest of the tunnel, Gyorgy broke.

"*Bene*," he said, tugging on his lacy sleeve with a sneer. It occurred to Joseph Carlo that this was as close to Gyorgy's real personality as they'd seen. "I want that." He pointed at the necklace that glinted just inside of Suchet's collar. Suchet grabbed at it, pulling the fabric closed over his collarbones.

"No," Suchet gasped, staring at Joseph Carlo in horror. "He can't . . . not for anything. 'Seppe, tell him!"

"No," Joseph Carlo stated. "You can't have that."

Pressed against Suchet's thin chest was the amulet that each Mauran boy received on his tenth birthday after he'd proven himself on the sea. Joseph Carlo could feel the small weight of his own medallion under his shirt. Honore would place the amulet around each Mauran son's neck, the pearl and gold chain giving way to a coin-sized medallion over the boy's heart. Stamped onto that coin was the Mauran family crest. To lose this would dishonor the family. Unthinkable.

"No," Joseph Carlo said again. "You cannot have that. Try again."

Gyorgy's grimace widened into a grin bereft of warmth, as if someone had fed the gypsy something terrible tasting and he was trying to convince them that it was indeed delectable. "Well then," he said, "what would you suggest for a fair trade?"

Joseph Carlo grabbed Suchet's arm, pulling the boy a few feet away and narrowly missing the puddle of vomit.

"All right, this is your game of bandy-wicket, what do you suggest? What are we going to trade him?" Joseph Carlo was half hoping that Suchet would raise the white flag so they could head home. The other half of him wanted nothing of the sort. He knew what mettle his cousin was made of, he always had. The roving packs of cousins often made fun of Suchet for his reticence. They thought Suchet was merely afraid but Joseph Carlo knew him better than that. What others mistook for fear was really caution that was almost frigid in its precision. Suchet did not jump without looking. He looked hard, and if he found the waters deep, only then did he jump. It took one look at Suchet's eyes to see that he'd indeed found the waters deep enough. He was going to jump.

"Do you have any money?" Suchet asked, although he knew the answer to that.

Joseph Carlo rolled his eyes at his cousin before shaking his head.

"So all we've got are our medallions?"

"Seems like it."

Suchet stood with one arm crossed over his stomach, his other elbow resting upon the arm while a hand plucked at his lower lip, a gesture Joseph Carlo knew well, although he doubted Suchet knew he was doing it. The bull's-eye lantern sat at his feet and threw his giant shadow up the tunnel wall and across the curved ceiling.

"The man *is* literate," he said, waggling the crumbling book still locked in his hand.

Joseph Carlo's eyebrows shot up to his hairline. "You don't think that he'd . . ."

Suchet paid him no mind. He stepped towards Gyorgy, whose face was now a calculating, non-descript mask, with a glaze of handsome. He looked ready to be lied to.

"It must get boring, waiting around for customers," Suchet began. "And with only a cat for company. Even one as charming as Gingilla, it must get dull."

Gingilla looked up with her saffron-colored eyes and meowed. "What's your game, friend?" Gyorgy cleaned his nails with a small piece of wood, his timpani tinkling musically. "If you have nothing to offer then I suggest we end our parlance now and resume our journeys."

"You're so clever, you must be starved for intellectual stimulation." Suchet's voice rang with youthful innocence and honesty as only a boy's could.

"Big words from such a small person," Gyorgy said, not looking up from his nails.

Suchet's head jerked back like he'd been clipped in the chin. He'd been expecting a refusal, but not cruelty. *Careful, cugino,* Joseph Carlo thought. *It's not just his pet who has claws.*

"We can't give you our necklaces. The only thing we have is this." He thrust the book towards Gyorgy. To Joseph Carlo it looked scrappier and more soiled than the man's coat, but one look at Gyorgy's face and it was obvious that he'd taken the bait. Whether or not the hook would set or slip remained to be seen.

"A book?" Gyorgy chortled. "Really? For shame, boys. I expected more. What's the title to the paltry offering?"

Suchet brandished the book, the golden threads woven into its cover glinting in the lamplight. Gyorgy's eyes grew wider. Even Gingilla was looking at it. "*I Racconti Fantasma del Sardinia.*"

"Ghost tales?" Not quite as dismissive this time. "I thought you boys would be too old for such nonsense."

"Well, okay, if you don't want it . . ." Suchet made as if he was going to tuck the book into his waistband.

"Wait! I didn't say no."

And the hook sets, Joseph Carlo thought.

"This book came from our uncle's library, he would not be pleased with me for trading his books to a fortune-teller." It was Suchet's turn to sound exasperated. "But I'm curious about my future. As they say: *Ho un mare di cosa da fare,* I have things to do. Either take the book or bid us goodnight. Negotiations are over." Again, Joseph Carlo marveled at the steel glinting through his cousin's soft voice. He sounded like a knight passing down a proclamation. Or a trading magnate making an excellent deal. He sounded, Joseph Carlo realized, like a Mauran.

"*Va bene,*" Gyorgy conceded.

"Trade?" Suchet extended his small brown hand.

"Trade," Gyorgy agreed, shaking it with his own, his many rings twinkling. The timpani were gone—he'd spirited them away to some pocket or another. He grabbed the book and flipped through pages as fragile as a newborn's skin before tucking it away under his cloak. It must have been hard for Suchet to see it go—it'd been his favorite book. *I hope it's worth it.*

"One book, two palms, that's my deal."

Joseph Carlo held out his right hand, but Gyorgy shook his head. "Right palm is your past, left hand's your future. I'd be happy to tell you where you've been, but I thought you were interested in where you're going."

Joseph Carlo swapped his left hand for his right. Gyorgy took it and motioned to Suchet. "Higher," he instructed. Suchet hoisted the lantern so the spill of light better illuminated Joseph Carlo's palm. Gyorgy leaned over. Gingilla also leaned over, as if she too had the gift.

Gyorgy traced the different lines sketched across Joseph Carlo's palm with a long and dirty pinky nail.

"Here you have your head line. This tells you where your mind wants you to go. This is your love line, self-explanatory. And yours! *Bravo ragazzo!* Quite a Don Juan, aren't you?"

Joseph Carlo blushed in the dim light.

"This here is your life-line, it signifies your journey through this world. And running parallel to it . . ." Gyorgy stopped short.

Suchet leaned in. "Running next to it is what?"

Gyorgy remained motionless for another beat or two and then shook his head, clearing it. "The line next to it is your travel line, it stands for any sort of travels you may have, in spirit or in body." Another long pause. "Or both, as we have in your case."

"What do you mean?" Joseph Carlo became aware of his surroundings: the drip-drip of viscous liquid, the smell of rot, the far-off sounds of claws on cobblestones.

"Nothing to get alarmed about, my young friend. You will embark on a journey, and soon."

"A journey? What kind? The kind you *actually* take or one you take, you know, in your mind. Like you said."

Gyorgy looked at Gingilla, as if consulting her. "Your palm tells me you will be going on both kinds. Your earthly journey if you will, will take you far away. Ocean travel, and you will see many new things. The other journey, the one of your spirit, will also take you far away. As far away from your true self as one can go. At the end, you will have a choice." He abruptly dropped Joseph Carlo's hand and took a step back.

"Do you remember the story of Orpheus and Eurydice?" Gyorgy's eyes were blazing blue in his lean face.

"Yes," Joseph Carlo said. "She died and went to the Underworld. He wanted her back and so charmed Hades with his lute playing. Hades said he could have whatever he wanted so . . ."

"So?"

"So Orpheus wanted Eurydice back," Suchet took up the thread. "Hades agreed under one condition: Orpheus must travel all the way out of the Underworld without turning back to check if she was behind him."

"*Di preciso*. He must not look back. And then?"

"He looked back," Joseph Carlo finished. "And she disappeared like smoke."

"He *chose* to look back," their new friend corrected. "And he lost what was most valuable to him forever. You, my young friend, will also be able to choose. Depending on your choice, you may lose what you value most."

In the pause after his words, Suchet thrust his hand out while shoving the lantern at Joseph Carlo. "My turn."

"Fair enough." Clearing his throat, Gyorgy bent over Suchet's hand, Gingilla once again peering at it from his shoulder. Suddenly, he gripped Suchet's hand harder, enough to make the boy cry out. A gust of wind barreled down the tunnel, and the flame in the lantern guttered low. Joseph Carlo twisted it this way and that, trying to get it out of the wind.

"*Dio*," Gyorgy whispered. He dropped Suchet's hand as if it'd scalded him. "Poor boy." He backed away. "You have no such choice," Gyorgy's words were clipped as he scuttled backwards. "You will make a journey as well, but at the end, there will be no choice." Gingilla was a mass of arched white fur on Gyorgy's shoulder, her claws digging into the man's coat. Dread dug its claws into Joseph Carlo's heart. The lantern flame guttered again.

"Get back here!" Suchet yelled after the retreating fortune-teller. He tugged on Joseph Carlo's sleeve, pulling him after Gyorgy. They followed the man and his cat, their circle of waning light coming with them. "You can't leave! You're not finished! You have to tell me!" Suchet's fists were balled at his sides. "This wasn't the deal!"

"Beware a man of bronze on a distant shore. He will be your undoing." Gyorgy's eyes burned in the darkness. For a moment, it looked as if Gyorgy and the cat had traded eyes: Gingilla's were as blue as a drowned man's fingernails and Gyorgy's as yellow as a beggar's teeth.

"Remember young travelers, beware the bronze man!" Gyorgy threw something like a child's ball over the boys' heads. It landed behind them, hissed, and turned on itself, and then issued a bang that made them both jump. A cloud of evil-smelling smoke issued from it, making them cough. When they recovered, Gyorgy was only a shadow in the tunnel, the clip-clop of his well-polished bootheels an erratic rhythm in the dark.

"Wait!" Suchet yelled after him. The rhythm of Gyorgy's boots did not slow, and then he was gone.

"Don't pay him any mind." Joseph Carlo gave his cousin's shoulder a shake. "He's just getting us back for not giving him the medallions."

"You think so?" Suchet's eyes still sought Gyorgy's shape in the darkness.

"What else is he going to do for entertainment? A man made of bronze? A fairy tale, nothing more. He's a liar, *burgiado*." Joseph Carlo spat into the darkness that'd swallowed their fortune-telling friend and his familiar.

"I guess so." Suchet stared into his own palm.

"What do you think, enough adventure for one night?"

"*Si, cugino*, let's go home."

Before they started their dark way back down the tunnel, Joseph Carlo fumbled for the pipe at his feet and heard Suchet whisper with wonder, "man of bronze."

Chapter Four

It felt as if they'd been gone for years. The sky was dark but beyond the silhouettes of houses, a pink and orange line of fire appeared on the horizon. Joseph Carlo blew out the long-suffering flame in their lantern, clanking the metal shutter shut. The wind off the mountains lifted the curls off Joseph Carlo's neck like cold fingers.

Each dawn, the wind shifted direction in Villa Franca, racing down the steep mountains that backed the seaside town and bringing with it the icy tang of snow and the deadened smell of burnt cook-fires. This was the wind that pushed ships out of the harbor. If they didn't get home soon, the household would soon be bustling and all their stealth would be for naught.

The boys traded a glance. Joseph Carlo could see the shadow of Gyorgy's words in the set line of his cousin's brow. He tried to think of a way to break the solemn mood.

"Race you!" Joseph Carlo bundled the lantern against his side as best he could and took off for home.

Suchet's footsteps were right behind him as they sprinted up the well-known route, bobbing like corks in a current and leaning into the corners. In the last stretch before they reached Casa Mauran, Suchet came abreast of his cousin, his forehead gleaming with sweat. Finding an extra reserve of speed in his arsenal, Suchet outpaced his cousin by one body length, then two, and then three as they rounded the last corner. The boys spilled up the steps, plummeting for the front door, and Suchet's pointer finger came to rest on the embedded coin first.

"I win!" Suchet wheezed.

"*Non e gusto!* I have the lantern! It's heavy." Joseph Carlo couldn't remember when Suchet had last beaten him in this race, one they ran at least once a week if not more.

"*Moito gust.* Very fair." Suchet reached out to push the front door open but Joseph Carlo stilled him with a hand on his forearm. Jerking his head towards the back of the Casa, he mouthed the words: "Fig tree." Suchet nodded. They went single file around the corner.

The fig tree's bark was like the skin of an ancient elephant, wrinkled and rough and hard as stone. For his whole life, he'd lived in the room next to the fig tree. That's how he defined his space in their busy household. The tree was a nursemaid of sorts, not quite human but loving enough, like having a dinosaur for a nanny.

Joseph Carlo left the lantern at the base, swung onto the first branch of his old friend, and began to climb. His cousin grunted as he pulled himself up to the first tier of tree underneath him. The cold dawn wind nipped at Joseph Carlo's exposed skin as he swung from one silvery gray branch to another. When he got to his jumping-off point, a tremor ran through his heart, as if something unseen was racing towards him. Being the stalwart lad that he was, fear was a foreign feeling to him. He had jumped this countless times since age eight.

He edged out onto the branch, holding onto one running parallel above, until he was four feet from the open window. Then he let go, holding his arms out for balance; the wind whooshed around him and he felt like a bat spreading its leathery wings. Feet braced one behind the other, he coiled into a tense spring of boy and jumped, powerful quad muscles propelling him through the air. With a *thump* he landed less than gracefully with his stomach on the sill, breath bursting out of him in a whoosh as his feet scrabbled against the wall for toeholds. One knee up, he torqued his body and with another grunt slid the rest of the way into the room.

As he was getting to his feet, Joseph Carlo heard a sniff from behind him. He turned, Suchet forgotten (which wasn't great for Suchet). Sitting on the bed in her neck-to-toe linen nightgown was Madalena, Lena to him and every other youngster in the Casa. Gone was the ready smile and sparkle in her eyes. The candle on the bedside table threw shadows on her face, making her seem much older than her twenty-four years. Maybe it wasn't the candle flame that'd aged her, he thought, but them—the boys.

There was a *whoomp* behind him as Suchet landed on the windowsill. Out of the corner of his eye, Joseph Carlo saw one long brown arm fling itself over the sill, followed by half a boy.

"*'Seppe? Help?*" Suchet whispered, gloriously unaware that keeping quiet was no longer a necessity as the person they were trying not to wake was sitting on the bed, fully aware of the goings-on.

Madalena pulled at her long black braid, her fingertips teasing out the end over and over. His heart broke at the sad expression on her face like violin strings snapping one by one: *twang, twang.* When she spoke, her voice was low, measured, and as impersonal as when she spoke to strangers. "Help him, Giu'Seppe. You always do."

Joseph Carlo turned to his younger cousin, limbs as heavy as his heart. Lena had used his proper name, Giu'Seppe. Usually it was 'Seppe, as the cousins called him, or Brunito. She must be very angry. He grabbed Suchet by the armpit and pulled. Suchet's eyes were huge in his face, and confused.

"'Seppe?" With Joseph Carlo's help, Suchet managed to drag the rest of his body into the room, never taking his eyes off his cousin. "What? Are you hurt?"

"No, Gufo, he isn't," Lena said from the bed.

Suchet spun, his face darkening with the same shame Joseph Carlo felt.

"Lena!" Suchet gasped. "Oh no! I . . . I'm so sorry . . ."

"Where were you?" she interrupted.

"We were in . . ." Suchet gulped. How stupid! They had never come up with a cover story! "We went to the Rue Obscure."

Anger washed over Madalena's face instantaneously, turning her formerly pale cheeks deep red. "You were in the Street of Shadows? Have you lost all judgment? People are murdered down there all the time! How could you be so . . . Why would you . . ." She didn't finish, just stared at them with a mix of horror and rage.

One look at Lena's glowering visage and Joseph Carlo could tell that pleading wouldn't do any good.

"We're going to your uncle," Lena said.

The boys exchanged horror-stricken looks: their Uncle Honore would consider this a smear on the name of Mauran. Two nephews scurrying around the Rue Obscure in the middle of the night like street rats? With real rats? For shame! This would not go down well with him, not at all.

"Come." Madalena rose. The stiff way she walked out of the room reflected her hurt. Another strand of Joseph Carlo's heart snapped, *twang*. They'd been in trouble before, but this was different. Usually Madalena would have pretended to be furious with the boys, all the while trying to tamp down a smile. This time she looked as she did at the funeral of their aunt. She looked as if someone had died.

Maybe we have, Joseph Carlo thought as he followed her out into the hall, Suchet one step behind him. *Maybe to her, we have.* The thought filled him with intense loneliness. Out of all of them, it was Lena he loved best, Lena who came to him when he was a child terrified by nightmares, Lena who'd wiped fever sweat off his brow. For Lena to disavow them, for them to have caused her that much pain, was unbearable. But here they were, Lena leading them to the kitchen in such a stilted gait she seemed more like sixty years old. This time there was no smile tucked into the corner of her mouth, no giggle bubbling up as she pretended to scold them.

She stalked into the wide kitchen with the pockmarked table at its center and a fire burning in the stone oven set back in the far wall. It smelled as it always did, of onions, rosemary, and baking bread. Copper pots hung from a trellis on the ceiling, their polished shapes throwing back the firelight. A basket of lemons sat in a large basin underneath windows that opened into the courtyard and let in the cool pre-dawn breeze. The chickens clucked sleepily in their coop out back and the fire hissed and popped as it kindled. Conchetta, their cook, was unaware she'd been joined by this sad trio as she shoved sticks into the fire, singing tunelessly, a row of the day's baking lined up on the table behind her.

Madalena cleared her throat, standing just inside the doorway with her hands clasped in front of her. Conchetta turned from the fire, her eyes widening as she took in Madalena and the two skulking boys in ratty clothing peeping out from behind her.

"Conchetta, *per favor*, *vattene*," Lena said with no inflection at all.

Conchetta scurried out of the kitchen without a word, giving both boys a dark look as she went. She even left the day's bread unfired on the table in front of them, the dough rising like cumulus clouds in their metal baking tins. She was about to disappear into the dark hallway when Madalena called her name again.

"And Conchetta, please wake the *signore* for me. Tell him he's needed in the kitchen."

Conchetta murmured a quiet, "Yes'm," and made fast her retreat.

With Conchetta out of earshot and Uncle Honore only minutes from arriving, Joseph Carlo decided to plead their case while he still could.

"Lena, please," he beseeched, tugging at his eldest sister's sleeve. She yanked it out of his grasp and walked to the table, spreading both hands on the scarred wood.

Joseph Carlo hazarded a glance at Suchet. Since Joseph Carlo's mother had died when he was too small to really remember her (a snatch of a half-hummed lullaby and lilac-scented hair),

Madalena had been both mother and sister to him. Mostly mother. She'd been too young for the responsibility that'd been thrust upon her, but it hadn't mattered. The weight of the household landed on Lena's shoulders even before their mother's funeral flowers had dried out. Ever since she'd upheld the order of the Mauran household with kindness when it was needed and caustic cleverness most other times. Her dark brown eyes constantly crackled with some inner joke as her diligent hands buttoned buttons or peeled clementines. She'd even foregone a family of her own, proclaiming her long tenure as Mama Madalena as more than enough family to last her a lifetime.

When Suchet had arrived from Sardinia, his own mother citing the poor educational choices on the island as the reason for his upheaval, Lena had welcomed him with open arms and a warm heart. Many of the other cousins and siblings were rough with him for his quirky Sardinian accent and bouts of homesickness. Those who thought to rib Suchet about his oft-sodden pillow would get whiplash from the rough side of Lena's tongue. She'd also fostered the bond between Joseph Carlo and Suchet, using Joseph Carlo's innate charisma to dispel the worst of the bullying. And it had worked, almost to her detriment it seemed as she was now faced with the newest offense of Joseph Carlo's and Suchet's alliance.

Joseph Carlo couldn't stay silent. He knew his Uncle Honore would have plenty to say on the matter when he got downstairs, but for now, he had to try to get Lena to say *something*. Her silence was far worse than any other punishment.

"Lena," he tried again. "Please talk to us. *Please.*" His voice broke on the last word.

She shook her head and tears spattered the well-used table top. "Street of Shadows? In the middle of the night? Have you lost all judgment completely? It was dumb, reckless, and dangerous. Really dangerous No, Giu'Seppe, not this time. This time you've gone too far."

Joseph Carlo hung his head. Shame sent a spurt of unspent tears down the back of his throat. He looked at his cousin, trying to think of some reassurance that this would be patched over, that they would all go back to being *simpatico* in no time. But Joseph Carlo couldn't lie; when he opened his mouth to speak nothing came out. But the tears did, streaking down his cheeks. He made no move to wipe them.

Chapter Five

By the time Honore joined them a few minutes later, Joseph Carlo's cheeks were dry. Suchet was still bewildered as only a well-behaved child can be when faced with the possibility of a hefty sentence, but Joseph Carlo had resigned himself to it.

Madalena had swung the kettle on its long arm over the fire and was measuring coffee into a metal pitcher when Honore entered. He had dressed hastily. His white linen shirt was half untucked and he was in the process of cinching his belt. His wispy gray and black hair stuck up around his ears but it would've been ill-advised for either boy to chuckle. His thick eyebrows, usually combed into some semblance of order, were wild and wooly, making him look untrustworthy, as if he might do anything. He finished buckling his belt and, without a glance for the boys, made his bow-legged way over to the table. He studied Lena's profile as she finished measuring the grounds, leaning in as she filled him in on his nephews' nocturnal activities. Joseph Carlo couldn't hear much but he did hear the words "Rue Obscure." Twice. When Honore looked up, Joseph Carlo's heart sank. His uncle's face was clouded with rage and his Adam's apple worked up and down in his throat.

"What have you done," Honore said. It wasn't a question; it was a condemnation.

"We didn't mean to, *Zio*," Suchet began.

Joseph Carlo sucked in his breath. *Idiota*, he thought.

Honore turned towards his young nephew like the swing of a mace. "Didn't mean to? Were you sleepwalking when you stole away to the Rue Obscure? Possessed? How could you 'not mean to' when it seems like every action you took went against common sense? Down there, being a Mauran can get you killed." He pounded a fist into his other palm.

Honore inhaled until his taut round belly pressed against his shirt, smoothed his wild eyebrows, and laid into them, flogging them with a verbal cat-o-nine-tails. He brought up the family crypt, as if the boys had shamed ancestors they'd never met, as if a score of skeletons sat in the Mauran mausoleum, shaking their bony fingers at the boys. He reminded them what it meant to be a Mauran, a family line that traced back to the Knights of Malta.

"You two," Honore said, ramping up to the meat of his argument, "were meant for better lives than those who dwell in the Rue Obscure. You were meant to take over the company. You could've been the most powerful trading magnates of the southern coast of the *Mediterraneo*, Joseph Carlo here and Suchet in Sardinia," he paused, "and yet you behave like imbeciles."

Although expected, it still hurt.

"You represent the Mauran family, but most of all," Honore's voice dropped to a whisper, "you represent me. And yet you're out on the street carousing with not a thought of who you might meet or what they might do to you? No, this will not stand."

What bothered Joseph Carlo the most was that Honore looked disappointed yet resigned, not a great sign for the boys.

"No," Honore continued in that deadly whisper, "this will not stand." He was no longer looking at them but at Lena. "We have no choice. You know this."

Lena poured out the strong coffee into two small blue cups but didn't touch hers. The boys weren't offered any. She nodded once, a crease between her brows.

Honore turned back to the boys, his face a hard, disapproving mask. "You've given us no choice: we're putting you to work. You'll learn some common sense. Obviously all this bores you, if you cannot keep yourselves to yourselves but risk your lives for fun." He flapped a hand at the kitchen and the courtyard and the rest of the Casa beyond. "The *Diligencia* leaves for Sardinia in an hour. You'll be aboard. You won't be there as family, you'll be crew. You'll have to earn it all back. Get your sea bags."

At the news that they'd be joining the crew, Lena looked up in surprise.

"Honore," she began haltingly. "You're right. These boys should be punished."

Honore waited, sipping his *po di caffe*. Madalena's hands twisted at her waist.

"Their punishment should teach them good judgment, which they lack." She paused, looking confused. "But the *Diligencia*, I . . . I don't know. It feels . . . off."

"Off?" Honore put down his coffee cup. "Lena, these boys have been on this ship countless times. It's almost a part of the family. A longer trip will give them a taste of what they would throw away."

"I know." Her eyes pleaded with him. "I just have a feeling. Please, let them stay. We'll find some other punishment. Clean Stronzo's coop for instance."

Honore uttered a sharp guffaw and shook his head. "I'm sorry Lena, you know I defer to you on what happens inside the Casa, but I cannot let this stand. Anything could've happened to them down there. No, this will not *stand*." To the boys, he said, "You have fifteen minutes to get your kit together." With that he stalked out.

When the boys appeared in the downstairs foyer fifteen minutes later with their canvas sea bags swinging at their sides, their uncle didn't so much as glance at them until he pushed the front door open. His hand hovered over the Mauran coin embedded in the door and he gave each boy a look, as if to say, "Look you well, those that go the path of evil."

Despite how upset he was (and Joseph Carlo was plenty upset even for an adventurous boy of thirteen), he heaved an inward sigh. This punishment wouldn't be easy or short. The sailing would be hard work, but stomaching their uncle's constant chastisements was going to be harder.

Lena had a woolen wrap of dark blue around her shoulders to ward off the morning chill outside. She grabbed the boys' hands, one in each of her own, and stared at them for a moment.

"Promise me you'll take care of him, Brunito," she said to Joseph Carlo. "Take care of one another." She smiled, a shadow of her usual grin but there all the same, and squeezed their hands once more before letting them go. Then her lips folded back into a stiff line.

Honore started down the steps. The cold, burnt-smelling wind had grown strong and hungry as it whipped around the edge of the Casa. It tugged at the boys' clothing and hair, as if anxious to be off. The Villa Francans called this dawn wind the *Mistral* as it carried everyone who wanted to leave, as well as some who didn't, out of the harbor on its cold spine.

The sun was behind a thick soup of clouds gathered on the horizon; orange, red, and purple beamed out from behind the mountain. The birds were at their morning songs, running through their notes sleepily; the cold wind rustled the trees as it raced down the hill to the harbor. Joseph Carlo had never before noticed the exquisite symmetry of the courtyards and the cobblestones under their feet. Even the potted plants waved to him as they walked by. It was as if the whole town had been created for their benefit, as if it was brand new. He looked back at the Casa before it disappeared behind the curve of the road. Madalena was a punctuation mark of white and blue against the terra cotta building.

Dark fingers of dread pinched his heart as they made their way down to the waterfront. Suddenly he heard something. He paused, searching the doorways and windowsills. It came again. This time he'd heard it more clearly: a rusty *miao*.

Behind a sewer grate a few feet away, yellowed eyes stared at him from what could only be one place—the Rue Obscure. He stared back in horror, wondering if their gypsy friend was going to further expand their uncle's knowledge of their evening out. The cat winked at him. Then she narrowed her eyes, leaned into the bars, and hissed. Joseph Carlo shook his head. When he looked back again, Gingilla was gone, but the dread remained, like a persistent chill.

Joseph Carlo trotted to catch up to Suchet, walking with his head down behind Honore. As they turned the last corner, the darker blue of the Mediterranean beckoned to him beyond the aquamarine of their harbor. A tinny timpani chime trailed after him like bubbles in a boat's wake.

Even though the town was just waking up, stretching its arms above its head, the harbor bustled. From this distance, the shirts of the sailors were bright in the gloom as they hoisted casks and rolled barrels up the gangplank. The thumps of the barrels were like bocce balls clunking together. He recognized the *Diligencia* tethered alongside the pier, her black hull a shadow in the half-light. Despite all that had happened since he and Suchet slipped off to the Street of Shadows, a thirst for the unknown unfolded in him.

A glance at Suchet's face told him all he needed, that the call to adventure hadn't yet hit him. The boy still followed their uncle with his head down.

"Psst," he whispered to his cousin, who looked at him with wet eyes. Joseph Carlo at first guessed it was the idea of working on the barque that was depressing Suchet. Sailing had never been his passion. Really, Suchet's passion was reading, his arms perfect for turning pages. But he hated hoisting, and this trip to Sardinia and back would mean a lot of hoisting.

Sardinia! Joseph Carlo slapped his forehead. Of course! Suchet's family was in Sardinia, and more specifically, Suchet's *mother* was in Sardinia. She was the most terrifying person Joseph Carlo had ever met. No wonder Suchet looked so upset. In a matter of days he would face the wrath of the smallest volcano on the southern coast. In her starched dress buttoned to the chin and a fan working overtime in her beringed hand, Luciana would undoubtedly have an opinion of her returning son's recent behavior, and not a favorable one.

Joseph Carlo said in what he hoped was a reassuring tone, "Don't worry, we have three days on the barque before we get there. Zio will be calmer by then."

Suchet gave Joseph Carlo such a look of scathing disbelief that Joseph Carlo had to resist reminding the boy that the Rue Obscure had been *his* idea. But that would've added insult to injury, so he stayed quiet and followed his cousin and uncle down to the family ship.

The *Diligencia* was about 120 feet long, square-rigged, a sturdy barque with three masts of different heights. She was crewed by seventeen seasoned sailors from Villa Franca. There were two cargo holds, one amidships and one forward, stuffed to the gills with the pots, boxes, bundles and urns that they'd need for the ten-day round-trip to Sardinia and back. Two or three to get there, a couple days to unload and load, and then a few days to sail back if the wind was right.

Honore and the boys reached the dock in the pre-dawn light that limned everything in luminescence. The first mate had assembled the crew in the waist of the ship to stand before their captain. They were olive-skinned, short, broad-shouldered, and thin-hipped. A lifetime at sea had roughened their skin and hardened their muscles. They wore sailor slops: billowing wide-legged trousers ending at the knee, buttoned shirts, straw hats held behind backs. All eyes were pinned on Honore.

"Men," he began, then stopped to look at the boys. He didn't say a word, just stared at them. At first, Joseph Carlo didn't get it. Then Suchet pulled on his sleeve, tugging him over until they were part of the assembled group. *You won't be there as family, you'll be crew*, Honore had said. What he hadn't mentioned was that the crew knew the boys as *primi figli*: the first sons of the Knights of Malta a la Mauran, and not *just* crew.

"Crew, these boys you know. They've been hanging off the spars like *scimmie* since they could walk. For this voyage I ask that you treat them no differently than you would any other wharf rat."

A murmur rippled through the knot of sailors and eyes cut sideways at the pair. Joseph Carlo could feel blood rise in his cheeks.

"I need your help to remind them who they are. I need you to teach them that carousing on the Rue Obscure," there was a collective hiss, "is not a worthwhile pastime for a Mauran man." An older tar spat on the dock and gave the boys a withering look, or maybe that was his naturally squinty expression. "Will you help wake the salt water in their veins?"

"Aye," the sailors said in unison.

A man in the back chimed in, "Once they're back from Sardinia, they'll be as salty as the rest of us!" There were a few chuckles. The man with the squinty eyes pounded Suchet on the back, making him lurch forward.

"Then we're off before *la Mistral* takes its leave of us," Honore concluded. "Men, to your stations!"

The sailors jumped to obey and shoulders ricocheted off the boys as they went by, followed by admonitions of "Watch it," and "Outta my way." Joseph Carlo had never seen Honore this way. Eyes gleaming, shoulders back, he was no longer their frazzled uncle with a million pieces of cargo floating around in his mind; he was a sea captain. Honore stalked by the two, not looking back. There was nothing to do but to follow their uncle aboard.

Chapter Six

THE FEEL OF THE DECK BENEATH JOSEPH CARLO'S FEET AND the creak of wood and rope were familiar. The ship rocked on the swell of waves in their protected quay, straining against her lines, ready to be off. The Mistral was gaining strength as dawn approached. The dry cold wind raced down the ancient peaks above town and through the streets, picking up the last hints of night jasmine as it went.

The boys didn't need to be told what to do once on board. In fact, they barely needed to think about it. They headed toward the bow across wide gray planks weathered to soapstone smoothness, lines of caulk running like veins down the length of them. Once there, they called through an open hatch to a sailor working in the hold, his face a lighter smear in the dark, and tossed their bags down to him. The crew slept in the fo'c'sle and they stored their kits below as well so they wouldn't get soaked by sea spray.

After stowing their kits, the boys went to the main mast. Luca, their uncle's first mate, was on the port railing sorting lines, sheets, and braces. There were a few things Joseph Carlo could think of that were as calamitous as a tangled line on board: a ripped sail, a punched hull, and, in some sailors' estimations, a lack of beer, but a tangled line as they ran out of the harbor with the wind at their stern could cause real problems: a sailor could step into the wrong coil, risking a broken ankle. There was nothing worse than being laid up with a broken ankle on one of these voyages, taking up space and unable to move freely around the ship. Being eaten by a shark was only a notch above it.

Luca had always been kind to the boys, which was unexpected from the old gnarled man. It was like a crab wanting to cuddle. Years of working on board had bleached Luca's hair as it had the *Diligencia*'s sails and darkened his skin so he looked like a man who had slathered himself in tar. An accident had left him with a bum hip and his body canted to the left. When a storm approached (or so Luca claimed), his limp was more pronounced. But, pronounced or not, it never hindered him. He was as spry as the youngest member of the crew, and more experienced. To top it all off, he had the loveliest singing voice in the harbor, even though he used it to sing the bawdiest songs on the sea.

Luca made his line fast and turned toward the boys. His dark eyes bored into each of them as his hands found the next mess of braces on the deck and coiled them with quick flipping motions.

"*Nave ratti*," he began in his smooth speaking voice, the same mellifluous voice he used to sing about Adriana's knickers. "It seems you're in a spot of trouble." The syllables all ran together like taffy. Luca's thick Sardinian accent was hard for Joseph Carlo to understand, but Suchet had no such problem. "Gettin' yer heads straight. That why he brought you along?" Luca said, jerking his head toward Honore. Suchet nodded.

Luca harrumphed, looking down at his scarred hands as they twisted the remaining rope into a neatened coil. "Seems to me he's right. Life comes at you hard and fast and it don't listen to reason." He slung the coil over a belaying pin. "Better get aloft before he catches you jawing around with me. You already in it deep, no need to make it worse."

Joseph Carlo opened his mouth to tell the old tar that *he* was the one who'd stopped *them*, but Suchet grabbed his forearm and yanked him towards the ratlines, the rope ladders that led them up to the first yardarm thirty feet above the deck.

Joseph Carlo swung himself to the outside of the ratlines with a withering glance at Luca's back. He knew he had a lot more guff to take but *per favori!* It was just one jaunt to the Rue Obscure! Grown-ups were so worried all the time, it was like they *wanted* to worry. Luca favored them with the litany he gave them every time they went aloft. "One hand for yourself and one for the ship; keep your eye on the job and don't look down."

"*Si signore,*" Joseph Carlo said while rolling his eyes. As he climbed, he rained whispered curses onto Luca's head as it grew smaller below him. He knew what to do already; he'd been sailing on this barque since before he could walk. When *he* was a grown-up, he reasoned as he reached up for the next stay, *he* wouldn't pitch a fit at every little thing his sons did. In fact, he concluded as he pulled himself up, if their sons decided to go meet some spooky gypsy in the middle of the night, he and Suchet would laugh about it. They would remember the time they did the same thing when they were young and clap their boys on the backs.

The ratlines quivered with Suchet's motion right above him. When they were almost all the way to the top, Joseph Carlo's head ran into Suchet's foot. Usually he would've stopped right below his cousin, but he was still thinking about his liberated parental approach. He leaned back to see what his cousin was doing. Suchet had stopped just below the crosstrees, the platform stationed halfway up the mast. One way to get to the yards and the sails attached to them was to climb up and around the outside of the wooden platform. This meant hanging upside down thirty feet above a hard deck while trying to put one's feet on the rope rungs. The other way was what was known as the "lubber's-hole," a small opening between the mast and the wooden platform itself, known as such because only landlubbers used it—landlubbers and Suchet.

Joseph Carlo grinned. Suchet did this every time. As Suchet weighed his options, Honore's voice floated up, calling, "Cast off the bow line!" The bright revolution of a rope spun through the air from the pier. The flying jib was raised, and the wind stretched the sail tight with a *crack*. The *Diligencia* strained against the remaining spring lines like an unbroken colt. She was itching to get out there, and as Joseph Carlo looked past the harbor to the mouth of the Mediterranean, he felt it too. The sea was calling, and both boat and boy were eager to answer.

Suchet made his decision as the rest of the lines were freed and the barque cast off from her berth. He went through the lubber's-hole, as Joseph Carlo assumed he would. Suchet hadn't yet climbed aloft without using the shortcut, inciting scorn from the other sailors. Even Luca stood aside when Suchet was being ribbed about using the easier method of getting to the yards; it was an unspoken rule on the sea: you use the lubber's-hole and take the verbal abuse, or you don't.

As Joseph Carlo began the nerve-wracking climb around the outside of the crosstrees, hanging from the ropes like an acrobat, Suchet slipped through the small aperture and continued his climb. Joseph Carlo pulled himself around the lip of the wooden platform and kept climbing to the uppermost sail on this mast, the t'gallant. The boys worked side by side, feet on the footropes hanging under the yard and hands on the gaskets, which attached the furled sail to the wooden yard. As the heavy canvas unfurled, Honore gave the final order from below, "Spring lines and stern lines!" Lines were thrown from the quay and the *Diligencia* pushed her way out, sailors running to jump onto her deck at the last moment.

Sails unfurled with a *flump*; the Mistral filled their canvas bellies and blew the *Diligencia* towards the sea. As the last gasket was loosened, the sun rose from the mountaintops and licked the outer harbor with gold. The barque picked up speed as orders were shouted from below. From their vantage point, the boys could see all of the deck and every man on it. Every sailor had a place and a job on the ship. From up here, the crew looked like well-trained dancers, spinning and twirling around cleats and lines. The boys would soon become part of it, taking their places in the intricate give and take that was life on board. But at the moment they were above it all with only one another and the wind.

The ship surged forward and Joseph Carlo's blood surged in response. There was nothing like being under sail, the canvas hooking its claws into the wind and hanging on as it took them where it would. The sun cleared the mountains and spilled a path of light in front of the *Diligencia* as she headed out of the harbor. They left the old fort to starboard, its unlikely spiral tower knifing into the sky in a stone salute. The Mistral sent an icy gust up the back of Joseph Carlo's shirt. He was enlivened by the tang of pine tar, the salty air, the creak of straining ropes, and the snap of the sails.

Despite it all—the rats, Lena's sad anger, Honore's punishment—Joseph Carlo had never felt more alive. The boys leaned out over the yard as the barque carved a path through the molten gold of the harbor. At the moment, this was the best place on land or sea to be.

Chapter Seven

Villa Franca fell behind in a patchwork pattern of rock and shadow, the stone fort indistinguishable from the hills and vales. It was hard to believe that somewhere back there, Lena was beginning her day, perhaps gathering eggs and risking Stronzo's wrath on her own. The bosun's whistle shrieked, waking Joseph Carlo from his reverie.

They began the climb down towards the deck. At the midpoint, Suchet squeezed through the lubber's-hole without hesitation. Joseph Carlo peered at the men scurrying on deck and saw Luca make a twirling gesture with his hand, meaning "Hurry up!"

With a sigh, Joseph Carlo laid himself flat on his stomach, and dangled his feet over the edge until his questing toes found the ratlines, wiggling backwards until he was over the side. The ratlines stretched out to make room for the platform and, directly below it, contracted back towards the mast. The odd angle made this a treacherous maneuver. *Got to get my sea legs back*, he thought as his feet trembled on the ropes. He glanced down and his stomach flopped. If he fell from here, it wouldn't be too bad, he thought, he'd only break his back on the hard edge of the rail. Suchet, already standing on the deck below, grabbed the ratlines and to Joseph Carlo's horror shook them, *hard*.

"Oy, *cugino*! *Smettila!*" Joseph Carlo's stomach did another flip-flop as the ropes jerked back and forth. "Quit it, Gufo!"

Suchet cackled up at him but he didn't let go of the ratlines, he just kept on shaking them. Luca and Honore sauntered up behind him and Suchet turned, swallowing his laughter. Joseph Carlo swung down the last few feet and jumped to the deck.

Luca gave them a perfunctory, "Your stations, boys." He looked over at Honore, who nodded. "Gufo, yer with the Captain. He wants you on the charts." Suchet shrugged at Joseph Carlo, and trotted after their uncle towards the captain's quarters.

Joseph Carlo harrumphed. Just like that kid to always come out on top, like cream in the milk pans.

"Jealous, Joseph Carlo?" Joseph Carlo didn't like the light in Luca's eyes. He shook his head. "I need you to scour the decks. Then you need to be about the deck to see if anyone needs anything. And *then*, if you find yourself at leisure, you come see me. I'll find you something to keep you busy." Luca grinned at him, revealing more spaces than teeth. "You'll be too exhausted to go carousing like a tomcat."

He's enjoying this, Joseph Carlo thought without surprise. But he touched his forehead in a gesture of respect before he made his way to the forward hold.

"Hard work is what'll do ya," Luca repeated from behind him.

Joseph Carlo barely suppressed a retort, but somehow, he managed.

The *Diligencia* soon found that sweet spot between water and wind and fell into the rhythmic pattern of a sailing vessel. Joseph Carlo set off to gather what he'd need to scour the decks from the deck locker, detouring around two sailors and the ship's cooper. As he walked past, the trio stopped talking and stared him down. He gave them a nod but only after many moments did the cooper nod back.

Their response troubled him. Normally, the sailors who worked the *Diligencia* were delighted to engage, teasing him like older siblings. The cousins were just two more ship rats among many. Today Honore had reminded them who the boys *really* were: two princelings of Mauran, half-grown boss-lings in the making. This was the point. Although Honore had told the crew to treat the boys like fellow crewmen, the message just under the surface was: *These boys are squandering their good chances. Let them know how you feel about that.*

Joseph Carlo and Suchet had opportunities the likes of which this crew would never be offered, nor would their sons. To watch these two waste their chances was like watching someone use florins as fishing bait.

As Joseph Carlo grabbed a bucket full of sand, a holystone, a mop, and another bucket, he thought admiringly of Honore. That man wasn't running a multi-ship trading company for nothing. But he resented the fact that Suchet sat with a sextant and a quill while he tied bandanas around his kneecaps so he could spend the next few hours on all fours, scrubbing and scouring.

He scattered sand across the ship's deck. He'd use it to scour the worn wood, washing it away with seawater when he was finished scrubbing. It didn't occur to him that Honore was serving the boys' innate natures. Suchet was small for twelve and not prone to exceptional athletic ability—a mess when it came to physical labor; however navigation and the like were right up his alley. Joseph Carlo was quick and dexterous as well as good-natured, an apt combination for a seaman about the deck. The boys, Brainy and Brawny, were the hope for the Mauran empire. One would gain the respect of his crew with strength and kindness, and the other would use his sharp mind to navigate the future.

Joseph Carlo lowered himself to his knees with a sigh, grasped the holystone with both hands, and started scrubbing.

Chapter Eight

THE ROUTINE OF THE WORKING BARQUE WAS THE PULSE OF LIFE on board. It was like the swell and ebb of the ocean underneath her hull: it gave shape to the men's days and wove them into a tapestry of common industry. Each time the bells pealed across the deck, the watch changed: four hours on, four hours off, like breathing. The machinations of the ship were completed at the turning of each watch, every four hours, so the off-watch crew would get as much sleep as was possible. Joseph Carlo slowly inured himself to living life on the watches, furious activity punctuated by stretches of too-short sleep and meager meals.

For his first watch, Joseph Carlo scoured the decks, which was a little like scrubbing the floors of a house if that house was a mansion, and that mansion was moving. The harder he worked, the more the men warmed to him as the morning grew towards afternoon. Watching him sweat cleaning the *Diligencia*'s decks made him one of them.

When he'd finished scouring the deck at the end of the morning watch, throwing buckets after buckets of water across the deck, the crew sat down to their midday meal. When they reached Sardinia they would be feasted, but for now their fare was simple: bread, cheese, olive oil, olives, a bit of chicken, washed down with beer, and for dessert, a fresh orange. Simple and satisfying, hard work was an exceptional relish.

They ate on barrels scattered across the deck with seabirds revolving above, hoping for scraps. Joseph Carlo was seated amongst the crew. Occasionally one of them slapped him on the back hard enough to make his eyes water; some made jokes about the pristine deck. He was one of them, his sins forgiven if not forgotten. Suchet, on the other hand, was seated by their uncle. As he watched Suchet and Honore out of the corner of his eye, Suchet speaking excitedly to the older man, he was struck by how much Suchet *looked* like Honore—not physically but in his mannerisms. This was a boy who would grow into a man who ran a company, perhaps even this one.

As for himself, he belonged with the men telling tall tales and ribbing each other mercilessly. He belonged here, with the crew. And in that moment, he could see it and he liked it, liked it very well indeed. He did not want to be the one with a sextant plotting a course; he wanted to be the one gripping the jug of grog while the noon sun baked his hair onto his scalp, whose knees still ached from a morning of scouring the decks. But by the time the two of them were grown, he promised himself, he wouldn't be scouring any decks.

The bells of the watch woke him from dreams of the future. Elbows jabbed and jostled him as the crew returned to their stations.

For the rest of the afternoon, Joseph Carlo had the unenviable task of pumping the bilge with three other sailors. The *Diligencia* was an old wooden ship, and she leaked. Without constant pumping, the stores they were taking to Sardinia would soon be soaked and worthless. Throughout the hot afternoon, Joseph Carlo worked the suction pump, pulling and pushing the stubborn lever back and forth, his arms screaming and his hair plastered in curls on his forehead. By the time the bells pealed again, signaling the start of the first dog watch, 4:00 p.m. to 6:00 p.m., he was longing for Suchet's position as navigator-in-training. He made his way back to his hammock to snatch an hour's nap, thinking of Suchet's blister-free hands as he studied the mess he'd made of his own. It was drudgery: pumping the bilge, scouring the decks, assisting anyone who needed help, all of it exhausting and forgettable, except for the the goat.

Like many merchant ships, the *Diligencia* had a small array of livestock on board. There was the usual: chickens, ducks, two pigs . . . and a goat. The goat had gotten out and no one knew how. Goats *were* innately good climbers and the stave could've been knocked out of the rickety pen at any point. However it'd happened, Joseph Carlo was the one to chase her down, capture her, and grapple her back into the pen. What Joseph Carlo found out in the two hours that he spent chasing her up and down the decks was that goats are quick and very nimble; that they don't like to have a rough blanket thrown over their heads as they are tackled by a burly boy; and that their horns hurt when used as weapons. A lot.

As the day began to wane in a spectacular sunset, Joseph Carlo realized that he hadn't thought of his tender state of punishment for hours. He also realized that the crew had forgotten any animosity towards him, probably because he'd risked life and limb to get their precious hooved cargo back where she belonged. And because now they had goat jokes to tell for the rest of the trip.

That night, the two boys snuggled into side-by-side hammocks in the fo'c's'le, surrounded by the whistling snores of the rest of the men. The hammock smelled of mildew and scratched Joseph Carlo's sore arms and kneecaps. His hands were covered with new blisters. He and Suchet might have linked their hands together in the space between the hammocks, but of course they didn't. The man-sized hammocks were too large for them and the sides curled up and over them like fiber cocoons.

"'Seppe?" Suchet said. His voice came from far away.

"Hmmm?"

"We've done all right, haven't we?"

Joseph Carlo opened his heavy lids and looked through the hammock's webbing to the ceiling. "I think we did, Gufo. How was your time with Tizio?"

"It was . . . interesting actually. I thought Tizio was going to yell at me some more but all he wanted to do was teach me stuff."

"What stuff?"

"You know, navigation techniques, how to use a sextant, how to plot a course." Wonder filled the boy's voice. The space between them was filled with the sleep sounds of the rest of the crew and the peaceful groan and creak of the *Diligencia* as she wended her way towards Sardinia. A chicken let out a sleepy cluck. The movement of the ship rocked their hammocks back and forth.

"Seppe?" Suchet's voice was clogged with sleep.

"Hmmm?"

"Today was pretty good?"

"Yes, Gufo. One of the best."

Chapter Nine

Joseph Carlo was disoriented when he was shaken awake in the dark. For a moment he thought that the figure leaning over him was Madalena. "Lena?"

A gruff laugh mixed with the pealing bells that signaled the change of the watch.

"D'ya hear that? Boy thinks I'm his nursemaid."

Joseph Carlo snapped awake and sat up in his hammock, setting it swinging; he gripped the sides to steady himself.

A shuttered lantern in the corner of the 'tween deck showed him a shadowed sailor dressed in his slops. "Time for yer watch, boys. The First said I was to come and wake ya, and if you didn't get up the first time, I's to turn you out your hammock." He shook Suchet's hammock, and Suchet uttered a groan which ended in a whine of "Don't!"

"There ya are, young master. Bright-eyed, bushy-tailed." The sailor grinned, his smile a white half moon. The other sailors' snores filled the 'tween deck like the buzz of bees.

Joseph Carlo succeeded in getting himself out of his hammock and leant Suchet a steadying arm to grip while he tried to swing his feet to the deck.

"Better bring something against the wind, the night breeze can bite." The sailor started for the short ladder that led to the deck as Joseph Carlo balled his jacket in one hand and headed after the man, Suchet on his heels.

The sailor was right. On deck the air was cold compared to the dank quarters of the 'tween deck. Joseph Carlo shrugged his arms into his jacket as they joined Luca near the mast. The sky was a huge black bowl above them, the horizon indistinguishable where sky and sea met. The only difference Joseph Carlo could tell was that one was made of waves and the other of stars. And what stars! Without any competing light, they saw the full showing. Straight away he recognized Leo standing guard on the horizon whereas Cassiopeia's chair stood empty halfway across the sky. He felt so tiny on the creaking *Diligencia* as she made way through the black sea, waves slapping her bow.

"Tired pups," Luca said.

Joseph Carlo grunted in response. Suchet swayed on his feet, and not solely from the movement of the waves. Joseph Carlo jabbed an elbow into his ribs and the boy jerked his head, eyelids flying up.

"Every man who works the *Diligencia* stands watch as lookout," Luca began.

"What are w—" Joseph Carlo's question was cut off by an enormous yawn that took over the bottom half of his face. "*Perdono*, what are we looking for?"

"Anything out of the ordinary. There must always be someone on watch. Farther north, near *Scosia o I'lrlanda*, we'd be watching for ice floes. Very dangerous for a small wooden barque like the *Diligencia*." Luca patted the mast. "There are also man-o-wars to watch out for, military ships. The war on the continent may be over, but that doesn't mean we shouldn't keep an eye out for the *Sanguinosa Britannico*, those bloody British, regardless of our Letters of Marque."

At the mention of warships, a chill snuck under Joseph Carlo's jacket. He glanced at Suchet and saw the boy was now wide awake. Their uncle had made journeys up north during the seven years of war but he'd never spoken much about it. Whatever had happened, it hadn't improved Honore's opinion of the British *or* the French. He carried his Letters of Marque, letters of fealty and protection from the King of Sardinia, with him on every journey, something he'd never done before his northern travels.

Joseph Carlo looked up the mast, plotting his course, and swung himself to the outside of the ratlines. He'd never climbed to the crosstrees in the dark. The ropes stretched above them, perhaps to the top of heaven itself.

"You boys did well today," Luca said, called after them. "Keep it up."

This time there was no crew to rib Suchet about going through the lubber's-hole. In Joseph Carlo's sleepy state of mind, he thought it best to use the lubber's-hole this one time, so as not to invite the danger of falling. It was really for Suchet's sake that he used it. He wouldn't want the poor boy to have to rescue him, Joseph Carlo thought as he swung hand to hand with only the diamond chips of stars to light his way. He squeezed through the lubber's-hole and out onto the platform to find two sailors waiting in the shadows to descend. Once the boys arrived, they swung onto the ratlines and started down without a word.

Joseph Carlo took a seat next to Suchet, who was sitting cross-legged and staring up into the infinite. He scanned the water for, as Luca put it, "anything out of the ordinary." There was nothing but the dark angles of the ship riding higher than the moving tapestry of the ocean. If the moon had been out, then they could have seen more, but as it was, they sat in almost complete darkness. Suchet only had eyes for those stars.

"Did you know—" Suchet sucked in his breath at the loudness of his words. Without the bustle of the ship's activities, voices amplified. He tried again in a much softer voice. "Did you know that stars are different colors?"

Joseph Carlo's eyes widened in the dark.

"It's true. You see those?" Suchet pointed to a group of stars four fingers above the starboard quarter. "The one in the middle." He waited for Joseph Carlo to find it.

"I see it! It's pink!" Joseph Carlo said in a whisper. "And that one looks blue to me, can it be blue?"

"Yep, you bet. That one," Suchet pointed, "is Centaurus. With it we can tell what line we're on, north to south. That's our latitude. One day, someone will figure out longitude."

Joseph Carlo steeled himself; Suchet's voice had taken on his teacher-tone.

"Longitude are the east to west lines."

Apple for your favorite pupil, Joseph Carlo thought.

"Without knowing what our longitude is, we could be any-where on the north to south line. But with it, we would know exactly *where we are*."

Joseph Carlo had to admit that was pretty great. He was, at heart, a pragmatist, one who didn't like being lost.

"That's longitude," Suchet concluded, "as slippery as a mer-maid and just as sought after."

Joseph Carlo burst out laughing. Between snorts he said, "Not only a navigator but a poet to boot." Suchet's smile was just visible in the darkness. "Do you tell your coordinates to Tizio in rhymes?"

"Not yet, but maybe I'll run it by him . . . on a whim."

Joseph Carlo groaned through his laughter. "Stick to naviga-tion, please."

The boys lapsed into silence, their arms hugging their knees, heads craned back to take in the never-ending stars. Now that Suchet had showed him the colors of the stars, Joseph Carlo couldn't *not* see them. It was like looking at a black velvet cloak strewn with sapphires, emeralds, and rubies.

"You really like this stuff, don't you?" Joseph Carlo tore his eyes away from the display above him and looked at Suchet's profile. He looked wise. He may not have looked it puking his guts out in the Rue Obscure, but with map and compass, Suchet was wise.

"I do, I really do," Suchet answered without hesitation, "and not just because Tizio wants me to like it. I'm good at it, *cugino*. Somehow it fits me, you know?"

Joseph Carlo agreed. "Yeah, I know what you mean."

The next day found the boys hard at work again, fully inaugurated into life on the barque. Once again, Honore had Suchet with him in the captain's chambers and Joseph Carlo toiled with the crew, this time on water duty. All morning long he transferred water from the storage casks in the hold to the barrels on deck, bucket after bucket, heavy, sloshing work as he slogged up and down two decks and through the narrow hatchways. By the time the bells pealed at noon, his trousers were soaked and his fingertips pruned. But the men would have water to dip into if they needed it. And Joseph Carlo was somewhat proud of that.

Late that afternoon, he caught a glimpse of Suchet during the quick turnaround between watches. All he could get out of the boy was that they'd set a compass course southeast, which took them to Pita Della Scorno in Sardinia on a lovely reach. Joseph Carlo left him at the rail, chewing on his tough biscuit and muttering to himself about hull speed, nautical miles, and knots.

At supper, Suchet came to eat with Joseph Carlo and the crew. He approached them shyly, one hand tucked behind his back and the other holding onto the wooden plate so tightly that even in the peachy light of the dying day, Joseph Carlo could tell that Suchet's fingertips were white under the pressure. Joseph Carlo motioned for his cousin to sit down, and Suchet did, awkwardly balancing his plate on his knees. And then, as if on cue, the goat bleated. Joseph Carlo started, dread rising in the back of his throat. That sound hadn't come from the pen below where the goat had been secured the day before. It had come from right behind him.

He swiveled his head and scanned the gloomy shadows underneath the crisscrossing ropes and the gray expanse of the sails still holding their ration of wind. He saw a glint of white peeping out from behind the mizzen mast, a glint of white shaped like an escaped goat's horns.

"No," he said softly. "No, it can't be."

"Yes, it can," said Nico, a sailor of about thirty but with the weather-worn skin of a fifty-year-old. "Oh yes, *fratello di capra*, it seems your *amante* has come for a visit."

There was a rumble of laughter from the rest of the dining party and various comments thrown around such as: "Got a new girlfriend, *nave ratti?*" And "That goat's got a taste for our Brunito."

Despite his utter dread of having to chase down the wily ruminant, Joseph Carlo felt a flush of pleasure at the sound of "our Brunito."

Suchet put his plate on the barrel next to Joseph Carlo. "*Cugino*, can I help?"

Joseph Carlo sighed and heaved himself off the barrel, placing his plate next to Suchet's. "Sure, Gufo, come meet our new Stronzo."

The goat didn't stand a chance against *two* boys who had dealt with the likes of Stronzo. The animal may have given Joseph Carlo a run for his florins the afternoon before, but now Joseph Carlo was armed with foreknowledge and an accomplice. Unless the goat summoned her feathered or snouted brethren from below, she was outnumbered.

Joseph Carlo and Suchet formulated a plan without exchanging a word. It was simple enough, Suchet grabbed a remnant of sail that had been used to patch the larger ones, slinked over to the mizzen mast, and became still as a statue. Joseph Carlo watched his cousin and waited. The brown goat didn't seem to mind Suchet's proximity but kept her eyes glued on Joseph Carlo, her *amante*, while stomping her small hooves and waggling her white goatee.

"She's only got eyes for you, Brunito!" came a hoarse yell from behind.

Joseph Carlo nodded to Suchet. The boy readied the three-foot length of canvas as Joseph Carlo took one big step towards the goat, flapping his arms like Stronzo in their kitchen yard back home. The goat stared at Joseph Carlo incredulously, her goat eyes gone wide. She took a tentative step backwards, her rump bumping against the mizzen mast that Suchet was hiding behind. Joseph Carlo approached, still imitating Stronzo, adding crowing noises to his performance. The goat looked positively alarmed by this and took another step backwards, but the mast prevented it.

She gave Joseph Carlo one more astonished look before she reared, swiveled away from the cackling boy, and bolted. And there was Suchet holding open the canvas exactly as a parent would hold open a towel for a child after a bath. The goat got three full strides away before Suchet collapsed on her. But he didn't quite cover her head with the sail, and the terrified goat dragged Suchet across the deck.

"*Cugino!*" Suchet hollered, desperately trying to keep his grip on the goat's bony back. Joseph Carlo lunged for the pair. He was faintly aware of the hysterical laughter billowing up from behind him.

Joseph Carlo managed to sweep the goat off her feet, wrapping her completely in the sail. He flipped her over deftly, cradling her as one would an infant, her head sticking out. As soon as Joseph Carlo noticed this comparison, the goat made a final *mehhh*, sticking out her pink tongue and sounding like a chastened *bambino*. This struck the collected crew as funnier than anything else and another gale of laughter swept over them. Luca was leaning on Honore's shoulder, who was trying hard to quell his own laughter but he couldn't help the tears running down his cheeks.

Suchet smiled at him as if his face would crack.

This sailing business isn't all bad, Joseph Carlo thought, listening to the men's laughter all around him. *Not bad at all.*

"Brrr." Suchet shivered, and Joseph Carlo scootched closer to him. Four o'clock in the morning, and the boys were back on watch. He scanned the dark water for anything out of the ordinary but saw only the different shades of gray and black undulating under the velvet sky. A glow emanated where the tip of the sickle moon, like the top of an animal's horn, pierced the dark line of the eastern horizon.

"Looks like the stars are about to have some company." Suchet pointed to a piece of moon like a glowing slice of melon pulling itself out of the dark.

As the boys watched, the moon slid up from behind the edge of the world, brightening their surroundings at the same time as it darkened them. The lines and rigging were in stark relief: what the moonlight touched was turned silver, and that which remained in shadow turned even blacker. As the moon rose out of the ocean, it spilled a silver path to the ship. Looking towards their stern, Joseph Carlo could see the dark crevasse of the ship's wake in the bright path of the moon.

"You know," Joseph Carlo said. "I feel the same way about working the decks as you do about navigation. I felt it right after the goat got loose."

"*Stronzo Dos*," Suchet said with a giggle.

"I was sitting with the crew and it just . . . fit. You know?"

"I sure do." Suchet's eyes shone silver in the moonlight. He paused for a few moments, looking towards the bow. "You know, it's going to be fun."

"What is?"

"The future. Running the Mauran fleet, you and me working together."

"Yes, yes it will," Joseph Carlo agreed.

The *Diligencia* sailed through the dark night on her silver course.

Halfway through the morning watch at six o'clock, the moon was a pallid shadow and a mist moved over the sea. At one point, a bird landed on the mast over the boys' heads, oblivious to their presence as they sailed through the gray haze of dawn. Joseph Carlo was body-sore from the unending circle of watches and punishing physical labor. But it was a good tired. He felt as if he needed tiny sticks to hold his eyelids open.

When they could see well enough, Joseph Carlo got up, young muscles groaning from disuse, and the bird at the top of the mast squawked in surprise, taking off. It circled them, as if testing whether the boys were created from its imagination. Joseph Carlo stretched, blood rushing from his fingers and to his toes.

"Come back at breakfast," he hollered as the bird winged away.

"You told him, 'Seppe," Suchet said.

The bells signaling the change of watch pealed, to Joseph Carlo's immense relief. He was a bone-tired thirteen-year-old. Suchet muttered, "*Grazie Dio*," under his breath as they watched the two sailors climbing the ratlines to relieve them.

The rope under Joseph Carlo's hands was wet from the mist as he went down hand over hand. He leaped onto the deck, landing with a thump, and headed for his hammock in the fo'c'sle. Although the hammock was nowhere near as comfortable as his bed at Casa Mauran, Joseph Carlo barely noticed the ripe scent of mold, the rumble of men snoring, or the scratchy rope as he settled himself. The rough ropes felt as soft as a princess's feather bed and his pillow of sail was as forgiving as moss. He was asleep before the hammock's swinging slowed.

He woke to more bells and broad daylight. He lay still a moment, letting awareness seep in. The ship creaked and the waves slapped against the wooden hull. Men moved around, rising for their day's work, and their boots clomped on the hatchway ladder. The hammock next to him was empty, Suchet already gone. Cookie, the ship's culinary expert, was making his way down the narrow ladder to the 'tween deck, his broad bottom moving from side to side and a canvas bucket clutched in one hammy fist.

"Ay there, boy, d'ya want some biscuit?" the large man asked, not in an unfriendly way.

Joseph Carlo swiped at his sleep-crusted eyes and nodded.

"Well, get your *culo* out of the hammock and get moving. Your friend is already at his sextant with the Skipper."

Joseph Carlo untangled himself from the hammock and stood, legs all pins and needles. The heat of the 'tween deck plastered Joseph Carlo's curls to his forehead. He was disheveled and out-of-sorts, and maybe a little grouchy, but he knew better than to take it out on Cookie. To do so would earn the wrath of the only man on board with access to steady nourishment.

Joseph Carlo pulled off the woolen jacket he'd put on the night before, plucking at the sweaty linen shirt underneath.

Cookie dug deep into the canvas bucket and produced a brown round biscuit about the size of his palm. He tossed it over to Joseph Carlo, who caught it one-handed.

Cookie's beefy dark arm once more disappeared into his bucket. "And this to keep you regular." He tossed an orange, the fruit making a vivid arc through the dank below-decks air.

"Thanks," Joseph Carlo said, sticking both offerings in the pockets of his slops.

"Just don't tell Luca about the orange, he might think I'm showing preference, *Capraio*." Cookie winked and grinned at him, showing an ample set of mismatched teeth.

Joseph Carlo grimaced. *Capraio*, he thought. *Goat-lover. Great.*

The atmosphere up on deck was well-ordered hustle and bustle and the sun was halfway to its zenith. It was a brilliant spring day, the sun intense as only the spring sun could be after a winter of lukewarm rays. The wind was strong but warm, pulling up white caps on the waves. The sky was a faded cornflower blue, the high clouds called "mares' tails" scudding along in the upper atmosphere.

After he'd relieved himself off the bow, Joseph Carlo stood blinking for a moment, wiping the sweat-stiff bangs off his forehead. The crew eddied around him on their business, throwing an elbow when he stood in their way. Suchet was somewhere with Honore, plotting the course to Sardinia.

Luca clomped towards Joseph Carlo. Without a word the older man grabbed his sleeve and pulled him across the deck to stand in front of a locker. He nudged it open with the toe of his boot and a hurly-burly of mops and buckets, extra lines, and scrubbing stones was revealed in the dark corner. Luca nudged a mop with the toe of his boot. It fell forward and Joseph Carlo grabbed it with his left hand. Luca hooked the handle of an empty bucket with his boot, swinging it forward and placing it with surprising dexterity at Joseph Carlo's feet.

"Swabbing?" Joseph Carlo asked as he leaned down to pick up the bucket. "Again?"

Luca grinned and walked on. Joseph Carlo scooped up the rest of what he would need and headed to fill a bucket with seawater to rinse off the deck. He leaned over the rail and lowered it by a rope attached to its handle. The sea was a deep teal with the white foamy cat's paws cresting on every other wave. They'd be in Sardinia's harbor by dark. The bucket slapped the surface, floated for a moment as it filled with seawater, and then sank. When it was filled, Joseph Carlo pulled the heavy bucket hand over hand towards the deck. He would do this over and over again in the next few hours.

He was almost done with the forward deck, on his knees with his shirtsleeves rolled up, when a shadow fell over him. He looked up, his wind-dried hair flying stiffly in the breeze like a brand-new sail.

"Morning, *Capraio*," Honore said, grinning like a schoolboy.

Joseph Carlo groaned and turned back to the holystone. His new nickname of "Goat Lover" had stuck.

"Brunito, the crew giving you a nickname is a good sign. It means they trust you. Just as I'd hoped."

"And Suchet?" Joseph Carlo asked, a droplet of sweat rolling down the side of his face.

"He's taken to the navigation like a fish to water."

"No swabbing for him then."

"No," Honore agreed, "but he's not as good swabbing as he is at plotting a course. You should see him, Brunito, he's a natural."

"I bet," Joseph Carlo said tersely, scrubbing the rough stone across the decks as hard as he could.

"Now, Bruni—"

From above came a call, "Sail ho!"

Their heads moved like marionettes attached to the same string. The sailor in the crosstrees was pointing over the starboard rail. Joseph Carlo stood, holystone forgotten at his feet, and squinted in the direction the sailor was pointing. There was a white smudge on the horizon.

"There? Is that it?" he asked his uncle, who had an odd mix of emotion playing over his face. At his nephew's questions, he marshaled his face into a mask of authority again.

"Yes. And what it's doing in our small neighborhood, I've no idea."

"Who is it?"

"Antonio will tell us more in a moment." Honore glanced at the sailor above focusing his spyglass on the white square flickering in and out of view. "But I can tell you that she's big, bigger than us. Hopefully not a warship."

"Isn't the war over?"

"It's never really over, *nipote*, not really. But don't worry, I'm sure she'll pass us by. Back to your task."

With that, Honore turned on his boot heel and walked back to his cabin, all the while staring over his shoulder at the tiny sail.

Joseph Carlo turned back to his job and forgot all about the small white scrap that would soon become a very big problem.

By midway through the fore-noon watch the sail was bigger. Everyone went about their duties, but with half of their attention focused off the starboard rail. Joseph Carlo had finished with the deck and was assigned to help the sailmaker, Sergio. He hunkered down by the older man's knee, learning the best way to worm, parcel, and serve a rope.

Over the next few hours, the crew's preoccupation with the mystery ship grew as did the frequency with which they glanced at the ever-growing sail. Every time Joseph Carlo looked up, the sail was bigger. Soon it became clear that they were only seeing the top royals of a much larger ship. The angle of the sails showed that the two ships were on converging courses, the *Diligencia* towards the reddened rough rocks of Sardinia and the other ship hopefully bound for Sicily. The wind had strengthened, playfully kicking up white caps on the tops of the waves.

At first Honore seemed intrigued yet calm, only looking at the sail once every few minutes. He'd brought Suchet out of his quarters, and the boy stood at the rail with a spyglass trained on the swelling sail. Joseph Carlo visited Suchet once at the rail, much to Sergio's chagrin, but what could he say to the little lordling? Joseph Carlo and Suchet stood side by side, eyes on the bluish-white square.

"He told me to let him know if anything changes." Suchet turned towards his cousin. "She's getting bigger. That's a change, right? Should I tell him she's getting bigger?"

"Suchet!" A sharp call came from the quarterdeck. Suchet whipped back towards the ocean, lifting the spyglass to his eye again. Honore stood at the rail, his face stern. He met Joseph Carlo's eye and jerked his head, wordlessly telling his nephew to get back to work.

Joseph Carlo made his way back to Sergio, noting the hour-glass that kept track of the watches on his way. It was almost the change of watch. Peals rang across the deck and for a moment, no one did a thing, contrary to the usual tumult of a watch change. The sail had hypnotized them all, turning them into stone like Medusa's stare.

The sailor aloft was about to head down, his replacement climbing up to relieve him, when he jerked the glass to his eye again. His body tensed as he leaned out, as if trying to get closer to the ship.

"Captain!" he hollered, his glass still trained on the ship.

Honore came to the edge of the quarterdeck, and the hands that gripped the rail were instantly white from pressure.

"*Que?*" he called up to the crosstrees.

"She's changed course!" the sailor yelled back, lowering the glass. The bluish smudges on the canvas had changed, the shadows now making the sails seem triangular instead of square. The ship had changed course, but in which direction, it was hard to tell.

"She's changed course!" the sailor repeated. "And she's making straight for us!"

Chapter Ten

EVERYONE IN THE WAIST OF THE SHIP FROZE. HONORE'S FACE registered a fleeting moment of fury, and then a still and deadly determination.

"Luca!"

The first mate trotted to stand at the ready below the quarterdeck rail. "We need to make full sail," Honore yelled at them. "We're going to outrun her. All hands! Every inch of canvas you've got! Bend on!"

Luca nodded and turned on his heel, belting out orders to every quarter. Joseph Carlo joined his uncle on the rail, and this time Honore did not indicate that he should go back to work with Sergio.

Honore looked at his nephew and what Joseph Carlo saw in his uncle's eyes frightened him. They were hard and glittery and very determined. He was hell-bent on outrunning that ship, despite the slim odds. The dark wooden hull and many sails of their pursuer became clearer and clearer as she bore down on them with every passing minute.

Honore sent all hands aloft to loose the gaskets on every sail: mizzen, main, and staysails. Joseph Carlo and Suchet climbed higher than ever before, and from that vantage point, legs balanced on the braces and arms slung over the yards, the stretch of water unrolled before them. The sea was the blue of a robin's egg in spring, a vivid surprise in the bottom of a nest. Then there was that ship with its dark hull and white sails, chasing them down, making to intercept the *Diligencia*. Its large frame cut through the ocean with the ease of a spoon slicing through *panna cotta*.

Joseph Carlo worked at the gaskets, loosening the sails with the same urgency he could feel from the rest of the crew. As more sails dropped and filled with wind, Honore drove them even faster, bellowing orders to Luca and the crew, not allowing a moment's rest. Every line stretched; every sail filled; every wire was like a too-tight guitar string, humming a high-pitched siren's song. The boat lunged through the waves towards the safety of red-rocked Sardinia. Honore switched his gaze from the approaching ship, to Sardinia, then back to the ship again.

From the crosstrees Joseph Carlo thought he could see the distance between the two ships widening. When he turned to look at the coast of Sardinia, he could now make out the depression in the sienna-colored rocks that was the mouth of the harbor. They were going to make it. They were outrunning her. As soon as they reached the island, they'd tuck into the harbor and the safety of the familiar town. But would they reach it in time?

"Honore's going to outrun her," Suchet said, skinny arms thrown over the yard and the brisk breeze blowing back his dark hair. "Once we make Sardinia, that ship will either turn back, if her captain's wise, or they'll deal with *la famiglia*."

A smile bloomed on Joseph Carlo's face as he imagined Suchet's diminutive yet terrifying mother standing at the end of the quay in Cagliari, shaking her finger at the ship.

After a few moments, Joseph Carlo looked again at their pursuers, and it did seem as if the *Diligencia* was getting away. Their wake fanned out behind them like a scar tipped with white sea foam, leaving the mystery ship behind.

"She wants something from us." Suchet's owlish gaze swung to Joseph Carlo. "I don't know what, but she wants something."

They stood side by side, elbows touching, and watched the dark ship falling behind even as it persisted in its unwavering course for the *Diligencia*.

For the first hour after the change of course, the *Diligencia* maintained a modicum of routine. After every sail on the small working ship had been loosened and trimmed for the most power. Luca positioned Joseph Carlo close to Sergio for the old man to keep an eye on him. Suchet was once again at the rail, spyglass trained on the ship, as was the sailor's glass above. The sailor stationed aloft, Marco, was an excitable sort, and yelled down updates every few minutes.

Honore paced the main deck, sailors scuttling out of his way as he wound round and round the masts. As he passed by Joseph Carlo hauling on one of the many lines running to the filled sails, Honore muttered, "*Chi cerca mal, mal trova.*" He who looks for evil, will find evil. A shudder went through the boy as his uncle passed by.

"S'all right, boy," Sergio said, eyes trained on the masthead fly, the flag that showed wind direction. "Yer uncle will steer us clear, always does."

The old man's words softened the dread lumped in Joseph Carlo's throat. But the lump returned when Marco called again from above. He could finally discern the nationality of the vessel by the colors she was flying. "She's an English man-o-war, sir!"

At this proclamation Honore set his jaw, adjusted his hat, and resumed his revolutions around the masts.

A cold sweat crept up the back of Joseph Carlo's neck. Sergio was hauling in on the forejib line, muttering too. But unlike Honore, Sergio was praying.

The wind from off the starboard quarter chilled Joseph Carlo's sweaty skin as he worked the constant pull and give of the lines. The *Diligencia* was at her hull speed, the absolute fastest she could manage. The stout loyal vessel trembled under the pressure of running all out. Any more and she would shake herself to pieces.

Despite the *Diligencia*'s brave attempt, the other ship was now closer. Perhaps it was a trick of the light, but it looked like she'd gained on them.

Honore noticed too. "Make smartly, lads! Signore Luca, drive her. Wring every knot of speed out of her." And Luca obeyed, pushing the sturdy barque through the wind, grinding the crew with orders to adjust the yards by even an inch.

The ship on their tail had more sails and she had put out every bit of canvas as well. There was no question, the larger ship was gaining. But Sergio, Honore, and the rest of them had been sailing this small sea all their lives and had seen war and worse. They weren't frightened, not yet. There still was a good chance that the *Diligencia* would duck into the mouth of Cagliari's harbor before the bigger ship came into hailing distance. Yet every passing moment and the black nuisance was that much closer.

At midday, the crew still pushed the barque as hard as she would go. Each man was engaged at his station with unwavering attention. It was a race against time; the larger ship had seen the *Diligencia*'s efforts to escape and had doubled her own, all her canvas in the wind. More sails equaled more speed. And it was working: the larger ship was closer.

Although Honore's crew was hell-bent on outrunning her, with an unlimited stretch of ocean before her, the *Diligencia* would be overtaken. But they weren't racing across the open sea; they'd almost reached the harbor. They could see the high white cliffs that marked the entrance. Cagliari had been a safe haven and accessible as far back as the Phoenicians; perhaps it could be again for the *Diligencia*. They just needed a little more time.

Honore still bellowed out orders—a line to be adjusted or a sail to be tended to—his voice hoarse from the stress, but his pains had been worth it. In another half-watch, the *Diligencia* would tack and reach the rest of the way into the Sardinian harbor. An eerie silence had descended on the crew, none of the usual ribbing or singing that went with the workaday routine. Even the ship herself seemed to be watching. Under full sail through the sapphire waters, she hummed under the strain. But the larger ship was still overtaking her, inch by nautical inch.

The men brought out their lunch rations and munched as they could, still attentive to their captain's orders. This was the home stretch; it wouldn't do to falter now. Joseph Carlo peeled his orange, flipping the rind into the ocean and watching the bright orange remnants bob in their wake. He mounted the quarterdeck, expecting a sharp rebuke from Honore, but there wasn't one. As he passed his uncle, he overheard the muttered conversation between him and Luca.

"That's as much as we can do, Captain."

"We've got all the canvas we can carry, Luca. The Brit's just faster."

"What do you think she wants?" Luca said, his eyes slits.

"I don't know. But whatever it is, it can't be good." Honore glanced at Joseph Carlo as the boy passed, seeing him but not seeing him. "Whatever it is, she's not going to get it."

Joseph Carlo joined Suchet and his spyglass at the rail, handing over half the orange.

"Thanks, 'Seppe," Suchet said, taking it. He shoved his half of the orange into his mouth and raised the spyglass to his eye again.

"See anything new?" Joseph Carlo asked, separating the segments and eating them one by one.

"Just her, getting bigger and bigger," he mumbled around a mouthful of orange as he handed over the spyglass. "Here."

Joseph Carlo lifted it to his eye and the large ship jumped closer. She was twice the size of the *Diligencia*. The Union Jack streamed from her mast as well as a series of code flags that Joseph Carlo couldn't read. And then he saw her crew. All of them, lining the deck, hanging off the ratlines, crowding the crosstrees and tops. There were hundreds of English sailors on the ship, all staring hungrily at the *Diligencia*. Some of them had guns. One man in particular, a dark brooding sort at the top of the mizzen mast, held a long musket slung across his chest. Through the spyglass, Joseph Carlo saw the man's fingers stroke the long stock. A chill raced up his spine.

As Joseph Carlo studied the crew, a hail came down from the sailor aloft. Suchet held out his hand for the spyglass, which Joseph Carlo reluctantly handed over. "What did he say?"

Suchet had the spyglass aimed at the other ship again, pointed high in the rigging for the code flags, which would tell them what the bloody British ship wanted.

"They want us to heave-to."

Heaving-to was a maneuver in which a fast-moving ship was brought to a standstill. The only reasons to heave-to were to ride out a storm or to stop because of a hostile ship's orders, as it was in this case.

"Heave-to? Why?"

Suchet lowered the spyglass, revealing his pale face, "To board us," he said, "or blow us up."

Luca and Honore were deep in conversation about whether or not to comply when Joseph Carlo felt Suchet tense up all at once, like he was about to spring up and over the rail.

"Tizio!" he shouted, his spyglass still pointed out to sea. "Tizio! She's going to fire!"

On the man-o-war, a puff of smoke appeared at the end of a bowchaser, a cannon that stuck out from the bow. The man aloft yelled, "Shot!" and pointed, moving his arm in an arc. The shot landed well in the water; they were going too fast to see the splash.

"Captain, they're firing at us again!" came the shout from above.

"Marco, which guns are out?" Honore asked.

"Too many!!" Marco replied, real fear in his voice.

Sure enough, the mystery ship's gundeck ports were all open and the black soulless cannons revealed. Smoke drifted from the port bowchaser. The men on deck were no longer watching the Italian boat but were scurrying around like ants, preparing. But preparing for what?

"What are they doing?" Joseph Carlo asked his cousin, but he thought he knew. The bowchaser on the foredeck was being filled with shot and gunpowder to have a spark put to its fuse.

"They're going to blast a hole in our hull," Suchet whispered, "unless we heave-to right now."

The bowchaser was aimed directly at them. Smoke puffed from its snout and a whistling object whizzed over the waist of the *Diligencia*. There was a splash on the other side of the ship where the shot landed. It had missed but just barely.

All hands turned towards the captain. Luca was staring at him, old weathered hands gripping a line, as was every single man on deck.

"*Capitan?*" Suchet hollered, not using *Tizio* or Honore, but the man's formal title.

Honore didn't respond; he was grim and tight-lipped.

"*Capitan!*" Suchet shouted again, louder.

Honore turned to look at the mouth of the Sardinian harbor, so close but oceans away for all the good it did them.

"*Basta!*" He cried as another cannon pushed its way out of the other ship's hull to join the long row of deadly weapons. "Heave-to!" he ordered, and the men jumped to comply.

"What're we doing?" Joseph Carlo asked.

Suchet's eyes were even larger than normal. "We're going to let them board us."

Chapter Eleven

As soon as Honore gave the order to bring her into the wind, the crew spun into furious yet orchestrated motion. Luca dropped the line he'd been gripping and vaulted off the quarterdeck, bawling orders the whole way. Although heaving-to was straightforward in theory, in practice it was a complicated maneuver that required training and skill on the part of the whole crew.

The lads in the upper yards clewed up the upper square sails and the fore course and main sail, shortening and shifting them to slow the ship down. Next, they backed the fore topsail but kept the main topsail full so the wind pushed the ship in two opposite directions. Grudgingly the *Diligencia* lost speed. She'd been barreling along and plainly did not want to slow. As the crew played with lines leading to sails both fore and aft, the ship began to shudder. The topsails flapped in the wind and the *Diligencia* slowed until she was no longer humming.

"That's it, lads!" Luca hollered. "Lower and hand in the fore jib!"

Honore yelled commands at Luca, who relayed them to the crew. The men moved so quickly it was hard to keep track of who was going where.

The *Diligencia* jerked along as she ceased slicing through the oncoming waves and began to slap them. The less-than-smooth progress was hard on the crew as well: the lines they were trying to haul in or ease out jerked unwillingly in their hands. Grumbles echoed from every quarter, not loud enough for the captain to hear but loud enough to reach the boys' ears. The lads did not want to heave-to *at all*. The back-winded sails began to push them backwards, an unnatural feeling.

Joseph Carlo and Suchet went to Luca for direction. He threw them a glance, his eyes as dark as the ship bearing down on them, looming like a cliff of wood and sail.

"When they board us," Luca instructed as a line whipped by his head. "Captain wants you out of view. *Feccia!*" He shook his fist at the English ship. With that he gave Joseph Carlo a push; the boy stumbled over his feet and collapsed on a barrel that was up against the quarterdeck. He tucked in behind it, and Suchet wedged himself into the small space a moment later. The corner of a crate of lemons jabbed Joseph Carlo in the ribs as his cousin shifted for more room.

With creaks and groans of protesting wood, the *Diligencia* became the only still thing on the ocean. The clouds scudded above and the sea heaved below, but the *Diligencia* bobbed like a cork. After the initial heave-to maneuver, there was nothing more for the crew to do but wait. Honore joined his men on the main deck as the other ship came into sharp definition. Its bowsprit pointed right at them as the behemoth grew so large that its white sails and black hull blocked out the bright Mediterranean sky. An eerie silence fell over the *Diligencia*, punctuated by the watch's updates.

"Captain, she's a fifty gunner!" the sailor reported down.

"That means she's got fifty guns on board," whispered Suchet to Joseph Carlo as they crouched between the barrel and a box of lemons.

Despite his growing terror, Joseph Carlo gave his cousin a withering eyeroll. Suchet didn't notice.

"She's probably a fourth-rate ship of the line." Suchet looked frightened, but also intensely interested.

The English ship, identified as the *Deptford* by the man in the crosstrees, came abreast of their barque and hove-to herself. Now the two boats were parallel to one another, rising and falling with the waves. The *Deptford* crew lowered a longboat and eight men rowed towards them on the ocean swell, one minute invisible from view and the next cresting the same wave that had hidden it. The white of the sailors' shirts stood out under their dark blue jackets. Indeed, they looked very English, especially the one standing in the stern with a tri-corn hat settled on his head. The sunlight flashed off the oars' wet blades as they surfaced. Although the longboat was intimidating, it wasn't as threatening as the broadside of the ship with the line of black soulless cannons.

At the rail, Honore leaned towards his first mate, whispering. Luca nodded and headed for the captain's quarters, returning a moment later with a sheaf of papers clutched in his hand. Luca tugged at his jacket, pulling it over the bulge at his hip.

"Those papers, they're Letters of Marque from the King of Sardinia granting any vessel under our uncle's command safe passage," Suchet whispered to his cousin hunkered next to him.

"Will the Letters make them leave us alone?"

"I don't know, 'Seppe. I don't know."

The longboat was soon eclipsed by the *Diligencia*'s rail. A few minutes later, a voice hailed them in English from the waters below and a sailor threw a rope ladder over the starboard quarter. The minutes stretched out as the whole ship waited, and then, all at once, there they were: two English sailors and an English second lieutenant. The lieutenant was tall with ginger-colored sideburns that disappeared under the black hat he wore battened down on his forehead. The man's compatriots were muscled and brown-haired: one had a sallow weasel-y complexion, generously stippled with pock-mark scars; the other had a wide jug of a face, cheeks reddened and roughened by life at sea and a nasty crooked scar threading up the side of his face, ending at the corner of his left eye, the white of which was blood red.

Honore stepped forward with Luca at his elbow. "*Benvenuto.* I welcome you to the *Diligencia*," he said in Italian.

The lieutenant said something in clipped guttural English. Joseph Carlo looked at Suchet, who understood the language a little, for a translation.

"The Englishman told Tizio to speak only English."

What followed was a brief but intense conversation between the newcomer and their uncle. A translation wasn't needed as the body language of the two men, tenser and tenser, plainly told the story. Honore brandished the papers under the man's nose and the Englishman snatched them up, his skin reddened with irritation. He scanned the letters and then let his gaze wander over the crew arranged behind the captain and first mate. The icy gaze glanced off Suchet and Joseph Carlo then moved on, only to snap back to them a moment later.

The Englishman held out the papers, shaking his head. Honore grabbed them, brandishing them under the man's nose. The Englishman bore this with dignity, although his skin continued to flush as Honore's voice grew louder and louder.

"Tizio is trying to convince the English that the *Diligencia* is a friendly and cannot be boarded or detained. The English doesn't seem to care," Suchet whispered.

"What does that mean?"

"It means they can take anything they want from us. Hopefully they won't blow us up."

"What?! Why would they do that?"

Suchet did not look surprised. "Because they're English and because they can."

Honore ceased his tirade but still held out the sheaf of papers. The breeze ruffled them, showing the mark of the King in red wax on one of the pages. Now it was the lieutenant's turn to speak. He didn't raise his voice, but the more he spoke, the more Honore's head shook back and forth. Beside him, Luca was as tense as a coiled spring, one hand under his jacket.

The unflappable second lieutenant stepped towards Honore, still speaking. Honore stood his ground, staring the English down. The two other sailors stepped up as well, Pock Mark grinning like a satyr. Honore lowered the papers until they were clutched by his side.

"Can you understand him?" Joseph Carlo asked Suchet.

Suchet shook his head. "No, I can't."

At that moment the Englishman's hand came up and his pointer finger shot right at the boys' hiding place. Honore turned and followed the finger's trajectory, his eyes widening in horror when he spotted the two boys amid the boxes and barrels. Scar Face walked over until his bulk blocked out the sun. The sun caught the side of his face and illuminated the ruddy orb that was his eye as he bent down to pick up the wooden crate of lemons to the boys' right. When Scar Face turned back towards the rail, there was Pock Mark, staring greedily at the boys. He said something in English.

"What's he saying, Gufo?"

The sailor jerked his chin up, indicating that he wanted them to stand.

Maybe there's another box of lemons behind us? Joseph Carlo looked over his shoulder as he gained his feet. That was when Pock Mark grabbed both of his wrists in one huge hand and yanked. Then he grabbed Suchet by the collar. Suchet squeaked in terror.

"Wha—?" Joseph Carlo started but the man cut him off by wrenching them towards the lieutenant at the rail, one boy in each hand. The other sailor was attaching the box of lemons to a bridle to lower it into the longboat.

"Tizio?" Joseph Carlo asked in a voice two octaves higher than normal. Honore's usually ruddy face was pale. There was a collective gasp from the crew as they began to understand what the English wanted.

The boys. The Englishman wanted the boys.

Joseph Carlo did not need a translation for what came next. Honore let out a stream of Italian invectives, interspersed with many "no"s. The lieutenant did not even seem to hear him, but continued instructing his two grunts. Pock Mark pulled the two boys over to the rail with the rope ladder as Honore's voice rose to a fever-pitch. Luca pulled the pistol that he'd been hiding under his jacket, but not fast enough. Quick as a comet, the lieutenant drew his own pistol, and pointed it directly at Honore's forehead. At the appearance of the gun, Honore's onslaught of blasphemy ceased. The lieutenant then spoke clearly and calmly, raising his voice so the whole crew could hear him.

"He says he will take two boys and a box of lemons," Suchet translated in a whisper. "Oh *cugino*, that's us! He says he will take these things or he will kill Tizio and then blow us to smithereens. He says he will kill everyone if Tizio refuses!"

In Joseph Carlo's mind, everything stood still, but in reality, it was he who'd frozen; his mind had stopped in shock. It was as if the English had already fired the gun and the echoing ring of it blocked everything else out. Pock Mark swung the box of lemons out into the space beyond the rail and began to lower it to the waiting longboat. Honore stood with the Letters of Marque a forgotten wad in one fist. Luca lowered his pistol, his lips working, his eyes pinned on the boys.

"Tizio!" Joseph Carlo sounded young even to himself. "Tizio, help us!"

Honore turned to his nephews. Suchet was whining like a kicked dog as Pock Mark forced him up and over the rail, one hand on his collar and one on his belt. Pock Mark slapped his hammy palm on top of Suchet's head and pushed. The boy climbed down and out of view. The lieutenant took no notice of the goings-on behind him but kept the nose of the gun aimed at their uncle's head. Pock Mark grabbed Joseph Carlo, who stood frozen behind him. The boy cried out; he couldn't help it. The sailor gave him a shake, his hard hand like a manacle on Joseph Carlo's neck. A call came from the longboat and Pock Mark man-handled Joseph Carlo up and over the rail, an evil grin on his face.

"Brunito!" Honore cried, taking an unguarded step forward. The lieutenant tisked, leveling the pistol until the muzzle was pressed against Honore's sweaty brow.

Joseph Carlo began to climb down the rope ladder on shaky legs. He caught a last glimpse of the stunned, frightened faces of the crew, Honore's front and foremost, and then they were gone. When he reached the longboat, a sailor pushed him to the floor where Suchet was already curled in on himself. All was still for a few minutes while the lieutenant, Pock Mark, and Scar Face made their way down the rope ladder and settled themselves. Then they were pulling away from the *Diligencia*, away from their family and everything they'd ever known.

Chapter Twelve

THE BOTTOM OF THE LONGBOAT WAS ROUGH AGAINST JOSEPH Carlo's cheek. His hands were jammed up by his collarbones and his legs were pinned by the box of lemons. His face was inches from Suchet's, and his cousin trembled all over, his face the color of candle tallow. When Joseph Carlo craned his head, he saw the sailors rowing, their bulging back muscles moving like snakes under their loose white shirts. The ginger-haired lieutenant was standing in the stern, making the bow ride high in the water and the craft more tender than usual—more liable to tip over.

The sun-washed blue of the Mediterranean sky framed the rowers as the boat surged over the waves in rhythm with the splash of the oars hitting the water and the creak of the oarlocks. Joseph Carlo strained to hear shouts or instructions, anything from the *Diligencia*, but there was nothing. He was puzzled until he remembered the snouts of the cannons pointed in the *Diligencia*'s direction, ready to punch holes in her hull and sink her at a moment's notice. They weren't out of danger yet. When their uncle could finally get underway again, would it be too late?

Suchet's trembling grew more frantic until his whole body spasmed. Joseph Carlo tried to calm him in hurried Italian. "*Calmati, cugino.* Tizio will come get us soon."

Suchet nodded, his face had taken on a particular chartreuse sheen. *Uh oh*, Joseph Carlo thought. Suchet was a puker, and he looked close to throwing up now. "And then, Tizio will blow these *idiotas* out of the water with—"

A painful kick to his ribs stopped Joseph Carlo's words with a *whuff.* The lieutenant's shadow fell across him as he tried to inhale with a painful whine.

"*Sta 'zitto,*" the man said in clear, accented Italian. "Shut up."

Joseph Carlo pulled in another painful breath, feeling his ribs. He waited until the man looked away and then glanced at Suchet again, noting his cousin's worsening pallor. With Suchet's panicky gaze pinned on him, Joseph Carlo just nodded, despite the ache in his side, hoping his cousin wouldn't barf all over the bottom of the longboat.

In what was probably a few minutes but seemed like an hour, a shadow fell over the boat as the English man-o-war towered over them, her dark wooden hull stretching up. It was taller than the lighthouse, taller than the tower at the old fort. It was the biggest thing he'd ever seen. At that moment, Joseph Carlo felt a jerk next to him and Suchet lurched to his knees. His face looked coated in yellow candle wax. He was going to throw up.

Oh no, Joseph Carlo thought as Suchet lunged for the rail. But he didn't get there in time, his head didn't quite make it over the gunwale when, all of a sudden with a horrible *glurk*, Suchet voided his stomach's unlovely contents all over the lieutenant's dark blue pants. Everyone froze, staring at the lieutenant's pants. From above came a snicker from an unknown sailor, hastily shushed. An angry red crept out of the lieutenant's collar and up his neck. When he jerked his head up to glare at Suchet, his eyes sizzled with hatred.

The officer said something deadly menacing to the boys in English as he twitched a pant leg with pinched fingers, trying to get some of the mess off. The sailor in the bow passed up the painter to secure the boat sideways against the ship as Joseph Carlo propelled Suchet away from the furious, vomit-covered lieutenant.

More shouts from above. Scar Face grabbed Suchet and pushed him towards a rope ladder leading up the man-of-war's black hull. Somehow, Suchet's hands found the ladder and he climbed. Joseph Carlo shot one more panicked look at the lieutenant, who had his hand hovering over a pistol at his belt as if deciding whether to shoot the boys on the spot, before Scar Face grabbed him by the armpit, wrenching him towards the rope ladder. The ladder shook in his grip as he climbed the side of the mammoth ship, one hand at a time. To his right and his left were the cannons, noses aimed at the *Diligencia*, barrels heavy and deadly-looking. He was only fifteen feet away from the many hands reaching out for him. He was terrified.

Soon those hands found purchase on Joseph Carlo's shirt, yanking him up. He went over the rail like a landed fish as shouts erupted from the crew. He was jostled to his feet, and all around him a blur of faces spoke rapid English as they pushed him into the waiting arms of an older sailor missing a left ear whose breath smelled like death. The old man ripped off Joseph Carlo's shirt, exposing him to the brisk breeze. Goose pimples stippled the boy's skin and a coarse brush ground caustic powder into his shoulders, turning the goose flesh into raw welts. Icy water bit his skin and the fumes from the powder stung Joseph Carlo's eyes. He heard a shout erupt from Suchet somewhere nearby.

"*Gufo?*" he asked, shoulders hunched.

"*Si, cugino,*" Suchet answered from behind.

Another bucket of seawater was dashed across Joseph Carlo's shoulders and with that, One Ear pushed him into a giant sailor with a pile of folded clothing. The purser, all stomach and beard, eyed the boy. He raised one finger in the classic "aha!" gesture and dug into the pile of white and brown fabric at his side. He thrust the clothes at Joseph Carlo, who hugged them to his shivering chest. The purser gave Joseph Carlo his endearing smile again as well as a sea bag and then shunted him aside.

Joseph Carlo looked frantically for the angry lieutenant and caught sight of the dark blue of his jacket and the copper of his hair behind a knot of cheering sailors and the box of lemons, headed towards the officer's quarters. He wondered what the furious officer would do to Suchet for decorating him with his breakfast.

Suchet shrieked in protest from beside him and Joseph Carlo whirled around. Suchet and One Ear were face to face, Suchet terrified but determined and the old man's face slathered in a greedy expression. They had their fists wrapped around something between them just below Suchet's nose. A small golden chain fed from the boy's clenched fist to thread around his neck. It was the Mauran Medallion and One Ear wanted it. Suchet yanked at the necklace in the hopes of loosening the old man's grip, but to no avail.

Just as Joseph Carlo was about to step in, a broad-shouldered man with a spill of black hair shouldered his way through the sea of brown and white shirts. The way that the sailors opened a path in front of him spoke of his status. A long black musket was slung over his back, the stock peeking over his shoulder. One Ear looked up at the man with the musket and began to speak defensively, yammering away like an angry bird. The man nodded until the old man had run out of steam. Then, with a swift movement, he pried the medallion free from the old man's fingers. Suchet jerked backwards, a hurt look on his face, and tucked the necklace into the safety of his shirt.

One Ear was indignant. He shoved his freed fist into the taller man's face and shook a wizened finger. The sharpshooter listened with the same calm expression. The older sailor seemed as if he was just getting started when a piercing whistle broke through his impassioned protestation. All the sailors rushed about in a mad scuffle until every toe touched the same line painted down the length of the deck. Shoulders were pulled back, hats doffed, and eyes pointed straight ahead. Someone man-handled Joseph Carlo into line with the others, Suchet two men down from him. When

Joseph Carlo stepped over the line to see where the dark-haired man had gone, he was yanked back until he stood abreast with the rest of them, like cattle awaiting branding. His shoulders still burned from the powder.

Another whistle and a called order made the men on either side of Joseph Carlo tense up. Making his way towards them was the captain and behind him was the furious lieutenant, pants still liberally smeared with Suchet's vomit. The bo'sun called out and the men pulled their shoulders back even further. As the captain stalked in front of his crew, they saluted him one by one, fists to foreheads. The lieutenant followed in his wake, and Joseph Carlo saw grimaces crease the sailors' faces as they smelled him coming. A snicker floated up and was quickly stifled when the lieutenant jerked his head around to glare at the unknown perpetrator.

The captain stopped halfway down the line, and looked out to sea. He had a long hooked nose and ruddy cheeks crested with white hair from his mutton-chop sideburns. His straight black brows topped eyes that brooked no nonsense. At his elbow was the ginger-haired lieutenant with a beet-red face. The captain turned a fraction towards the lieutenant and sniffed, keeping his gaze pinned on the ocean. The lieutenant sketched a salute, ignoring the look of disgust on his captain's face, and began speaking. The older man's gaze shifted towards the two boys, who squirmed under its cold intensity. Some of the officers leaned forward to get a better look at the boys.

When the lieutenant finished, the captain stepped towards Joseph Carlo, who pulled his own shoulders back. The sailor to his left jammed the sharpest elbow he'd ever felt into his ribs. Joseph Carlo grimaced and moved a step away, but the sailor just dug the elbow harder into Joseph Carlo's side. He suddenly understood and brought his fist to his forehead. The captain nodded, satisfied, and his voluminous white wig swayed with the movement. He then launched into a long preamble directed at the two Italian boys. At times he spoke to a midshipman with an unruly rat's nest of bright red hair. The captain's speech seemed to be of great importance and Joseph Carlo understood exactly none of it. At a certain point, the red-headed midshipman snapped a salute, crying out, "Yes sir," which Joseph Carlo understood just fine.

The captain then pointed his speech back to Suchet and Joseph Carlo and his voice rose to a resonant boom. The lieutenant stood in his stinky pants, a look of incredulity replacing the rage on his face. With one last unintelligible directive for the two new members of his crew, the captain spun on his boot heel and headed back to the quarterdeck with encouraging cries from his crew following in his wake. The lieutenant trailed after him, firing a death look their way as he passed, the nauseating smell of vomit trailing after him.

"What?" Joseph Carlo yelled in Italian to no one in particular as the group broke up. "*Che cossa?* What did he just say?"

The red-headed midshipman turned to him with a wicked grin and replied in perfect Italian, "He said, 'Welcome to the British Navy.'"

Chapter Thirteen

The last coherent thought Joseph Carlo had while watching the *Deptford*'s sails fill with wind and pull away from the still-stopped *Diligencia*, his uncle and crew lining the rail, was, *We're never going to see her again.* He meant the *Diligencia* and Villa Franca, but most of all, he meant Lena. No one waved on the *Diligencia*, they just stared. Joseph Carlo watched the *Diligencia* shrink to the size of a child's toy on the deep blue of the Mediterranean as the *Deptford* returned to her course.

He wasn't given much time to watch the last of his childhood disappear from view because, all of a sudden, the red-headed midshipman appeared in front of him, Suchet just behind his shoulder. Joseph Carlo pulled his gaze away from the *Diligencia* and stared at the boy in front of him.

On closer scrutiny, Joseph Carlo didn't think he *was* a boy. Although he was a full head shorter than Joseph Carlo, he carried an air of maturity that indicated he was merely small for his age. His pointed chin and slanted blue eyes gave him an impish air while the thatch of red hair and smattering of freckles sprinkled over the bridge of his nose suggested someone young. His smirk, a slight lifting of the left side of his mouth, seemed to be his face's permanent resting expression. Joseph Carlo took this all in and then shifted his attention back to his family's ship growing ever smaller on the horizon off the *Deptford*'s stern. The midshipman caught the wistful glance and gave Joseph Carlo a look of sympathy.

"I'm Tomaso, *paisan*," he said in perfect Italian, "and Captain Hollwell has given me the distinct pleasure of training you boys up. Do you speak any English at all?"

Joseph Carlo shook his head, eyes still pinned on the small ship bobbing like a bath toy in their wake.

"Does he speak at all?" Tomaso asked Suchet, half-teasing. Suchet shrugged and looked at his feet. Tomaso sighed.

"I'm going to be honest with you boys, this will be hard on you. What are you, aristocrats?" He grabbed Suchet's hand. "Soft and perfumed, as I thought." His smirk widened into a downright grin at the boys' irritation. "C'mon, get off the line, you need to see the rest of the ship." And away he went, both boys numbly following him.

Tomaso kept up his narrative as he showed them around their new home (the fact that he kept calling the ship "their new home" did nothing to improve the boys' outlooks), filling them in on shipboard life as well as his own personal history. The ship spanned the deck under their feet to three more below them. Above them was a spider's web of lines and yards, with men stationed at different points like well-trained birds in a very large tree. Some of the other sailors had been unwillingly pressed into service, like Joseph Carlo and Suchet. Some, like Tomaso, had joined up, and others, such as the captain and the officers, were career Navy.

Tomaso had inherited his excellent and fluent Italian from his mother, a Venetian beauty with a superb singing voice. Tomaso had her slanted eyes, although hers were green not blue; they'd earned her the nickname *Canto Gatto*, singing cat. She'd married a Scottish laird, hence Tomaso's odd name: Tomaso McDougall. His father had also begrudgingly gifted Tomaso with his English and a stout hatred of the old man. Since Tomaso's mother had died, the dour Scotsman had been left alone in his falling-down castle with only his drink for company. His drink and Tomaso, or at least until Tomaso had had enough. His father had surfaced from his drunken stupor long enough to buy his youngest son a midshipman's position in the Royal Navy. That done, he'd once again submerged himself in Highland whiskey, and Tomaso left him to it.

Three years later and Tomaso was steadily and surely climbing the naval ladder.

"You see, boys," Tomaso told them while picking his way through the claustrophobic space of the 'tween deck, "the Royal Navy is the one place a man like me can make it on me own." He stood before them, hands on his hips, the perfect product of his parents. He could either break into a glorious Italian aria or a stream of blasphemy in a Scottish brogue.

The ship was huge compared to the *Diligencia*. It was like living in a small town all one's life and suddenly being plunked down in the middle of a large city. A city made up of three hundred common sailors and their officers. There were men everywhere, men and lines. And everyone was at work, which the boys would soon find out was the state of affairs on board the *Deptford*. You were either working or sleeping, and if you weren't doing either of those, you were whacking the weevils out of your biscuit or pouring grog down your throat. There was not a lot of leisure time.

The boys would be ship rats, Tomaso informed them as he stopped by the pen of chickens, a pig, and two goats. (Joseph Carlo's heart ached when he saw the goat. What he wouldn't give to be running after Stronzo Dos right now.) When they went into battle, the boys would be powder monkeys, Tomaso told them as they made their way to the gun deck.

Suchet spoke up for the first time since the dark-haired man had rescued his medallion. "Powder monkey?" he asked as they ducked through a hatchway. The gun deck was dark and smelled of gunpowder and oil, which kept the guns running in and out of the ports smoothly. Between the time Joseph Carlo had climbed up the side of *Deptford* until now, the guns had been pulled back into the belly of the ship and the gun ports closed. They headed towards the fore hatch that spilled a shaft of brilliant sunlight through the dust motes.

"You get the gunpowder to the cannons," Tomaso answered as he patted one of the large black cannons as one would thump the family dog affectionately on the rump. "All right, me foine fellows, first things first, you'll have to learn English. That is, if you want to avoid being flogged or keel-hauled."

Joseph Carlo's stomach dropped. On top of everything else, they were going to have to learn a new language to avoid being tied up, thrown overboard, and dragged through the barnacles on the bottom of the ship: *keel-hauled*. Great. The lucky keel-haul victims sank just enough when they hit the water to avoid being sliced to ribbons by the razor-like crustaceans underneath. Of course, they also drowned, but it was better than having your skin mutilated by crustaceans and *then* drowning.

Tomaso started up the wooden ladder to the deck. "And don't worry about being keel-hauled, first you have to worry about how you're going to pay me for English lessons."

Tomaso's top half disappeared through the hatch until only his scrawny legs, also liberally freckled, were still visible.

And just like that, the boys were inaugurated into the crew of the HMS *Deptford*, a fifty-gun fourth-rate ship of the line, serving King and Country at the tail-end of the Seven Years' War.

Suchet and Joseph Carlo did pay Tomaso for their English lessons. The Mauran medallion hung on a golden chain, as One Ear had noticed. It also had pearls strung onto its length to signify the Maurans' connection with the sea. They were small pearls, not like some of the big beauties Honore brought back from trading ships in Sardinia. But they were still pearls, five to a side. It was these that Joseph Carlo used to pay Tomaso for the whispered lessons conducted on the 'tween deck, between the crew's hammocks swaying back and forth to the rhythm of the sea. One pearl for each week of tutoring was the steep cost for Tomaso's services. And he wasn't the most patient teacher; his taciturn Scot father would show through when one or the other of the Mauran boys failed to pick up the current lesson. His cheeks would redden and his voice would lower to a gruff growl as he repeated himself.

In a few days Joseph Carlo began to understand the shouts and calls that surrounded him as he worked on deck. At first, he'd followed the sailors' tacit hand gestures: the sailmaker mimicked sewing and then pointed to the seam that needed mending; the carpenter aped sanding motions and then thrust the coarse sander at Joseph Carlo, usually throwing his hands up in exasperation if he had to demonstrate more than once. It seemed as if every other sailor on this ship was constantly exasperated with him, and for Casa Mauran's Golden Boy, this was quite a change.

Everything ached from the first minute of his working day to the last moment before he passed out at night. His back throbbed from the long hours of manual labor and his mind was sore from the strain of learning a completely new language from a less-than-patient teacher. After a day of swabbing, sanding, and sewing while all around him English words swelled and faded like the tides, Joseph Carlo found his brain was tired of English. He needed Italian, to speak it, to hear it, just for a few moments. Italian brought him closer to home. It was this longing for his native language that got him in trouble with the captain and his ginger-haired lieutenant, Jameson.

It was three weeks after they'd been impressed into the King's navy. The *Diligencia* had been left far behind; the *Deptford* was finally making for Gibraltar at the mouth of the Mediterranean. The talk aboard was that they were headed back to the shipyard in England. Frankly, Joseph Carlo couldn't be bothered. If they weren't headed home, he didn't care where they went.

Suchet looked as if he cared even less than Joseph Carlo, although it was hard to tell. Suchet had been mostly silent since they'd first encountered the *Deptford* off of Sardinia. Even under the cover of night, tucked next to Joseph Carlo in their too-large hammocks, he still was buried within himself. Joseph Carlo would later blame what happened on his desperate attempt to reach out to Suchet who had, to Joseph Carlo's growing horror, become an empty husk. They'd counted themselves lucky that morning (little did they know!) to be stationed with their holystones next to one another. A familiar ache arose in Joseph Carlo's knees as he worked the rough stone in concentric circles, scouring the deck. His arms, well tanned and toned by now, fell into the rhythmic motion with ease. His body was becoming used to this life even if his mind was not.

He paused for a moment, watching Suchet's lank hair hanging in his face and his still-skinny arms jerking the holystone to and fro on the deck. A familiar fear gripped his heart as he wondered, for the hundredth time, where his cousin had gone.

"*Cugino, dove sei?*" Joseph Carlo muttered out of the side of his mouth, continuing his circles while at the same time watching Suchet. He continued in gentle Italian, "*Where have you gone?*"

Suchet's scrubbing paused for a moment. "*Non lo so,*" he replied. "*I don't know.*"

Joseph Carlo continued to speak to him in a soft soothing voice. *Dios,* it felt good to speak with the rounded vowels and rolling consonants of Italian. "*Cugino, no si preoccupa. Don't worry. It's like I told you when we were taken, Tizio will come and get us, and when he does, these cani inglese will be sorry.*"

Joseph Carlo had been so focused on Suchet that he didn't notice the booted foot that stepped in front of his holystone until he jammed it into the leather-capped toe. His heart leapt into his throat as he followed the line of the boot up to a knee and on to the dark blue coat with golden buttons. Golden buttons and golden epaulets. A coat worthy of a captain. And that's exactly who was wearing it.

He took in the captain's glowering countenance in a panic and hoped the captain didn't speak Italian. Why would he? The rumor was Captain Hollwell (or All's Well among the crew) was a war dog, a soldier and sailor with only one thing on his mind: winning battles at sea. At this, he was an expert. He didn't need Italian to help him pin down the enemy, did he?

Joseph Carlo had almost convinced himself that although the captain would be angry that the boys were speaking Italian (he'd forbidden it as soon as they arrived on board), he wouldn't know that the boy had just called him an "English dog." At that moment, the ginger-haired lieutenant stepped abreast of the captain, shot a wicked look Joseph Carlo's way, and whispered into the captain's ear. The captain's frown turned into an outright glower as the lieutenant reported to him what the Italian ship rat had said.

"Sailor," the captain snarled, "is what Lieutenant Jameson says true? Were you insulting the captain and his Majesty's Royal Navy? And were you doing so in Italian, even though you were expressly ordered not to speak any language except English?"

Joseph Carlo opened his mouth to answer but it seemed his words, both Italian and English, had deserted him. Miserably, he nodded.

"For disobeying my orders, you will receive five lashes from the cat." The captain's eyes blazed as he leaned forward to make his point. "And the next time I hear you speaking Italian on my ship, I will hang you from the yardarm myself. Do you understand, sailor?"

Joseph Carlo managed to answer him in a trembling voice. "Yes, Captain," as he offered a weak salute.

The captain whirled on his heel and stalked off, Lieutenant Jameson trotting at his heels like a well-trained dog.

"Maybe this'll teach you to keep your mouth shut," the captain threw over his shoulder. "You're not in Italy anymore."

No, I'm not in Italy anymore, Joseph Carlo thought.

Chapter Fourteen

AFTER THE CAPTAIN'S PROCLAMATION OF JOSEPH CARLO'S PUN-
ishment, events occurred in quick succession. As with most things
on the ship, all looked like chaos, with sailors running here and
there, but really everything followed a well-ordered ritual. Joseph
Carlo supposed he should feel lucky that the captain had been
convinced to alter the vehicle of the punishment: he would still
receive five lashes but he'd be whipped with the boy's cat, a smaller,
lighter cat-o-nine tails. It had the same weighty handle and its
lethal bouquet of ropes, but the boy's cat only had five "tails"
whereas the cat used on grown men sported nine. Additionally,
they were made of smooth whipcord, not the rough nap that cut
more easily into the skin.

Every able-bodied seaman would be present for the flogging,
as was required for all punishments on board. A sailor roughly
delivered Joseph Carlo into the hands of the master-at-arms,
the officer in charge of weapons and judicial proceedings. He
was stout and shorter than the other officers, his thinning gray
hair secured beneath a hat. Professional in every aspect of the
punishment (he'd handled many before Joseph Carlo), his anxiety
betrayed him only in the pulsing muscle of his jaw. He seemed
sorry for what was happening to "the wee boy-o," as he called him.
The bo'sun's mate, whose muscled arms would deliver the lashes,
set to work making Joseph Carlo's wrists fast to the eye hooks
where the port gangplank had been. As the mate tied his ankles

to the grate he stood on, Joseph Carlo asked him why this was necessary in halting English.

"It's so if you faint, you won't slip off," the man replied as he gave a good yank to each of the bindings.

Joseph Carlo controlled himself up until the ship's surgeon, Dr. Dover, cut off his shirt. He'd seen the mate bring out the cat and check each of its lashings. He'd heard stories about other floggings. He *knew* what was about to happen to him, but he didn't know it in his bones yet. How could he? He'd never even been spanked. Maybe swatted with a wet dishrag by an annoyed Lena, but that was the extent of it.

When the sea breeze hit his naked shoulders, panic flooded his mind and all rational thought fled. He craned his head to look for Suchet and just caught a glimpse of him, standing next to a grim-looking Tomaso, before the bo'sun's mate stepped forward while at the same time freeing the cat. Time slowed as the long leather tentacles unfurled, each long lash dragging on the ground behind him tipped with a knot the size of a baby's fist. Joseph Carlo turned to stare out to sea, his shoulders tingling in anticipation. The crew was completely silent, all of them.

From his place next to the surgeon the captain made his proclamation. He called Joseph Carlo's slip-up "a transgression against Crown and Country, for which the seaman will receive five lashes to punish his soul." Joseph Carlo wondered if he'd pass out before the full measure of lashes. A buzzing vibrated his skull and his muscles jumped underneath his skin. He pulled at the bindings but the bo'sun's mate had tied them true, they wouldn't budge. The only sounds were the wind through the rigging and the flap of the canvas above them.

The captain called out "One!" There was a whistling sound, and then a crack. Pain exploded across Joseph Carlo's shoulders and emanated outwards from a burning streak of fire running down his back, pulsing through him and turning everything red. He hung his head, which still echoed with the crack of the whip. His shoulders were too numb to feel if they were wet with blood yet. It didn't matter; they soon would be. He hadn't cried out, but he didn't think he'd be able keep quiet for long. It hurt too much.

The captain yelled out "Two," and the whistling noise of the whip cut through the air. The second lash cut across the first one with a *crack*, making an agonizing X across his back, and wetness coursed down his spine. A belabored sigh rose from the crew; even the saltiest of the tars didn't relish watching a boy getting a beating. Through a red haze he thought he heard Suchet's scream. Each lash jolted him forward, his bindings pulling taut against his wrists. He hoped that his shoulders and back would go numb, but the time between the lash strokes wasn't long enough. With each awful, agonizing lashing, Joseph Carlo's vision swam in a red and black haze. But he didn't pass out, and the lashes seemed to go on and on. When the captain called out for the fifth lash, Joseph Carlo couldn't help it, he shrieked in pain when it hit him. His knees buckled, and his arms wrenched above him. Spittle hung from his mouth and tears coursed down his cheeks as blood coursed down his back.

From very far away, the surgeon spoke with authority. "That's quite enough. Cut him down and bring him to my quarters."

Joseph Carlo was vaguely aware, in his place between unconsciousness and white-hot agony, of his wrists being cut loose. Someone hoisted him up and carried him. He would later learn it was the same man who'd whipped him: the bo'sun's mate. He looked for his cousin and found Suchet among the others. Suchet's hand clutched at his throat, his eyes bulged. He looked like he might vomit again. If it hadn't been for Tomaso's restraining hand on Suchet's shoulder, the boy would have bolted through the crowd to his cousin's side. But Tomaso had a firm grip; he wasn't going to let Suchet go anywhere.

Then there was only a pulsing red river of pain across Joseph Carlo's back. Each step jolted new agony through him. He couldn't feel the individual wounds anymore; his whole back was a mass of fire. By the time they got him to the surgeon's quarters, he'd finally passed out.

He woke up to pain and an unfamiliar room. After a month of shipboard duty, it felt odd to be on a bunk instead of in a hammock. He was also on his stomach, another oddity. An immediate surge of white-hot pain rose. The memory of the flogging, tinged with disbelief, was eclipsed by the screaming nerves in his back. This pain was worse than the lashes. To stave off infection, the surgeon was packing salt into his wounds. The screaming of his mutilated skin and torn muscles was now joined by the sting of salt in new wounds. He moaned, and the noise seemed to come from down a long tunnel. He craned his head to look at the surgeon working over him, his white coat stained with streaks of blood. Before he could indicate that he was awake, the surgeon put something on his back; an immediate and all-encompassing agony overtook Joseph Carlo. More salt. He tried to scream, but all he could manage was a rusty groan. His last thought before he fainted again was that the blood on the surgeon's coat was his own.

When he awoke again, it was nighttime and he was still on his stomach. The ship rocked back and forth, back and forth. Darien, Dr. Dover's assistant, slept in the corner, slumped over a barrel, a flickering lantern hanging from a hook over his head. Joseph Carlo was so thirsty. He tried to speak but his tongue was wet sand stuck to the roof of his mouth. He cleared his throat and croaked.

The sound woke Darien. He stood up too quickly and whacked his head on the lantern.

"Thirs . . ." Joseph Carlo tried, but the word unraveled into a coughing fit.

Darien grabbed a tin cup and dunked it into a small barrel next to the one he'd been slumped over. Up it came, filled to the brim with delicious-looking liquid. Joseph Carlo didn't even care about the green scum on the surface or that it was probably beer. Fresh water on these ocean journeys went bad in mere weeks. He tried to prop himself onto his elbows and was immediately thanked by new rivulets of pain tearing across his back. He cried out and Darien stopped just in front of him with cup in hand. Joseph Carlo hung his head, feeling the tears start up in his eyes and trying not to let them fall. He reached out one hand for the mug, which Darien deposited there without a word.

Joseph Carlo drank the bitter-tasting beer, sputtering while gulping it down. It sloshed around his empty belly, but he was thankful to feel anything other than agony. A wave of nausea hit him and he almost disgorged all the beer onto poor Darien's feet. He waited, counting his breaths, until it passed.

"*Grazie . . .*" he began, and then sucked in his cheeks. Speaking Italian had gotten him into this. He wouldn't make that mistake again. "Thank you."

He eased himself back down under the watchful eye of Darien and closed his eyes. Sleep stole him away to a dreamscape filled with pulsing red light and the image of a nightmare whip, long and black, chasing him down a shadowed street. When he found the courage to turn and face his tormentor, it was the ginger-haired lieutenant, laughing, whip in hand.

Daylight streamed into the crowded surgeon's quarters when he woke again. He concentrated on Darien, who stood behind the white-coated torso of the ship's surgeon. It wasn't exactly Darien that caught his eye, but the filled mug in his fist. Joseph Carlo reached out for it and Darien darted forward, delivering the mug into his waiting hand. Joseph Carlo drank, sputtering with over-eagerness.

"Take it slow, boy-o, ease it down."

Joseph Carlo recognized the master-at-arms' voice. He propped himself up, as painful as it was, and turned to look at the source. Although the pain was omnipresent (Joseph Carlo couldn't actually remember a time when he *hadn't* felt like this) he was glad that he didn't think he was going to immediately throw up or pass out. An improvement, small but measurable.

The master-at-arms held his hat in his hand and his thinning gray hair dusted his head. His anxious face betrayed that he didn't like meting out punishment on the younger sailors any more than Joseph Carlo had liked taking it. Beside him stood the surgeon, Dr. Dover, tall, stately, and concerned-looking. He regarded his patient with a detached interest. The ever-present Darien hovered like a worried beagle watching over a litter of pups.

"How are you feeling, sailor?" Dr. Dover asked, hands clasped in front of him.

Joseph Carlo was glad that the doctor had changed out of the blood-stained jacket. It occurred to him that Dr. Dover didn't know his name. For some reason this incensed him. He could be beaten to within an inch of his life and they didn't even know his name?

The master-of-arms sensed this and stepped forward. "What's your name, boy-o? I have a boy about your age back home."

"My name," he choked out, "is Joseph Carlo." Speaking took incredible effort; he waited for the nausea to pass. It was hard to believe that this man meted out punishment and distributed weapons when needed. He was like a pistol-toting Father Christmas. "My name is Giu'Seppe Joseph Carlo Mauran, first son of Concetta and Timon."

"Well, Joseph Carlo, I'm Master-of-Arms Dunkirk. I'd like to say that you were one of the bravest sailors to get a lashing I've seen in all my years." Dunkirk looked to Dr. Dover for confirmation and the doctor nodded without hesitation.

"I cried out. I couldn't help it." Joseph Carlo's cheeks burned.

"We all do," Dunkirk said. "All of us has gotten the cat at one time or another. And we all cry out." Dunkirk reached out his hand as if to pat Joseph Carlo on the back, thought better of it, and withdrew. "Seeing your bravery, an idea came to me. I put it past Captain Hollwell, who's agreed to it."

Despite the furious pain in his back, Joseph Carlo's curiosity was piqued. He struggled to a sitting position with the surgeon's and Darien's help, his legs hanging off the bunk and his back on fire.

"Yes, sir?"

"I thought you'd like to apprentice with one of our sharpshooters, seeing as you've got a right steady heart. Pace!" Dunkirk shouted over his shoulder, "come on in."

A man ducked to get through the doorway, and the already-small surgeon's quarters felt three times smaller. To Joseph Carlo's surprise, it was the dark-haired man who'd saved Suchet's necklace from One Ear. His long Brown Bess musket slung across his back indicated he was still on duty.

Dunkirk turned back to Joseph Carlo. "Pace is one of our best sharpshooters, and he needs a powder monkey to keep him stocked with powder and shot in battle. You'd train up to be a sniper yourself. It's a lot of time aloft and a lot of time running up and down the ratlines. How does that sound?"

"Yes, Master-of-Arms Dunkirk," he answered, darting a glance at Pace.

"Fine, my boy." Dunkirk turned to leave. "I mean Joseph Carlo." With that he left the quarters, Pace right behind him, but not before the sharpshooter gave Joseph Carlo a nod. Despite his stinging, screaming shoulders, Joseph Carlo felt the kindling of hope.

After the two men had left, all the energy that had held Joseph Carlo in a sitting position flooded out of him. He slumped, teetering on the edge of the bunk, and both the doctor and Darien lunged forward to steady him. They eased him down onto his stomach and he cringed when his shoulder blades shifted. Joseph Carlo was worried that it was time to change his bandages and thus to pack more salt into his wounds, but Dr. Dover made no such indication. Joseph Carlo fell asleep with the workaday sounds—sailors' shouts and the flapping of loose sail—drifting through the open hatches. Pace's long musket stayed in his mind as he began to doze, leaving him with this last thought: he was going to be a sharpshooter.

The next thing he remembered was voices, voices he recognized, piercing the red-tinged darkness he was floating through. It was hard to surface this time; he had to unwrap his mind from sleep's mantle as if he were drugged. When he gained consciousness, he lay still for a moment, listening to voices go back and forth. The conversation was dominated by Tomaso, speaking English and Italian. The other voice, Suchet's, was barely a whisper.

He opened his eyes. Tomaso and Suchet stood by the port-hole in the twilit cabin and hadn't yet noticed that he was awake. Outside, the yellow sky heralded sunset's beginning. Both boys looked worried, Suchet downright despondent.

"*What if he dies?*" Suchet asked in Italian in a tragic voice, perhaps louder than was prudent, given Joseph Carlo's situation.

Tomaso seemed to sense this as well. "Shhh, Suchet. English only, *per favori*. He won't die, the doc said so. Hey! Look who's awake!"

Tomaso and Suchet took a few steps toward him as Joseph Carlo propped himself up on his elbows. His back still hurt hor-ribly. The skin and muscles felt like ground meat, but his head felt clearer.

"Hello," Joseph Carlo said.

Suchet broke the momentary silence in halting English. "How . . . how are you?"

After another pause, Joseph Carlo burst into painful chuffing laughter. "I feel about as good as I look, *cugi*—" he corrected him-self, "Suchet. How do I look?"

"Terrible," noted Tomaso with a half-grin.

"Really?" he asked.

"Yes," both boys said at once.

Joseph Carlo grimaced as he swung his legs stiffly over the side of the bunk. Tomaso and Suchet gripped his upper arms as he put first one bare foot then the other on the wooden planks of the floor. He tipped himself forward until all of his weight was on his feet for the first time since he'd been flogged. When he caught his balance, he looked at Tomaso, who was studying Joseph Carlo's uncovered back with a face that was pale under its freckles.

"Bad?" Joseph Carlo asked, swaying on his feet.

Tomaso snapped his gaze to Joseph Carlo's face again. "About what you'd expect."

Joseph Carlo took a faltering step towards the porthole, then another, and another. He grabbed the edges of the small round window, leaning forward until he could see out into the sunset. There was no land in sight, only sea.

"When do I go back to work?" Joseph Carlo asked.

"As soon as you can. You're lucky. Dr Dover has requested that you have more time. Usually they put you back to work the same day."

"How long have I been out?"

"Tomorrow morning will mark the fourth day."

Joseph Carlo's head was murky, making it hard to think. He finally noticed Suchet's expression of abject despondency. "Suchet, are you all right?"

The other boy scuffed the wooden planks with one booted toe. When he looked up at his cousin through his lank hair, his eyes were filled with tears. "*Cugino*," he whispered. "'Seppe, I'm so sorry." The tears made tracks through the dirt on his face.

"What? *You* didn't flog me."

"It's *my* fault. You were trying to help,"—the word came out like *chelp* in his thickly accented English—"trying to make me feel better. That's why you spoke Italian. It's my fault you got flogged."

Joseph Carlo shuffled forward to put a hand on his cousin's arm, the best he could do without breaking the new scabs on his back. "Stop. It *wasn't* your fault. It was stupid to speak Italian. I understand now, I'm not a Mauran, I'm not Brunito, I'm only a ship rat in the Royal Navy." He paused, making sure Suchet understood. "Like you."

Suchet's eyes went wide.

"The sooner you get used to it, the better it'll be for you. *Tizio* isn't coming for us. No one is. We must survive. And that means no Italian. Do you understand me?" Joseph Carlo gave him a shake. The boy blinked and nodded. "Then say it. In English. Tell me who you are."

Suchet said in halting English. "I am not a Mauran, I am a ship rat in the navy. That is all."

Joseph Carlo dropped his hand from the other boy's arm as a wave of exhaustion and nausea rolled over him like the incoming tide. His knees buckled. Tomaso caught him before he hit the floor.

Chapter Fifteen

Joseph Carlo stayed in the sick cabin for one more day, and then he was sent back to normal duty. He would visit Dr. Dover periodically to change his dressings and check his wounds. Thankfully, there would be no more salt. His wounds were healing without the bright red streaks that indicated blood infection, so the ship's surgeon could forego it for now. The duties assigned to him were less strenuous than the tasks he'd been used to before the flogging. He imagined that Dr. Dover had something to do with that. While working on the boy's mutilated back, Dr. Dover had a habit of muttering under his breath, maligning the treatment Joseph Carlo had faced at the end of the cat.

"Barbarous," the man had muttered while unwinding the blood- and lymph-stained bandages. "To think they want me to patch up what they'll simply take out and break again. Barbarians, that's what they are, little more than barbarians. Goes against my Hippocratic Oath."

Joseph Carlo took comfort knowing that the good doctor wasn't on board with the Royal Navy's corporal punishment. As for himself, he'd be avoiding any and all encounters with the spiteful Lieutenant Jameson. He wished that the lieutenant had never laid eyes on Suchet or him. And that Suchet hadn't thrown up all over him, humiliating him in front of his crew, not that there was any love lost there. Joseph Carlo couldn't think of one sailor who had a good word to say about Jameson. Accident or not, the lieutenant had it out for them now. Any time he had a clear view of the boys he was glaring at them with such intensity that Joseph Carlo could feel the gaze even on his back.

When Joseph Carlo was sent back to duty, his back wasn't healed; that would take weeks. With the healing came an unbelievable itching that Joseph Carlo couldn't scratch, not unless he wanted to rip the newly formed scabs off and open his wounds again. The itch wormed its way through his healing skin. At night on the 'tween deck, lying on his side in the rough confines of his hammock, Joseph Carlo was beset with the urge to scratch. During the day, going about the business that Tomaso assigned him, he could ignore it. But at night, he couldn't ignore it, as there was nothing else to distract him. He gritted his teeth and listened to sailors sleeping, snoring, grunting, and farting, with both hands trapped between his thighs.

The other crew members treated him with a new deference. The purser gave him an extra shirt so when his only one soaked through with blood, he'd have something dry to change into. Suchet and Tomaso slipped him parts of their rations but, much to Joseph Carlo's surprise, other sailors did too. And the looks he caught from the other men spoke volumes about how he'd comported himself at the end of the cat. A few times, he'd felt a pricking on the back of his neck whilst going from one task to another and looked around to catch sight of the sharpshooter watching him from high up in the rigging.

Since the surgeon's quarters, he hadn't heard a thing about his apprenticeship with Pace, or the Nightjar as he was called after the small predatory birds. Once or twice he'd decided that he'd dreamt the whole thing up in his pain-induced stupor, but then he'd feel that pricking on his neck and he'd look up to catch the black eyes in the rigging. He'd give it a few more days, he reasoned one late night while trying to keep his hands off the maddening itch in his back. If they'd reached the shipyard and he'd still heard nothing about his apprenticeship, he'd ask the master-at-arms himself.

The *Deptford* passed the Rock of Gibraltar at dawn on what would have been the middle of their sixth week aboard. A chiseled cliff spiked into the air, marking their last sight of the Mediterranean and their first of the Atlantic. High in the rigging on watch, both boys turned to look behind them as the ship sailed into the Atlantic. Never had the Mediterranean looked so lovely and so inviting.

They left southern Spain to starboard and northern Africa to port. The immense ship made her way through the small stretch of sea with the leonine mountains of Africa matching the heaving waves. Ahead of them, a straight line crossed their watery path. The half they were sailing on was the familiar turquoise of the Mediterranean, but on the other side were bristling white caps in a steely ocean as unfamiliar as it was inscrutable. The iron gray waves crashed against their Mediterranean counterparts with ferocious power, creating a frothy border between the two seas. Gone were the tranquil warm waters from which dolphins burst with glee. This ocean was deadly serious.

They crossed the line with a jolt of the waves on the hull. Even plowing through these Atlantic waters felt different to Joseph Carlo. The sea wind that hit his face was colder and much, much saltier. This was the ocean of the English. They pulled through the strait on a northwestward course towards an unknown shipyard in England, and Joseph Carlo looked back from high up the main mast. The last speck of turquoise disappeared around a corner of land. Joseph Carlo's heart clenched.

Tizio's boat can't sail this ocean, she's not built for it, he thought. *That's it then, we're lost to them.*

When he turned to the Atlantic that stretched before them, he felt years older than he was. He was now a sailor of a colder ocean, not a boy of thirteen playing in the warm waves of the Mediterranean. He did not look back again.

It took them a few weeks to get to the shipyard that carried the same name as their vessel: Deptford Navyyard. The welts on Joseph Carlo's back had begun to turn into scars that he'd carry until he was an old man, if he lived that long. Suchet also had come back to a degree; he was no longer vacant and silent. After Joseph Carlo's flogging, Suchet had decided something: he'd decided to live. There was no more banter in a foreign language between the two cousins and the half-Italian Tomaso. The flogging had whipped the Italian out of the boys. But there was still banter. Suchet committed to learning English, practicing all the time and with anyone who would humor him. Fond of English sayings, he used them at the most inopportune times, saying they were left "high and dry" when they stood in a pelting rainstorm.

The farther north they sailed, the grayer the landscape became. Since Gibraltar and the last glimpse of the sea that Joseph Carlo had called home, the weather had declined from fair to foul. The boys kept their oilskins at the ready for every watch. Even the seabirds ratcheted back their forays above the deck as the rain pelting their wings overpowered their hopes for a scrap of food thrown into the air.

When the *Deptford* sighted the shipyard, the boys were completely unprepared for the chaos that awaited them. No matter that they were deeply tanned by their time on the *Deptford*, could speak English competently, and could scramble up the ratlines in a half-second. They were still two young boys from Villa Franca. Their small jewel of a harbor was nothing compared to the hustle and bustle of this harbor. As they sailed towards the long piers and many warehouses that made up the watery city of the Deptford Navyyard, all they saw were masts from one end to the other. Ship after ship tethered to the docks, with men scrambling around them unloading and loading, mending, repairing, and refitting.

The spire of St. Nicholas staked its claim in the middle of it all, the dome of the Royal Observatory nearby. Once the *Deptford* had sailed in as far as she could go, smaller boats towed her through knots of ships to her berth. Some of the docked ships were as large as or even larger than the *Deptford*, and their attendant sloops and boats darted about them like gnats around an elephant herd. As they passed through the forest of spars and lines and yards, sailors shouted greetings to the men of the *Deptford*. Joseph Carlo stood with eyes wide and mouth agape, the line he was parcelling forgotten in his hands.

Jonas, a salty career navy man, poked the boy in the ribs with the iron hook that now served as his hand. "Ever seen anything like it, boy?" the older man asked him.

Joseph Carlo shook his head.

"Get used to it. We'll be here a while." The man lifted Joseph Carlo's line with his hook. "And get back to work."

Joseph Carlo took the line back.

If the boys had thought life at sea was rough, they were now surprised to learn that life in port could be rougher, but for different reasons. For one, it was at the shipyard that they learned what was to become of them. One long day just after they'd arrived, Joseph Carlo was still unloading empty barrels and casks and loading ones filled to their brims with rations as Suchet watched from the fo'c'sle. The amount that was being stored in the *Deptford*'s hull was immense, enough to make Joseph Carlo curious and a trifle nervous. This did not look like the rations of a ship bound back to the Mediterranean. Although he hadn't admitted it to even Suchet, Joseph Carlo had been harboring a small hope that the *Deptford* would, after stopping at the boatyard, pop back out and make her way to their home port, depositing them back into the lap of their family with only a little convincing. What was so obviously happening was that the captain and crew of the *Deptford* were instead preparing for a long journey.

Joseph Carlo asked Tomaso for verification. Even though it was against Navy protocol to share tactical information, Tomaso had become a friend and confidante even though he was their superior. The fact that he let them in on certain information was a secret that the three boys guarded carefully.

They sat near the fo'c'sle after a day of lugging and sewing and sanding. Sailors were forbidden to leave the ship during stays in port to keep them from deserting. The boredom was some of what made their stay in the shipyard so trying. There was enough to do while on duty, but after work, there were too many long hours playing cards and ignoring the other men's carousing. Faced with the very real threat of sailors deserting, an armed Marine manned the catwalk—the narrow walkway off the side of the ship—as a reminder of what would happen if any sailor disobeyed the orders to stay on board. The *Deptford*'s Marine paced the small length of the catwalk, eyes alert and rifle at the ready. Joseph Carlo wondered, watching from the foredeck, if the Marine would *really* shoot a sailor trying to escape. The idea of escape had become a pulse in Joseph Carlo's mind in the last weeks, stronger now that they sat in the shipyard, the anonymity of a bustling port so close and yet so far.

Tomaso agreed with Joseph Carlo that the amount of rations meant their final destination was far away. How far? Tomaso didn't know for sure, but he'd find out at the next shipyard they'd stop in, the one in which Captain All's Well would leave their esteemed company and a new captain would come on board along with orders as to where they'd head next.

"I think we'll be going for sugar," Tomaso said, using his sail knife to whittle a crude whistle out of a piece of wood. The Mediterranean sun had burned his fair skin a bright pink under the orange freckles; he never tanned, he said, only burned.

Joseph Carlo hunkered down next to him. "Sugar?"

Tomaso looked up at him with his ever-amused cat's eyes. "Sure, *paisan*, the sugar trade. You know, the Colonies? Well, this is further south. I'm thinking it could be Jamaica, Cuba, Hispaniola."

Joseph Carlo's last hope was extinguished like a lantern in a monsoon. Hispaniola, that definitely meant across the ocean. "Really?"

"What'd you think, we'd be taking you back to fair Italia?"

Joseph Carlo shook his head unconvincingly. Tomaso's eyes filled with sympathy, then hardened. "Remember what you said in the sickroom, *paisan*. You're not Italian any longer. You belong to the Royal Navy."

Joseph Carlo nodded once, gave him a weak salute, and headed for the ratlines, his mood as gray as the sky above him.

After repairs and refitting at the Deptford shipyard, they traveled down the Thames into the channel and around to Portsmouth. If Deptford was a city of masts and lines, then this was a whole country of them. They passed piers where hundreds of ships were tethered. Giant pines that would soon become masts floated through the air on pulleys and ropes. Great ships were raised out of the water in order to scrape the barnacles off the bottoms of their hulls and some were being re-coppered, their hulls glowing red-gold. The creak of wood and rope was punctuated by the sounds of shouting and pounding hammers. Underlying it all was the sound of the sea and seagulls. Cannons were hoisted to the gun decks by pulleys in jerks and lurches, their dark, deadly sides gleaming in the intermittent sunshine. This was the place they'd bid *arrivederci* to Captain Hollwell and *buongiorno* to the new captain.

Joseph Carlo imagined the captain's departure would occasion some fanfare, but he was wrong. He was working aloft that morning, tracking the cordage, lines that connected the sails to the spars and masts. The gray English sky spat rain, seemingly at him personally. He'd never get used to this weather, he thought, he would have this bone-chill the whole time he was in this drafty country. The rain pitter-pattered against the back of his oilskin, the treated sailcloth so stiff and unmanageable that it jabbed into his still-sore back.

The bo'sun's whistle shrilled and he peered down through the latticework of lines to the deck below. There were a few seamen re-tarring the deck, and the new tar, black as pitch, looked like veins running through the woodwork. Captain Hollwell strode out of his great cabin, voluminous blue coattails flapping; Lieutenant Jameson followed him, lugging his sea chest. Joseph Carlo smiled as the lieutenant struggled to get the cumbersome chest onto the gangplank, and he downright chuckled when the chest almost ran over the captain on its way down, much to the lieutenant's horror.

Joseph Carlo went back to his work, thinking only that Captain Hollwell would be back for a farewell ceremony. But that was the last he'd ever see of the man. As Hollwell made his way down to the dock, he again heard the shrill call of the bo'sun's whistle. Coming up the gangplank was a man wearing the blue greatcoat and gold buttons of a captain. Younger than Hollwell, he had a snubbed nose and square jaw that suited the large tri-corn hat that topped his brown hair. He didn't wear a white wig as Hollwell had. He jumped down onto the deck and stood for a moment, looking around the ship that was to be his new home.

The bo'sun blew his whistle, summoning the crew topside for an announcement. Joseph Carlo shimmied down the ratlines and found Suchet. After a few minutes of controlled chaos the men amassed around the port gangplank in two rows: officers with their toes on the line and lower ranks behind them. The boys, jammed behind a bunch of sailors in back, only got glimpses of the proceedings up-front.

Joseph Carlo jumped onto the rail and pulled Suchet up next to him. From that vantage point, the boys had a clear view over the heads of the other sailors to the group in front. Another officer and three civilians had joined the captain. That was all very interesting, but not as interesting as the ornate box on a trestle that a pair of marines had carried to the deck. They flanked the box on either side, guarding it. The new captain stood with his hands clasped behind his back, nodding to his new crew. When all three hundred had assembled, the captain thanked the bo'sun.

"Crew of the Deptford," he boomed. "I am Captain Dudley Digges, your new commander."

A murmur ran through the sailors.

"This is first lieutenant J. Seward . . ." a young man with a good amount of gold on his blue jacket stepped forward, "and William Lyttleton, governor designate of Jamaica." The murmur from the crowd grew louder; so Jamaica was to be their final destination. Joseph Carlo caught Suchet's eye. His cousin's face looked as downcast as he felt.

"We also have aboard John Robison, astronomer, and William Harrison, horologist, who has brought along his father's stroke of genius: the H-4." Robison was a tall man with a striking resemblance to a crow enhanced by the all-black outfit he wore. Harrison had an aquiline nose and extraordinary blue eyes, visible even from this distance.

"We are honored to have them with us, in particular, William Harrison. Harrison, would you address the crew?"

Harrison stepped forward. "Gentleman, I would like to introduce you to the sea clock, or the Watch." Harrison gestured to the Marines and they wheeled the trestle forward. A rustle arose from the crowd like a southerly breeze as the men shifted, jostling one another to get a better view. "What is the Watch, you may be wondering? It is an invention of my father's, a man of solitary genius and singleness of purpose." He lifted the lid, revealing what looked like a very small clock or a compass embedded in velvet. "The sea clock may solve the question of longitude, and it may do it on this journey." With that Harrison shut the lid of the box. The murmurings from the crowd grew as Harrison followed the captain and the rest of his party into the great cabin. Joseph Carlo didn't know what Harrison meant by the question of longitude, but he knew whom he could ask.

That night, Joseph Carlo was awoken by bells for his watch. (It seemed superfluous to have to stand watch while they were docked in Portsmouth and not on the open sea, but the order remained.) He grabbed his oilskin and climbed the steps to the deck, slipping the coat on before mounting the first ratline. Although the night looked fair, English weather was finicky in its best moments. When he reached the lookout a few minutes later, heart pounding, he found Suchet already there, and Joseph Carlo hunkered down next to him. He didn't even have to ask what was on Suchet's mind. Since the new captain's announcement, it was apparently all the other boy had been thinking about. When Suchet began speaking, he was so eager that his new English words tumbled over one another and he had to take a breath and start again, more slowly.

"Did you hear him, 'Seppe? Did you?"

Joseph Carlo wasn't sure what he meant. He was preoccupied with the information that their destination was Jamaica. How would they get home from across the Atlantic Ocean?

"What are you talking about? Jamaica? Or longitude?"

"Longitude! The question of longitude! I mean, this has baffled navigators for centuries! Tizio told me about it just before . . ." Suchet trailed off. They bobbed on the dark docked ship and thought back to the fair days before the *Deptford* had sailed into their lives. "Longitude is as important as learning that the earth is round, or locating the North Star. Some sailors think it's even more valuable than finding the lost city of Atlantis."

"*Why* is it so important, Gufo?"

"With longitude, we can pinpoint our exact whereabouts *in the middle of the ocean!* So, all we know is our latitude, the lines running north to south. But when you add longitude, then . . ." Suchet waited for Joseph Carlo to pick up the thread like a patient tutor waiting for a slow student.

"When you add longitude, you know where you are east to west and you get an X to mark the spot," Joseph Carlo finished. Despite his black mood due to the announcement of their new marching orders, he had to agree with his cousin, this was pretty exciting.

Suchet nodded. "With longitude, we can figure out *exactly* where we are. We can predict where our enemies are. It will change exploration, trade, you name it!"

Suchet stopped speaking and his enthusiasm dimmed. The last thing he'd said smacked of Honore. The boy had probably heard it on the *Diligencia*.

"And the Watch, what is it?" Joseph Carlo pressed. "What does it do?"

"The Watch is a sea clock, a tiny one though. An important part of finding longitude is exact time, hence the clock."

A raindrop hit the end of Joseph Carlo's nose.

"To know *where* we are," Suchet went on, "we first have to know *when* we are. And time in Villa Franca isn't the same as it is in Portsmouth, is it?"

"True," Joseph Carlo agreed.

"So we need a clock that won't lose *any* seconds or minutes on an ocean voyage. To think we may be part of the test that pinpoints longitude . . ." His voice hitched with excitement.

They sat in silence for many moments until Suchet spoke again. "Tomaso says there's a contest. Whoever creates and tests a device that can pinpoint longitude wins *ten thousand pounds*."

"Wow."

"This may be the trip that proves it, 'Seppe."

As it turned out, the sea clock would prove its mettle well before the *Deptford* sighted Jamaica.

Chapter Sixteen

THE FIRST DAY OF JOSEPH CARLO'S AND SUCHET'S TRANSATLAN-
tic passage, the weather was horrible. The *Deptford* made its way
out of Portsmouth Navyyard in a gray miasma of November
rain and ferocious wind. As boys growing up on Italy's golden
coast, they never could've imagined such despicable weather. It
was downright malicious, blowing and raining so hard that the
raindrops dashed sideways. Even the woolen jacket underneath
Joseph Carlo's oilskin did nothing to alleviate the biting cold;
tendrils of icy wind raced up his sleeves and his fingers felt numb
underneath the coating of tar left from the lines.

Each sailor made his own oilskin from sailcloth and water-
proofed it with linseed oil, which smelled like a dog's armpit.
They also had lashings at wrists, neck, and ankles, drawstrings to
tighten against wind and rain. The one at a sailor's waist, his "body
and soul" lashing, was known to "save a body," hence the name.
You could grab a sailor by his body and soul lashing to stop him
from being dragged overboard by waves or wind. The body and
soul lashing had saved some men from a watery grave and made
heroes out of others.

Joseph Carlo had never made rain gear, so his lashings were
loose and the rain ran down his forearms and dripped down the
back of his neck as he worked. When the tide turned, the captain
gave the order to weigh anchor and set off down the Solent to the
open Atlantic Ocean beyond.

The *Deptford* gained speed, her bow breaking through the icy barrage of waves. Joseph Carlo leaned over the rail and looked back. He could hardly see through the sideways rain, but the towering masts of the shipyard loomed through the icy haze. For the first time in many months, Joseph Carlo's gut spoke to him. It told him that this was his last view of England. He was not disappointed. A permanent crease furrowed his brow and his eyes were guarded. No longer the golden boy from Villa Franca, he was a ship rat in the Royal Navy. He picked up his line and faced the Atlantic.

They'd had no sight of land for three days when things went wrong. And they ran out of the one thing the sailors claimed they couldn't live without—beer. The food was always wretched on board. Beyond wretched, it was like the English weather: malicious. As always, the fresh water on board was undrinkable now after only a few days. A green scum formed a skin on the surface as it festered in its barrel. When a sailor cracked the lid, a wave of fetid air would envelop the poor soul, sending him coughing or retching or both.

Instead the crew drank grog—watered-down rum—or beer. For non-liquid foodstuffs, there was biscuit, made of only flour and water and so dense that when thrown at one's head, it left a mark. It was double and triple baked to ensure that it wouldn't go bad on the long journeys. Despite this, the weevils loved it. Before each meal, the sailors whacked their biscuits on the long wooden tables to dislodge the many tiny beetles who had diligently made themselves at home. It sounded like a hard rain on a tin roof: *rat-a-tat-tat*. Although dislodging bugs from your food was a trifle hard to get used to, the biscuit was the most palatable of the victuals on board. The salted pork was so hard and processed that it would actually take a polish and gleam if rubbed hard enough. When it became too hard to eat, which was quite often, the men carved sculptures out of the cured meat. It wasn't unheard of to find tiny pork figures of naked ladies rolling around the 'tween deck.

Crickmore's shout—a mighty sound of outrage—came mid-morning from the cook's quarters. It included some well-chosen words in a thick Cockney accent but the gist was clear: something had gone wrong in the galley. By the time Joseph Carlo got there, Captain Digges was already investigating, jammed in the tiny space with Crickmore, his head bare of his official hat and nose crinkled against the smell.

"What is it?" Joseph Carlo asked the sailor next to him.

"Cookie's found bugs in the flour . . ." Double yells of dismay peppered with colorful commentary issued from the galley. "God in heaven I hope that's not Himself finding out the beer's gone bad," one of the sailors said, crossing himself for good measure.

But the beer *had* gone bad. Before they tipped the whole lot into the heaving Atlantic, the captain asked a few of the sailors to smell it so they'd know that the stuff was skunked. Not a fortuitous way to start off a very long journey, but it led to Harrison's sea clock proving its mettle.

Captain Digges' guests were present for the official dumping of the beer and heard the groans of the crew. Lyttleton, the imminent Jamaican governor, suggested in a loud voice that the captain's steward should liberate some bottles of wine from the captain's stores in order to replace the beer. This was met with a smattering of unenthusiastic applause as wine was not much favored among the common working sailors. Nonetheless, they appreciated the generous gesture. Then the new captain announced that the *Deptford* would alter her course to stop at Madeira, an island famed for wine and women, to reprovision. This announcement brought a round of riotous cheering. Pillared by the crew's newfound confidence in him, Digges led his guests to his cabin to chart their new course.

The news spread across the ship like a grease fire in a galley: the captain was using Harrison's Watch (along with traditional means of navigation) to plot their course to Madeira. Harrison insisted that the Watch could get them to Madeira quicker than any captain or sailor would believe. Although Digges agreed to this, he didn't seem altogether convinced. When they spoke of it later that night, Suchet guessed that Digges had chosen to humor Harrison as any mistakes in navigation should be easily corrected at this point in their journey.

Digges, Harrison, and Dunkirk were on their way back to the captain's quarters when they passed close to the boys repairing the port ratlines. At first Joseph Carlo thought that they were merely going to walk on by and mount the steps, but then Suchet stopped them.

"Excuse me, Captain Digges," Suchet said, handing a frayed end of the line to Joseph Carlo and saluting his captain.

The men stopped and turned towards the pair, Captain Digges surprised and Master-of-Arms Dunkirk downright angry at the boy's interruption. He stepped forward to rebuke the boy, but Digges' hand stopped him.

"Yes, sailor?" Digges had a wide mouth and when he smiled, which he did now, it changed his whole countenance.

"I'm sorry, Captain, I don't mean to bother you." Suchet looked at the deck beneath his feet.

"That's right, boy. You shouldn't be bothering the captain with your blather." Dunkirk glowered at Suchet.

"Quite all right, Dunkirk, quite all right." Digges leaned down to catch Suchet's eye. "What is it, m'boy?"

Suchet glanced at Dunkirk with trepidation. "Well sir, I was wondering how the sea clock deals with temperature?"

The captain looked puzzled as he turned to Harrison. "Would you like to answer that question, my good man?"

"Yes, I would," said Harrison. His bright blue eyes reminded Joseph Carlo of a predatory bird like an osprey. Joseph Carlo wondered what Harrison saw when he looked at his cousin, so diminutive of stature and so formidable of intellect. "I'm surprised you know about sea clocks and fluctuations in temperature. What's your name, boy?"

Suchet squirmed under the man's observation. "Suchet, sir."

"And Suchet, how did you hear about sea clocks?"

"My uncle taught me navigation, sir. Before I . . . before the Navy, sir."

"Did he? Interesting." Harrison's sharp eyes became even sharper. "The problem of temperature plagued my father, but the solution is simple. And keeping time is vital to determining longitude. Do you know why?"

Suchet didn't hesitate this time. "Yes sir. In order to figure out our longitude, we must first know the latitude," he ticked off the points on his fingertips, "the height above sea level (which doesn't much change when you're on a ship), and the correct time."

A smile curled Harrison's mouth. "Exactly right. The more changes in pressure and temperature, the more seconds a sea clock will lose, until seconds become minutes and the minutes become hours. What my father did with this chronometer, which he hadn't done with the other three, was to insert bands of different kinds of metal *inside the Watch*. Why do you think that works?"

Suchet thought for a moment. Then he grinned. "Different metals are affected differently by temperature! The different metals regulate it!"

"That's right, you sharp boy. That's exactly right. With different metals, the Watch won't lose time. And as we say in the business: *tempora mutantur . . .*"

" . . . *et nos mutamur in illis*," Suchet finished for him.

Harrison's mouth dropped open and the sly look fell off his face. When he could speak again, he addressed Captain Digges. "Well, well, captain, I had no idea the Royal Navy employed ship rats who speak Latin. What a wonderful surprise."

Both Digges and Dunkirk looked as surprised as Harrison. "I didn't know we did either," Digges responded.

"Captain, I have a request." Harrison said. "Actually"—here he raised his finger in the air—"I propose a wager."

Digges smiled. "Absolutely."

"If the *Deptford* makes Madeira in record time using the Watch, then the ship rat becomes my cabin boy."

"And if we don't?" the captain returned.

"And if we don't, the boy wastes his Latin on the 'tween deck." The captain looked from Harrison to Suchet and finally stuck out his hand. "It's a bet." They shook, Harrison clapped Suchet once on the back, and the group continued on to the captain's quarters.

Suchet looked after them with worry and longing. "Oh *cugino*, I hope we make Madeira in time!"

He needn't have worried.

When the *Deptford* sailed into Funchal's main harbor on a lively wind, Joseph Carlo was in the rigging. After Britain's gray sodden landscape, Madeira soothed his color-starved eyes. The smell of gardenias and jasmine hit them before they caught sight of the island (other sailors had told him that in Madeira, as well as in their transatlantic destination, flowers bloomed all year round). Madeira's sea cliffs were rounded and browned from the sun, looking like flanks of a mammoth animal lying on its side. As the *Deptford* reached into Funchal's welcoming harbor, the bright purple of the bougainvillea on white-walled houses freckled the brown mountains.

As they sailed closer to the piers where they would find the provisions they would need for the next six weeks, Joseph Carlo spotted Captain Digges and Harrison standing on the quarter-deck with their spyglasses. As they drew closer, Digges clapped the other man on the shoulder, gesturing towards the harbor with the spyglass and grinning. They had made Madeira two whole days before they thought they would, meaning that the Watch had done something extraordinary. It seemed as if this ship, her captain and crew, and her illustrious cargo would soon make history.

Harrison's success was cemented on the twelfth of December in Funchal. For three days the crew unloaded the rotten stores and loaded up on passable essentials. Digges ordered more beer and an extra ration of rum for each man, upping his popularity. The crew called him "a sailor's sailor," which sounded a lot to Joseph Carlo like one of Suchet's mixed-up aphorisms. Regardless, the crew liked Digges better than they'd liked Captain All's Well. After they'd loaded up on all they would need, Captain Digges gave his men leave to enjoy the port town. Although the Royal Navy would have looked down on such lenience since men could desert by jumping on a merchant ship bound for England, Digges felt confident that his men weren't going anywhere but the local rum shacks.

As Joseph Carlo and Suchet got ready to leave the *Deptford* for the first time since they'd been pressed into service, a shout came from the rigging. Digges popped out of his cabin, spyglass in hand, and raced for the quarterdeck, coattails flapping. Most of the sailors who remained on deck rushed to the starboard rail.

The *Beaver* was sailing into Funchal's harbor. The merchant vessel had left Portsmouth shipyard ten days before the *Deptford* had weighed anchor, and here she was, arriving three days after them. Harrison joined the captain on the quarterdeck, borrowing his spyglass and crowing with delight as he made out the ship's name and nationality. This proved it then. Without a doubt, plotting a course with the help of the Watch had gotten them to Madeira faster. Joseph Carlo looked over at his cousin waiting for him next to the port gangway. Suchet was Harrison's boy now.

Relief and sorrow warred with one another in Joseph Carlo's heart as he and Suchet made their way down the long wooden pier to the cobblestone streets. Being Harrison's cabin boy would give Suchet the protection that he needed. He'd been almost invisible during their voyage from the Mediterranean to Great Britain, making himself inconspicuous and thus not a target for other sailors. Joseph Carlo knew his cousin wouldn't survive much longer on the bottom rung of the Royal Navy's ladder, and if Suchet was flogged, Joseph Carlo thought it would kill him. He was already too thin for his age and prone to random sickness. He could never gain an ounce of muscle, even with Lena's rich foods back home. It didn't help that he'd rather read than eat, and Lena had to prod him at the table. With the poor nourishment and wretched living conditions on the *Deptford*, it was only a matter of time before sickness or punishment got the best of Suchet.

All that would change now that Suchet was officially Harrison's cabin boy. At meals Suchet would serve Harrison, the captain, and the other officers, and it wasn't just biscuit and salt pork for that lot. He would eat the officers' leftovers, ensuring the most nutritionally balanced meal to be had on board for a common sailor. He would work for Harrison and tend to the man's every need; no more scaling the ratlines and dragging barrels topside. At night, the cousins would sleep swinging side by side with the rest of the crew, hammocks so numerous on the 'tween deck that they looked like bats roosting on a cave's ceiling.

As they shakily made their way to the main thoroughfare (they hadn't found their land legs yet) Joseph Carlo listened to his cousin go on about chronometers, longitude, and navigation with a twinge of sorrow. Suchet's appointment also meant that the boys would be split up. Different stations, different duties. Suchet hadn't realized that yet. For him it was pure excitement to be under Harrison's wing. But for Joseph Carlo, it felt as if someone he loved had taken leave of his company without bidding him goodbye.

Madeira swarmed with European nationalities. It was a Portuguese island, stuck in the sugar trade because of its tropical weather and its geographic location—due east of Morocco. English, Spanish, and French ships used it as a jumping-off point as its position off the coast made it an excellent port for restocking provisions. In addition to the mobs of European sailors, large numbers of African slaves farmed the sugar cane in the countryside. Walking the streets of Funchal arm in arm, the few shillings they'd earned clinking in their pockets, Joseph Carlo and Suchet heard snippets in at least five different languages. Squawks of birds interrupted chatter in Portuguese, and the smell of night jasmine and cooking fires hung over the narrow streets.

Land felt odd beneath Joseph Carlo's feet. He was used to the heaving deck of the ship and the streets' solidity made him feel unmoored and agoraphobic, as did being able to walk in any direction for as long as he wanted (or until he hit the ocean again). Nevertheless, he was thrilled to be exploring a different culture, far from home, without any supervision. He felt no eyes watching the little lords of Mauran on this rock. But there *were* eyes on Madeira, both looking to cause them trouble and keep them out of it.

Chapter Seventeen

Suchet and Joseph Carlo were eating honey cakes watching a street performer and his monkey when a voice spoke English behind them.

"And what do we have here?"

The voice was familiar, but Joseph Carlo couldn't place it until he turned and saw the ginger-colored hair curling above Jameson's blue coat. He dropped the last piece of his honey cake in the dust.

"Since when do ship rats get shore leave? And Italian curs no less. Well, well, well," Jameson sneered. His smug face flushed even more than usual. He looked drunk. This was not good.

The hair at the nape of Joseph Carlo's neck stood on end. Although Jameson was no longer stationed as lieutenant on the *Deptford*, having departed with the rarely missed Hollwell, he still sported the blue and gold of an officer in the Royal Navy. Disobeying Jameson could still result in disaster for both boys.

Joseph Carlo grabbed Suchet's arm and pulled him backward, trying to melt into the crowd, but he backed into another blue coat with gold buttons: Jameson's cohort. The smell of rum rolled off the man. Joseph Carlo held onto Suchet's arm, readying himself to dart with his cousin into the crowd and disappear, but Suchet gave a yelp as his arm was wrenched from Joseph Carlo's grasp. Yet another blue coat hoisted Suchet by his armpits. Jameson looked on with approval, his arms crossed over his chest and his face blotched from drink.

"There's a lot of danger lurking in port towns. Didn't you know, boys?" Jameson asked. The sailor that reeked of rum grabbed Joseph Carlo by the shoulders and steered him after Jameson down a dark and narrow side street, behind the other sailor and his captive. "Thieves, pirates, murderers. You should be more careful."

Joseph Carlo stumbled along the cobblestones, trying to twist free of the drunk sailor's grasp. "What do you want with us?"

Jameson turned with a surprised look on his face. "Oho! Your English has improved! A good flogging can be just the inspiration a boy needs. And your friend? How's his English?"

The three men clustered into a tight triangle on the dark street, boys caught in the center like a sadistic game of Monkey-in-the-Middle. Suchet opened his mouth to respond but nothing came out; both English and Italian had deserted him.

"Boy," Jameson said as he rolled up the sleeve of his greatcoat. "Don't you know that when an officer of the Royal Navy speaks to you, you answer? You don't want to be punished for insubordination, do you?"

The third sailor put Suchet down on the cobblestones.

"Say it." Jameson snarled. "Say insubordination."

The slip of a boy looked up at Jameson. "Insubor—" he began, his voice shaking on every syllable.

Jameson punched Suchet hard in the stomach. The boy doubled over with a *whoof.*

"Sorry dearie, not quick enough. Looks like we've got an insubordinate ship rat to take care of. I'll teach him some respect." He drew out the last word mockingly as he unlatched his belt buckle, pulling the long strip of leather free from his pants. He cracked it experimentally on his thigh with an evil *smack.* "Turn him round," he ordered, "and hold him still."

Suchet gave a strangled cry as the third sailor spun him around and threw him over a wagon with a broken wheel lying sloppily on its side. The sailor yanked at the boy's clothes, ripping them to expose Suchet's bare back and buttocks. Joseph Carlo stepped forward, fists clenched. "No!" he shouted.

Jameson jerked his head towards the second sailor and the man wrapped his arms around Joseph Carlo's chest from behind in a fierce hug and squeezed, lifting him off the ground. All the breath whooshed out of him and he couldn't draw another.

Suchet whimpered next to the broken wagon as Jameson approached him with his broad belt. Joseph Carlo kicked his feet, hoping to connect with the sailor's shins, anything to make him let go, but his legs only pinwheeled in the air.

Jameson was flexing the belt back and forth, smiling. "Bring the other one here, Hutchins, make him watch." Hutchins shuffled forward with Joseph Carlo trapped in his arms like a gnat in a Venus flytrap. He tried to say his cousin's name but Hutchins squeezed him harder, grinding his ribs together.

Jameson pulled the arm holding the belt back behind his head as Suchet made a high-pitched keening sound. The bursts of talk and commerce coming from the marketplace seemed far, far away. The belt whistled through the air, bringing Joseph Carlo back to his time at the business end of the cat-o-nine-tails. It connected with a smack of stiff leather on soft flesh . . . but not on Suchet's naked back. The belt had fallen on the broad forearm of the Nightjar. Joseph Carlo had no idea where he'd come from or how he'd snuck up on them. Jameson tried to pull the belt back but it was still wrapped around Pace's beefy forearm. Pace grabbed it in his fist and yanked, *hard*. Jameson was pulled forward, his feet stuttering on the uneven cobblestones. He fell to one knee and lifted his head in time for Pace's other fist to connect with his jaw with a sound like a hammer striking a side of beef. The man crumpled to the ground without a sound and lay deathly still.

Did he kill him? Joseph Carlo thought in a panic. *With a punch?*

Hutchins let go of Joseph Carlo and backed away. Pace regarded the unconscious man on the ground before turning to Jameson's accomplices. He lunged towards them, teeth bared, brandishing the belt. One of them yelped and then both of them ran hell-bent down the dark alley, disappearing into the gloom.

Pace turned towards the boys. Suchet was crying and pulling at his clothing. When Pace looked at Joseph Carlo, the boy feared that Pace would take the belt to him, so dark was the man's gaze. Pace must have seen Joseph Carlo's expression because he dropped the belt, turned his back on the unconscious Jameson, and made his way down the alley towards the marketplace. Suchet followed Pace, holding his ripped pants up with one hand.

Before following his shipmates, Joseph Carlo stood over Jameson. The lieutenant was curled on his side on the cobblestones, not moving, not making a sound. Joseph Carlo took a look around to make sure he wasn't observed and kicked Jameson in the ribs so hard it hurt his foot. The man made a *whoofing* noise but didn't wake up. Joseph Carlo ran after Pace's lumbering silhouette and Suchet's slight shadow stumbling at his heels.

They followed Pace through the crowded marketplace like ducklings after their mother. All the thrill and adventure of the place had disappeared with Jameson and his gang. It now seemed like trouble in blue coats was lurking behind every corner. Joseph Carlo kept expecting to come upon Hutchins and his friends leading a troop of armed guards to arrest them for striking an officer, so he focused on Pace's broad back to keep himself calm. Pace looked different somehow; he was still intimidating in his height and breadth, yet he seemed diminished. Only after a number of turns through the labyrinthine alleys did Joseph Carlo figure it out: Pace didn't have his musket for the first time since Joseph Carlo had met him. Every other time he'd encountered the man, his Brown Bess lay across his back like an unspoken warning.

They reached the pier that led them to the *Deptford* without further incident. The soles of their leather shoes slapped on the wooden planks in counterpoint to the hollow echo of Pace's boot heels. The ripe smell of low tide, rotting fish, and seaweed wafted on the humid night breeze.

Joseph Carlo had never been so glad to see the *Deptford*. It had been his nightmare, his prison, and his classroom, but this was the first time he had ever felt as if it were his home. When they reached the gangplank, Joseph Carlo sighed with relief, louder than he'd intended. Pace turned halfway up the gangplank and grinned. To Joseph Carlo's astonishment the Nightjar had dimples.

Both boys spent a restless night expecting the shrill bo'sun's whistle to summon them to whatever fate Jameson and the Royal Navy chose to mete out. Joseph Carlo wondered what punishment he'd earn for kicking an unconscious officer. He hoped Jameson wouldn't remember, but he couldn't be sure, not fully. In the long night, Joseph Carlo convinced himself that Jameson *would* remember and hold Joseph Carlo accountable for that kick to the ribs.

When the bells came, both boys started in their hammocks so violently that they knocked together, struggling to sit up. When Joseph Carlo gained his feet, the two started towards the hatch, and a shadow appeared against the light. The boys stopped short.

Master-of-Arms Dunkirk's tall boots were making their way down the ladder, all business. Short of stature, he didn't have to stoop when he reached the last step and faced the two boys, who had their fists to their foreheads in trembling salutes.

"You two, this way." With that, Dunkirk started up the ladder again.

On deck, the pre-dawn mist cloaked the ship in gauze, hiding the harbor from view. It was like being on board a ghost ship, the air and the sea matching one another completely in color and opacity.

Dunkirk led them to the quarterdeck where Captain Digges, Harrison, Tomaso, and Pace were waiting for them. The only one who smiled at them was Tomaso, and a quick look around stifled that.

Joseph Carlo raised his fist to his forehead in fearful deference. He elbowed Suchet and watched out of the corner of his eye as Suchet did the same.

The captain inclined his head, acknowledging the boys. Pace, Harrison, and Dunkirk all looked grim. A sea creature splashed out in the mist.

"Boys," Digges began, "I've been told that you found some trouble on your shore leave."

"Yes sir," the boys said in unison.

"You ran into Lieutenant Jameson, Hollwell's first mate."

"Yes sir," they said again.

"He gave you a hard time." Digges paused, his face solemn. "I've heard of the unfortunate circumstances surrounding your initial meeting."

A silence stretched between the Englishmen and the Italian boys until Joseph Carlo stepped forward.

"Permission to speak, sir."

Digges gave him a quick nod.

Joseph Carlo turned to the Nightjar. "Thank you, Mr. Pace, for saving us."

Smiles bloomed on the faces all around and Tomaso lifted one hand to hide a chuckle. Pace met the boy's eyes, holding them with his black gaze, and nodded. Ghosts of his dimples graced his cheeks.

"Well then," Digges took control of the conversation. "Now that that's been said, let's get down to business. I've been speaking with Dunkirk about you two. He seems to think that you're *not* normal ship rats."

Joseph Carlo was confused. He looked at Suchet, who mouthed the word "Latin" at him.

"Your compatriot is correct; the Latin was a clue," Dunkirk agreed. "As was the name you gave after your flogging."

At the mention of the flogging, Joseph Carlo's shoulders tightened.

"At this point, there isn't a way to promote you to midshipmen, no matter your breeding or education. The naval hierarchy doesn't work like that. But we *can* apprentice you, Suchet to Harrison here, and . . ." Digges raised his eyebrows at Joseph Carlo. "And you with Pace. Your apprenticeships will ensure your safety until we make Jamaica. Although Tomaso has done a right job by you boys, it's time for different training. And, of course," the captain finished, smiling, "Harrison will be happy to speak Latin with you, Suchet."

Dunkirk stepped forward. "Do you boys understand what your captain is asking of you?"

"Yes, sir." They both said together.

"And how do you respond?"

Suchet spoke first. "Yes, sir. I'll be Harrison's cabin boy. Thank you, sir." Suchet again raised his closed fist to his forehead.

"Your meals will be a sight better, lad, although I can't say as much about the company," Digges put in, much to the continued amusement of Harrison.

Dunkirk's direct gaze was pinned on Joseph Carlo. "And you, boy, what do you say? Would you like to be a sharpshooter's powder monkey?"

Joseph Carlo didn't answer right away. Off the starboard bow, the dawn was inching in, the water particles in the mist reflecting and refracting the rising sun's rays so they were caught in a sparkling nimbus. Bits and pieces of his life from before came to him: the smell of the lemon tree in the courtyard of Casa Mauran, Stronzo's raucous crow, the scurry and shrill shouts of twenty different cousins underfoot, the moonlight glancing off the fig tree's tough skin. The last thing he remembered before he replied to the master-of-arms was Lena's frightened whisper, *Promise me you'll take care of him.*

Joseph Carlo squared his shoulders and looked straight at the Nightjar as he answered his captain, "Yes sir, I'll be the sharpshooter's powder monkey."

Chapter Eighteen

WHEN THE *DEPTFORD* LEFT MADEIRA ON THE EIGHTEENTH OF December on an ebb tide at the end of the old year, Joseph Carlo sat high in the crosstrees again. This time his companion was not his cousin but Pace, musket stretched out between them. Unlike Suchet, who chirped like a wren whenever they were stationed aloft, Pace was silent. He didn't speak about his past or how he had come to be a captain of the Marines on an English man-o-war. He said nothing, just sat with his long legs folded under him, staring out to sea or at the musket, picking it up from time to time and handling it with delicacy that belied his taciturn manner.

They sailed the unfurling teal waves out of the sweet-smelling port of Funchal in their floating city. They would not see land until well into the next year, and 3,328 nautical miles later. Land was out of sight by midday and then all around them was the endless ocean.

For the six months that Joseph Carlo had been aboard, this was as close to being alone as he'd gotten. There was *always* someone around, and most likely, more than one person. Wherever you were on board, you knocked elbows with someone else. Even if you couldn't *see* another sailor, you could *hear* one: laughing, singing, talking. Even while doing your business in the head, you could often see slight movement through a porthole, and sometimes, a face staring back.

Soon, the ship and the men who worked on it fell into a syncopated rhythm not unlike the sea itself. The strict routine of the

Navy became something that Joseph Carlo could lean into. Over the rails was the undulating stretch of deep dark blue, sometimes crested with tips of white, sometimes jagged and fearsome, bubbles churning across the face of each wave, sometimes surging in great hills of water, the sea swells rolling out in front of them. And so it was on the ship.

Some of Joseph Carlo's routines had changed. He worked more with Pace, learning how to take apart and clean the Brown Bess, climbing the ratlines with first one, then two, and finally three of the long muskets strapped across his back. During battle, Pace's job was to pick off key officers on the enemy's ships and three muskets meant that he could get off three shots without having to reload.

But much of Joseph Carlo's workaday life was the same familiar routine he'd become accustomed to: he swabbed decks, mended sails, and parceled lines with the rest of the swabs. At mealtimes, he was one in a long line of sailors whacking their biscuits on the tables as the ship pitched and the square wooden plates slid around and bumped into men's elbows. He learned sea shanties and sang them with gusto, he got drunk off grog and regretted it, he laughed and cajoled with the others when Jemmy Ducks, the sailor who was in charge of the livestock, took the Duchess—a Tamworth pig—for her daily stroll around the deck.

Although just livestock in any other setting, in this isolated environment the Duchess had attained celebrity status. She had become the sailors' pet. Brown with bristly hairs that grew longer on her chin, she boasted satiny soft ears (her best feature), and a beguiling, upturned snout. Her honey-colored hide had patches of darker brown, her "beauty marks." The sailors loved her, and she basked in their adoration. They fed her bits of salted meat and biscuit, carved tools to scratch those hard-to-reach places high up on her bristly back, and one sailor even sewed her a pillow on which she could rest her considerable haunches. For these favors, she bestowed a porcine grin and grunts of encouragement. On many occasions she poked a sailor with her snout in greeting, her nostrils flaring in and out as she snuffled.

They all knew why she was there; she was like the gardens that captains maintained along their trade routes: a food source. But the crew didn't like to be reminded of this. Whenever Crickmore commented on how tasty a particular part of her was going to be as she was led around deck for her constitutional, he was roundly yelled at and sometimes swatted for his pains. Despite her dubious fate, the Duchess was good for morale.

Another bright spot in the unending tapestry of sea, sky, and ship was that Joseph Carlo and Suchet were able to maintain their nighttime watches aloft. Up there, high above the deck, bundled against the cold, basking in white-blue starlight, the boys talked for hours on end as their eyes scanned the dark moving waters for anything out of the ordinary. They spoke mostly in English, as was their custom at this point, but they also spoke softly in Italian. Neither one feared that another sailor would overhear them and report them to Captain Digges, or that they'd have the skin flayed from their backs for it. But the boys were still careful. They only let themselves switch back into the welcoming sibilant consonants of their native language when they were high above deck in the darkest part of the night. And even then they whispered.

So it went. Most of the routine was drudgery, but it was a drudgery that Joseph Carlo knew. His hands hardened with callouses and his skin browned from countless hours under an unrelenting sun. He sewed some better-fitting clothes for himself and wore them with his sail knife dangling from his rope belt. Even Suchet's scrawny arms (*braccia de pollo* was what the crueler cousins used to call him) had beefed up with muscle and he'd gained weight under Harrison's watch. Suchet's mental state had improved as well in his new station as cabin boy. Some nights it was hard to get him to shut up about all the navigational techniques he was learning. According to Suchet, Harrison called him the Map Maker for his ability to digest and spit out accurate navigational courses in record time.

Both boys could still climb the ratlines in mere minutes with Joseph Carlo maintaining that *he* would be the winner if they raced.

"I have to climb with *muskets* on my back, *cugino*," Joseph Carlo informed his cousin one starry night on the morning watch. "You just can't compete with that." Suchet did not disagree. But to his credit, he no longer used the lubber's-hole.

If Suchet was learning all about navigation, latitude, longitude, and celestial observations, it was matched by Joseph Carlo's tutelage under Pace. Joseph Carlo was becoming a sharpshooter and, if target practice was any indication, a darn good one. Every afternoon aboard the *Deptford* there was a drill, usually martial. They varied from drills which tested the crew's readiness for battle to timed drills on the gun deck to exercising the great guns. And all the drills were run by Master-of-Arms Dunkirk. The drills specifically tailored for the sharpshooters were, of course, Joseph Carlo's favorite thing to do. What thirteen-year-old boy *wouldn't* love shooting at things like rotten food, garbage, and crockery?

The first time they had a shooting drill from the crosstrees was well into the second week of their voyage. The gray skies had been spitting and drizzling for days but on that day, it'd stopped raining. The wind had laid down and the clouds had cleared to reveal a sky that was as pure blue as a nun's habit. Pace had found Joseph Carlo at work on the aft deck and requested that the boy join him aloft in true Nightjar fashion. He had walked up to the boy as he was parcing a line and waited until Joseph Carlo looked up from his task. Then he had jerked his chin and left.

Joseph Carlo caught up to him at the bottom of the main mast where Pace had gathered two Brown Bess muskets and a bucket filled with shot and twists of gunpowder. Pace twirled his finger in the air, indicating that Joseph Carlo should spin around. The boy complied and Pace threw a leather strap over the boy's shoulder, securing it so it lay in a diagonal line across his chest. Joseph Carlo felt a heavy weight drag at the strap and, when he took a step, the musket bumped into the backs of his calves almost at his ankle bones. Pace strapped on his own Brown Bess, which reached to just below his hips. He slung the bucket of powder and shot over his arm and climbed. Climbing with the musket was much harder than doing it without, and Joseph Carlo couldn't imagine doing it in a battle with shot whizzing all around him and with not one but two more muskets added to the first.

When they reached the crosstrees, Joseph Carlo gasped at the vista, which was so very different in the daylight. The ocean lay before them in great moving patches of turquoise, teal, and navy. The clouds were flecks of fluff floating just out of reach on the salty breeze. A pod of dolphins swam close to the wake of the *Deptford*, which cut through the blue like a wound bleeding white foam. They leapt and danced over the ridges of waves, their dark forms matching the ship's speed as they raced under the skin of the sea, each waiting its turn to leap and flex its muscular tail in the air.

A *whinging* sound broke through Joseph Carlo's reverie and he glanced behind him. Pace was down on one knee, Brown Bess in his hands, tracking a flying thing in a smooth arc. He pulled the trigger just as the object began its downward trajectory. Directly above Pace's trigger finger on top of the musket, the steel hammer rocketed down, slamming the frizzen, the spark of flint against the steel, igniting the gunpowder-covered plate, creating the charge which then shot out the musket ball with a loud *tchock*. The object off the port quarter exploded into smithereens as Joseph Carlo watched, awe-struck. Pace didn't even look up to check his aim, he just reloaded the musket, holding the twist of gunpowder in his teeth while his hands were busy. Musket loaded again, he handed it to Joseph Carlo and stood, arms crossed over his chest, while the boy approximated the man's kneeling stance. When he felt as ready as he'd ever be, he nodded and Pace signaled the men on deck.

The *whinging* sound came again and another object flew into the air above the port quarter. Joseph Carlo sighted down the end of the musket, trying to remember all the things Pace had told him about shooting in the seconds before the object was going to hit the water. At the last possible moment, Joseph Carlo pulled the trigger, sending the flint into the gunpowder with a crack. The musket butt jammed into his shoulder with a jolt, but the object—a broken plate—dropped into the sea untouched. Joseph Carlo hung his head until he felt a hand on his shoulder.

"You fired the weapon. That's better than most," Pace said. "Soon enough you'll be hitting what the lads send up."

Pace was right. By the end of the afternoon, Joseph Carlo had hit three of the seven intended targets. He didn't think it was all that impressive until he got a look at Pace's face after he'd hit his third, this one a jug. As the ceramic vessel shattered into shards, he heard a gruff, "Bravo," behind him. He lowered the smoking muzzle and turned to Pace. The man regarded Joseph Carlo with an unmistakable look of admiration, his dimples peeking through. Joseph Carlo's heart leapt.

"Knew it," Pace said as he took the musket from Joseph Carlo. "You have what it takes."

Joseph Carlo stopped gathering the twists of unused gunpowder. "What it takes?"

"Yep," Pace fiddled with an odd-looking instrument at his belt, securing it. "To be one of us, a sharpshooter."

The blood rushed to Joseph Carlo's cheeks. Emboldened by the praise, he asked, "Mr. Pace?"

Pace raised his eyebrows.

"What *is* that?" Joseph Carlo pointed to the whistle he'd seen at the man's waist. It looked kind of like a flute but not. "Will you play it for me?"

Pace's face darkened. He grabbed the whistle where it was secured by a thin line to his belt and flipped it to the inside of his jacket, hiding it. He swung himself to the outside of the nest, taking the ratlines down two at a time and dropping out of sight in a half second.

Joseph Carlo scuffed a toe on the wooden boards beneath his feet. "*Stupido*," he said, then followed the Nightjar down to the deck.

Chapter Nineteen

THE OLDER SALTS SAID THEY KNEW THE STORM WAS COMING when they woke in the morning. It had something to do with the heaviness in the air and the color of the sky.

"You know the old mariner's rhyme," said an old tar as he dug around in his sea bag and pulled out his foul weather gear. "Red sky at night, sailor's delight; red sky at morning, sailors take warning." He nodded his grizzled head towards the hatch and the strange red sky beyond it. The sea was an innocuous gray with no swell at all; it stretched like a languid cat and shimmered like oil, reflecting a sky which rioted with billowing bubbling clouds, tinged red by the odd light.

"You'd best get yours out as well. If my old bones are correct, we're in for a blow." With that the old man left Joseph Carlo on the 'tween deck rummaging in his sea bag for the stiff smelly jacket he'd made for himself. The linseed oil he'd coated the canvas with was still fresh, and it stank. He jammed it under his arm as he stowed his hammock, tying it to the ceiling with the others.

Joseph Carlo felt the heaviness in the air as he climbed the narrow ladder to the main deck, as if the air were pushing him back. No breeze blew and it was hot for January. The leaden atmosphere felt like an overheated, sodden blanket. The amassing cloud bank was just off the stern. Since their course was west southwest, they sailed with the fearsome wall of bronzy-green clouds just behind them and catching up fast. It was an impressive sight. The cumulus clouds stacked on top of one another were the color of unripe pumpkins. The weird hue remained even as the sun climbed to its zenith and after other clouds would've lost the rainbow tint of sunrise. As the day wore on, the mass of orange clouds faded to a bruised purple, and the sea and wind stayed at a dead calm. The *Deptford*'s sails dangled limply, and the Union Jack lay so still on the gaff that you could barely make out the red and blue of the design.

As the day wore away, Joseph Carlo felt tension seep into his bones like the flu. Bending his mind to the task at hand and staying at it proved difficult. His eyes dragged away to study the ins and outs of the cloudbank. He noticed Digges, Seward his first mate, and Harrison grouped in a nervous cluster on the quarter-deck, watching the sky. The other sailors ranged around the deck had their oilskins close at hand; Jemmy Ducks took the Duchess for her constitutional earlier than was his habit (she oinked indignantly at the change in schedule).

Suchet was harried, walking fast between the various lines and crates scattered about the deck, when he bumped into Joseph Carlo.

"*Cugino*, what's happening?" Joseph Carlo said, standing up.

Suchet stopped, swiping the sheaf of dark hair away from his forehead. It had gotten long. Joseph Carlo's fingers went to his curls, which had been bleached a tawny gold from the sun and, when pulled to their full length, reached well below his shoulders. He had them tied in a tight bun at the nape of his neck.

"'Seppe!" Suchet's face was conspiratorial. "'Seppe, have you heard?"

"Yes, a storm is catching up to us. A big one."

Suchet shifted from one foot to the other, anxious to be off on his errand. "The glass is falling, Mr. Harrison says. The barometer, the mercury in it is falling, which means that the air pressure is falling, which means there's a storm coming. It is falling very fast, which means that the storm is big."

The boys regarded the mass of boiling clouds, changing color and shape from one minute to the next. They were mesmerizing.

"I've got to go to the galley for Mr. Harrison . . ." Suchet began. "Brunito, promise you'll take care?" Suchet used his cousin's nickname for the first time in many months.

Joseph Carlo's mouth quirked into a half smile; the irony of Suchet watching out for *his* well-being was not lost on him. "I promise, Gufo. Tomaso says if I'm aloft I'll be lashed in."

"Okay then." Suchet took a step to leave, but then turned back and grabbed Joseph Carlo, pulling him into a fierce hug with his wire-strong arms. He let go quickly and walked away.

Both the old sailor's rhyme and the barometer proved to be right. By evening, the air had become even heavier and the bank of clouds acquired an ominous purple black on their swollen bottoms. The interiors of the massive clouds lit up with unspent lightning every few minutes and sheets of rain swept across the seascape as the dusk came down around them. The storm was coming and there was nothing to do but ride it out.

Captain Digges was on the quarterdeck just after four bells at six o'clock, giving the orders to batten down the hatches and lash down every non-essential item. Joseph Carlo headed up to the yards to shorten the topsails as the setting sun cast an eerie light on a mass of turgid thunderheads directly behind them. It seemed that they would ride out this storm at night. Wonderful. Although the wind had been nonexistent all day, Tomaso swore on his lovely mother's grave that this wouldn't last.

"You'll feel it kick up," he said. "When you feel the wind you'll know the storm's hit us." He thought for a moment, his face looking younger than it had any right to. "And when the wind sounds like banshees are bearing down on us, that's when you know we're in trouble."

The main sails were taken in as well as the t'gallants. They would sail under the jibs and the lower topsails only. The winds could be strong enough to rip their larger sails in two, but they needed the smaller ones to hold onto some semblance of control. Joseph Carlo was at the yard, gathering the tough sail and furling it as best he could when he felt the first licks of wind on the back of his neck. It wasn't much at first, just a few playful cats' paws batting at his curls and finding their way up the uncinched sleeves of his foul weather gear. Then the playful licks of wind became stronger, turning into short bursts that felt like a giant's paddle. Joseph Carlo swung with each one, his feet on the rope and his arms slung over the yard as he gathered the uncooperative canvas. He was jumpy and nervous, as if a low charge of electricity ran over his skin. When he'd finished lashing the gaskets, he made his way to the crosstrees and threw his body-and-soul line around the girth of the mast, securing himself to it.

The wind grew stronger, the bursts turning into a constant blow. Many of the unanchored lines flew sideways. Joseph Carlo watched as the sea began to take shape, rolling swells lifting the *Deptford* and slapping her back down. They climbed one rolling hill after another. The wind moaned, high-pitched and eerie, like a woman singing. Above that Joseph Carlo heard another sound, a haunting melody, and caught sight of a figure in the mizzen top twenty feet away. He'd recognize Pace's silhouette at any distance. Pace was playing his whistle, the same whistle Joseph Carlo had asked about during the shooting drill. Around his waist, a rope tethered Pace to the mizzen mast. The sea began to heave harder, surging underneath the ship with a behemoth's strength and dropping her into the waves' troughs with terrifying speed. Still the Nightjar played on, his own intricate melody accompanying the howling of the wind.

The rain kicked up as day became a blue-gray nightfall. Needle-like raindrops turned Joseph Carlo's fingers into unresponsive sticks. It took him a while to cinch in the neck and wrists of his foul-weather gear. The ship groaned with each gust, a horrible sound that rose to a wooden shriek as the wind bore down on her frame. A high-pitched whistle cut through the wind and rain. On Pace's platform, the big man was waving at him. When Pace saw he'd caught the boy's attention, he pointed at the rope that anchored him to the mast and yanked it in an over-exaggerated gesture. Pace cupped one hand around his mouth and yelled something instantly lost to the wind.

"What?!" Joseph Carlo screamed with all his might, the rain pelting his face in what seemed a hostile onslaught of a thousand tiny daggers. The *Deptford* climbed the face of a mountain of water four times the ship's size. All around them the angry sea churned under a boiling purple bruise of a sky. It was hard to tell which was which. The ship slammed down into the trough of the wave with the finality of a guillotine blade. Through the sideways rain, Joseph Carlo saw Pace reset his feet into a wide stance and cup his mouth with one hand again.

"Check it!" Pace's yell was no match for the screaming wind. Joseph Carlo barely heard him. *Banshees*, he thought fearfully, *The wind sounds like banshees.*

Pace pointed at his anchor again. "Check your knot!"

Both hands wrapped around his tether in a death grip, knuckles white, he gave the knot a good yank. One line shifted, giving the other room to wiggle. Not good.

Oh no, Joseph Carlo thought as he untied the bowline as quickly as his numb fingers would let him. He'd be untethered for a moment, and that's all it would take for the storm to grab him and throw him into the angry sea. The ship began yet another climb up a wall of water, the air full of both rain and sea foam frothing off the churning wave. Suddenly, a particularly strong gust of wind batted Joseph Carlo sideways. The end of his tether yanked out of his grip and he slid towards the edge of the platform, the vertical angle of the ship's climb threatening to dump him out. His feet fought for purchase on the wet wood and suddenly they were scrabbling in air. Slithering off the platform up to his belly, he threw his arms out for anything to stop himself from falling. The *Deptford* crested a mammoth wave and tipped forward into her headlong fall into the wave's trough. Gravity pulled him in the opposite direction and he realized he was going to fall off the opposite side of the platform after sliding across again.

As he skittered across the platform, he caught the smooth surface of the mast with one hand as he went past. He pivoted his body, trying to hold on, but at the last moment lost his grip. His legs went over with slippery speed and then his hips were off the platform. His hands grappled blindly in one last attempt to save himself and then he was over the edge, dropping into nothing. He screamed, his voice matching the howl of the storm as he fell into the maelstrom.

Suddenly, a sharp yank at his waist stopped him. He was hanging off into space inches below the top as the *Deptford* began to climb yet another mountain of water. His body-and-soul lashing had caught a cleat, its slack taken up in his free fall from one side of the platform to the other. He gripped the rope and prayed that his stitches in the oilskin would hold. He pulled himself up by inches, hand over hand, until one knee could lever over the lip of the platform. He yanked on the lashing as the ship crested a wave, flipping his body over the edge to skate across the wet wood again. But this time, he grabbed the mast in a ferocious bear hug, pressing his cheek to its cold grain.

When his breathing slowed and his heart ceased to feel as if it would explode, he slid himself up the mast, never letting more than a quarter of an inch between himself and the wood. When he was upright, he passed his tether around the mast with shaking hands, taking care with the knot, remembering what Honore had told him about the bowline being the most important knot he'd ever learn.

"It may save your life one day," his uncle had said many years ago.

Joseph Carlo unwrapped himself from the mast, both hands tight on his tether. He stood with his feet wide apart and looked towards the mizzen mast nest again. Pace was at the edge of his platform, one hand on his own tether line. It looked as if he was going to launch himself through the space between the two masts. Joseph Carlo gave him a shaky wave and Pace stepped back, putting one hand on the safety of the mast. As the *Deptford* began another long climb up the face of a wave, Pace once again cupped a hand to his mouth.

"Hold fast!" Pace yelled into the unrelenting wind. "Hold fast!" And Joseph Carlo did just that for the rest of the night.

The Duchess was missing.

Besides everything else—ripped sails, a damaged spar, several cases of fractured ribs, and one broken collarbone—her absence depressed the men's rebounding spirits more than anything. Jemmy Ducks swore up and down that he'd secured her with more care than the rest of the livestock.

"On me honor, boys," the poor man attested, twisting a cap between his calloused hands, "I put her in her crate and lashed it with four lines. Not one, not two, but four!" He held up four twisted fingers as proof. "I loved her as much as the rest of you, I did." No one had the heart to blame him.

The crate in which the Duchess had been secured lay broken in the livestock pen, its wooden canes breached in two places. There was a spatter of blood on one side, and this upset the investigating sailors most of all.

The mood on board was an odd mix of jubilant relief and depression. As to the weather, once the monster storm had blown itself out, the day had broken with a scrubbed clean sky and a middling wind. When Joseph Carlo and the rest had set the sails to the captain's orders, he made his way down to the deck on shaky legs. Dawn's streaks of red and purple illuminated a sky free of clouds. He'd never seen anything so beautiful.

Suchet had ridden out the storm with Harrison, protecting the Watch in its padded box. Harrison was terrified that the Watch would get wet, thus spoiling its accuracy. Other than a few bumps and bruises, all three of them—Suchet, Harrison, and the Watch—were fine.

The *Deptford* had sustained her fair share of injuries during the storm as well. Everywhere you looked, there were frayed lines and splintered wood. Her hull and rig had held, despite the beating she'd taken, and the men were proud of that. If only they could find the Duchess.

For much of his day watch, Joseph Carlo was at the bilge pumps, bailing out all the seawater that had inundated the ship. It was a laborious process that took a lot of men and took a lot out of them. Exhausted from a violent sleepless night, the constant pumping and bailing taxed them more than usual. Joseph Carlo worked shoulder to shoulder with men twice his age and three times as strong, and their labored breathing matched his own.

The ship's bells sounded, signaling the end of the watch, and Joseph Carlo let go of the pump he'd been working for hours. Blisters had risen on his hands and broken, only to have risen again. The man next to him, a heavily muscled lad straight from Ireland, sighed and stretched, hands plastered to the small of his back. He inspected his raw red palms.

"My blisters have blisters," he said, with a little pride.

Joseph Carlo climbed up the narrow stairs to the 'tween deck behind the rest of the bailing crew, thinking only of a good dose of grog and a dreamless sleep in the scratchy cocoon of his hammock when he heard it underneath the ladder, somewhere in the depths of the storage. He paused, watching the rest of the men tromp up the ladder, all of them too tired to question why he was hanging back. When everyone had left the lowest deck, he sloshed through the murky seawater to the bow storage area, and listened. There was only the swish of the water running by the *Deptford*'s hull, the accordion-like whoosh of the pumps, the steady drip in the bilge, and the creak of the ship's wooden bones. Nothing else. It felt as if he were in the belly of some great wooden beast. He gave up and walked back to the hatch, dragging his feet.

When he reached the stairs, though, it came again. It wasn't a snort; it was an *oink*. It was faint, but it was an *oink*. He'd grown up with all manner of animals living close at hand. He knew the sound of a pig when he heard it.

He hurried back to the shadowed depths of the storage area, scanning the random angles and shapes of the crates and sacks.

"Duchess? Are you there?"

Nothing.

Joseph Carlo pushed through the jumbled cargo. Before the storm, this had been orderly and lashed down, but a night of ferocious winds and waves had thrown this space into disarray.

"Duchess?" he said again.

Still nothing.

He shunted some of the crates around. A broken piece of wood stabbed his sore legs as he shoved his way through. He hefted bags of sodden grain out of the way, each time hoping to uncover a frightened Tamworth pig. He'd reached the end of the storage and put one hand on the inside of the ship's hull, inches away from the energy of the ocean rushing by.

Still no Duchess.

Defeated, he turned to make his way back through the jumbled clutter of crates and sacks.

"*Oink?*" It sounded like a question.

Joseph Carlo spun, ripping away the last of the broken crates. There, huddled against the front of the storage area in a space too small to accommodate any crate, was a brown pig. The Duchess's eyes glinted in the light of a lantern hanging by the hatch. A smudge of blood stained her snout. Joseph Carlo voiced a quick prayer. He moved as slowly as possible, taking care not to startle the already frightened pig. As he approached, he tripped over one of the smashed crates, lunging to keep his balance. The Duchess let out a squeal and shoved herself even further back into the bow, hooves skittering on wood. Although he hadn't wanted to scare her, he was glad to see her react so fast. It meant she wasn't too wounded to move.

Without being aware of it, he began crooning an Italian lullaby that Lena used to sing to him.

"*Fa la ninna, fa la nanna,*" he sang. He crouched only a few feet from her. Her labored breathing sped up as he reached one trembling hand to her forehead. He stroked the place between her ears where he knew she liked to be scratched, avoiding the injured side of her head. She jerked her face away from him at first but then, as he continued with the lullaby and his gentle attention, she relaxed, her eyelids slipping to half-mast.

"*Fa la ninna, bel bambin.*" Go to sleep, lovely child, he sang. The Duchess's trembling slowed and with his other hand, Joseph Carlo slipped a loop of rope around her neck. She jerked but she was too late by a second; she was caught.

"Come on, Duchess," Joseph Carlo said in a soothing voice. "Let's get you fixed up. The boys will be happy to see you. We thought we'd lost you."

Joseph Carlo reached out a hand to steady her as she reluctantly poked her way through the wreckage and the two waded to the hatch that led up to the 'tween deck. When they got closer to the lantern, he paused to study her. There was a nasty gash on the side of her head but other than that, she seemed all right.

They made their way laboriously up to the 'tween deck, and then, Joseph Carlo still singing to her, they climbed to the upper deck. She had difficulty climbing the wooden steps on her own and, once, her hoof slipped on the wet wood, making Joseph Carlo's heart clench in his chest. She regained her footing with a scrabble of hooves and continued to follow him, the rope stretching between them. When they reached the main deck, he stood for a moment in the last light of the day, unnoticed by the men swirling around him. All of a sudden, there was a shout and the Duchess tensed against his leg.

"It's the Duchess!" a sailor yelled, pointing at them.

In a split second they were surrounded by ecstatic sailors laughing and yelling. There were even a few teary eyes. He reluctantly gave up the Duchess's lead, and a group of sailors walked her to the surgeon's quarters where Dr. Dover would give her a good once over. She trotted with them like an obedient schoolgirl, the wound on her head forgotten, and looked back once at Joseph Carlo with an expression of gratitude.

After she'd been delivered to the surgeon's, Joseph Carlo resumed his path to his hammock. On the way, he received quite a few back pats, an equal number of bear hugs, and a slug of grog. He went to sleep with aching muscles, a warm fire burning in his belly, and a light heart, listening to the crew's raucous shouts of, "Long live the Duchess! Long live the Duchess!" He'd survived his first storm at sea, and even better, he'd found the crew's heart in the belly of the ship. It had been a good day.

Chapter Twenty

AFTER THE STORM AND THE SUBSEQUENT RESCUE OF THE DUCH-
ess, Joseph Carlo enjoyed an elevated status on board. It seemed
that lasting the night in the rigging during a terrible storm ("I'd
give it an eight out of ten," Tomaso intoned) and then rescuing
the *Deptford*'s adopted mascot meant that you got your back
slapped and head nuggied for many days afterwards. The Duchess herself enjoyed an elevated status after her brush with death.
Dr. Dover bandaged the left side of her face in quite a fetching
manner and Captain Digges made her an honorary member of
the crew. For the remainder of the voyage, she'd be safe from
Cookie's butcher's knife, and they *did* have three chickens and a
goat, if it came to that.

Soon after the Duchess became an able sea-pig, the crew
learned that during the storm, they'd lost a man overboard. Darien,
the boy who'd provided Joseph Carlo with water after his flogging,
had been on the wheel (it took two to four men to control it during
a serious blow) when he was washed overboard by a strong wave.
The other man on the wheel reached for him and almost had him,
but the boy's lashing slid through his fingers and Darien slid out of
reach. The poor man recounted watching helplessly at the wheel as
he fought the sea for control of the ship while Darien was pulled
into the maelstrom. He couldn't have gone after him for fear of
losing control of the helm; that would've meant certain death for

all three hundred sailors aboard. Life on board was often about choosing between two terrible options.

The *Deptford* rode the trade winds as the crew set to repairing broken or frayed gear, bailing, sewing the sails, and rechecking every sheet, line, and halyard on board, as well as hanging the sodden sails out to dry. They sailed another three weeks and three days before the island of Hispaniola appeared off to larboard. The trades blew steady and warm as they pushed the *Deptford* along at a quick clip on a broad reach towards Jamaica.

Once there, they'd leave Harrison after establishing Lyttleton in his gubernatorial seat on the island. They'd reprovision and press more men into service before heading to Cuba, their *actual* destination. The men they'd invite on board (a generous term for it) would be native Africans who now worked the English sugar plantations on the island as slaves. Pressing the slaves into service was not a popular tactic amongst the Englishmen who ran the plantations.

"Pressing them into service, especially with the promise of freedom, gives them too many ideas, the slavers think," Tomaso told him as they checked the lines in the topmasts. "Beyond the loss of their workforce, they don't want their slaves learning how to use muskets. They don't want another Tacky's rebellion."

Villa Franca and the rocky shore that rose above her sapphire harbor seemed like a child's dream to Joseph Carlo, and he was hardly a child anymore. His hands were like polished mahogany, and his muscles hardened from constant work. He had a thousand-yard gaze from scanning the horizon and he had the peculiar rolling gait common to sailors used to walking on a heaving deck. He and Suchet kept up their meetings on the dark night watches in the crosstrees. They were the only times that Joseph Carlo felt that he could really be himself, stuck somewhere between childhood and adulthood and fully in neither.

Suchet thrived under Harrison's tutelage. The watchmaker's son had found an eager student in the young Italian and poured all the knowledge he could into the boy's sponge-like mind. In the crosstrees, Suchet told Joseph Carlo that he felt torn. Harrison would leave the *Deptford* in Jamaica and probably wouldn't take Suchet with him. Joseph Carlo sensed that Suchet held out a small flame of hope against all rational thought that Harrison would decide to take him on permanently.

Honore was right, Joseph Carlo thought. *He would've been the perfect brain to my brawn.*

As Joseph Carlo slipped comfortably into the routine of his ship life, his mind was free to drift home on the other side of the ocean. And, more often, to thoughts of escape. How was he going to get them off the ship? If he could do that, could he do it without getting them killed?

Much to many of the sailors' dismay, they learned that after landing in Jamaica, the *Deptford* would sail on to Cuba as a part of the English naval fleet. They were to attack Castle Morro in Havana, wresting it from the Spanish and delivering it into the hands of the English.

For Joseph Carlo and Suchet, the terrifying prospect that a battle lay ahead came with one glimmer of hope: it would give the boys the opportunity to escape. Suchet still hoped that Harrison would take him back to England, but Joseph Carlo was sure this wouldn't happen. In Joseph Carlo's mind, they would flee the *Deptford* in the chaos of battle, make it to Spanish-occupied Cuba, and find a ship bound for Italy.

"*There are plenty of ships in Cuba that we could get back home on*," Joseph Carlo assured an anxious Suchet in Italian, days before arriving in Jamaica. They whispered less because they were speaking Italian and more because they were speaking of desertion.

Suchet thought about this, while he watched the brilliant spill of stars overhead. Finally, he voiced what was worrying both of them the most. "*Cugino*, without Signore Harrison, I don't know if I'd survive." He said this with no inflection, matter-of-factly.

Joseph Carlo thought of Lena's face if he returned to home without Gufo. He couldn't bear to fail her. So he promised himself that, if for some reason Suchet didn't make it, he wouldn't return home either. He couldn't, not without Gufo.

In the top, he responded to his cousin without a pause. "No way, *cugino*, you'll be fine. You've learned more than you think you have. You'll see." Suchet didn't seem to notice the transparency of the other boy's confidence. He continued studying the constellations reeling above him. Then he nodded.

"*I can do it. I'll have to,*" he finished in Italian. Joseph Carlo believed it himself with the suspension of reality peculiar to the young.

The *Deptford* spotted the small island of Port Royal and the mountains of Jamaica rising behind it on the morning of January 19th. The dark blue of the mountains stood out against the faded denim of the morning sky, the yellow sand of Port Royal stretching out in front. A fort stretched across the spit of land, curving around the turquoise bay, creating an arm of fortified protection with Port Royal standing sentry amidst the ruins.

This island had been a pirates' paradise until an earthquake sank almost every building on it at the end of the last century. The husks of buildings still lurked here and there, canted in odd directions and half-mired in the quicksand that swallowed up the whole town in a matter of heartbeats. The English had hopped over from Kingston and rebuilt, turning the island into a working piece of Her Majesty's Navy; the harbor boasted a naval yard, a cooperage, sawpits, a canteen, and a hospital.

By midday, they were sailing into its harbor. The *Deptford* was towed to a dock in a harbor bristling with masts, most of them English man-of-wars, all there for the same reason: to get more men. In the battle for Castle Morro, more men meant more guns, and more guns were better.

The atmosphere on board was filled with sailors' stories about Port Royal. It became a contest of sorts to see which sailor had the most outrageous story about previous exploits on the island and who had the highest expectations this time around. The most intriguing stories were about the earthquake that had swallowed up the pirate city that was once Port Royal. In a matter of seconds in 1692, almost all of the town had disappeared into the sand. Some said the underwater wreck of the pirate town was haunted, and any who disturbed the remains would be cursed. Others dove for treasure, sliding rings off the fingers of underwater skeletons.

The hectic quality of the men's claims also related to the next leg of their journey, when they would head to Cuba, guns at the ready. Joseph Carlo had a hard time forgetting that fact as he scrubbed, swabbed, and worked the rigging. It was still festive, threat of battle or not; the Union Jack flew in the brisk breeze, which smelled of cooking fires, coffee, and flowers. Joseph Carlo even caught Pace laughing, dimples on full display.

Joseph Carlo had just reached the deck when he spotted Suchet trying to navigate the stairs that led down from the quarterdeck to the main deck with an immense box in his arms. Joseph Carlo raced up the stairs to meet him.

"Here, *cugino*, give it over."

Suchet stopped on the steps above him, craning his neck to see around the wooden crate. "'Seppe, that you?"

As a reply, Joseph Carlo grabbed the crate from Suchet, who smiled with relief. "Thanks, 'Seppe. Hold on, will you?"

Without waiting for Joseph Carlo's response, Suchet mounted the steps at a trot and disappeared into Harrison's cabin. He returned in a few moments with bags and charts as Joseph Carlo balanced the large crate awkwardly on one knee.

Suchet pushed past Joseph Carlo and led the way to the port gangplank. Sweat beaded on Joseph Carlo's forehead as he tried to manage the cumbersome crate and keep up with his cousin. "What is all this stuff, *cugino?*"

Suchet picked his way across the narrow gangway to the pier. "Mr. Harrison's kit. He and Mr. Lyttleton and the astronomer are going to set up a lab." They'd reached the clunky wooden hand cart on the pier. Suchet deposited his load next to the other boxes on its bed and made room for Joseph Carlo to do the same. "They'll test the Watch as soon as they get the tent up."

Joseph Carlo tried to look thrilled. Suchet made a derisive sound in the back of his throat.

"This is momentous! If the Watch hasn't lost any time, we'll know Master Harrison did it! He'll have found the key to longitude."

Joseph Carlo screwed his face into a more enthusiastic expression. "Better?" He asked through his clenched teeth.

Suchet took one look at his older cousin and broke into a gale of giggles. "You look like you're telling Crickmore you love his lobscouse stew."

Joseph Carlo grimaced. "Lobscouse, ugh," he shuddered.

The boys made three more trips until Harrison's cabin was empty. On their final trip, Joseph Carlo noticed that Suchet's sea bag bumped against his thigh as he carried the last of Harrison's things to the waiting cart.

"Are you going with them?" Joseph Carlo asked.

"Just for the test. Then I'm back on board," Suchet answered.

Suchet stored the rest of the gear in the back of the cart, tossing a tarp over the top and tying it down with a rope.

"But I get to stay in the barracks while we set up." Suchet waggled his eyebrows at Joseph Carlo. "Only the best quarters for Master Harrison."

"I'm jealous." This was only partially true. Joseph Carlo was *not* an officer's cabin boy and had become quite used to life as a sharpshooter's apprentice. He wouldn't have traded places with Suchet. The one good thing about the fancy quarters was that there would be mosquito netting, unlike the 'tween deck where they slept in the open air. The netting kept the mosquitos at bay and, from what Joseph Carlo had heard from other sailors, Jamaican mosquitos were not only fearless, vicious, and ravenous, they were also thought to be deadly. Ships had lost two-thirds of their men to yellow fever, and flying abominations like moths and mosquitos were thought to carry the disease.

The boys gave each other brief heartfelt hugs at the end of the gangplank, and Joseph Carlo reboarded the *Deptford* to go aloft again. When he reached the crosstrees at the tippy-top of the mizzen mast, he looked down at the pier. He barely flinched at the deadly drop to the deck.

On the pier, the cart trailed two men onto Port Royal's Harbour Street. Harrison strode in front, and Suchet, tiny compared to the rest of them, trotted behind it. Joseph Carlo put two fingers in his mouth and whistled shrilly, a trick he'd learned from Pace. Suchet heard him and looked up at the *Deptford*'s rigging. He found Joseph Carlo and waved before turning back to Harrison, following him into the fort.

Chapter Twenty-One

IT WAS A DIFFERENT SUCHET THAT RETURNED TO THE *DEPT-ford* six days later—disconsolate and quiet. Word on deck was that Harrison had left that morning on the *Merlin*, headed back to England. He'd taken the successful results of the test and the Watch with him, but he hadn't taken Suchet.

To cheer him up, Joseph Carlo and Tomaso had gotten Suchet added to the water party headed ashore that afternoon. The island had many fresh water rivers, the sweetest in the Indies, and it was the water party's job to row across the harbor from the *Deptford* to Jamaica, fill up the water casks, and get the heavy cargo back on the ship. Joseph Carlo thought an adventure to Jamaica would be just the thing to lift his cousin's spirits. He wouldn't say it aloud, but he was glad that Harrison had left Suchet behind.

They boarded the longboat just after the midday bell. The day was hot and still, a combination that made Joseph Carlo's head swim. During target practice, he'd missed three out of the five targets Pace had set for him, not up to his latest standard. Pace wasn't the type to admonish, but Joseph Carlo could tell that the Nightjar had been less than pleased with his performance.

"No worries, boy," Pace had said, shaking him gently by the shoulder. "You'll take another crack at it tomorrow. It's that bleeding sun."

Lips compressed, Joseph Carlo had slung the musket across his back and climbed back down to the deck.

On the longboat, eight men rowed and five others huddled together in the stern. The majority of the boat was taken up by the water casks, around twenty wooden barrels, each standing to Joseph Carlo's hip. They'd beach the longboat, hauling the stubborn craft onto the shore, then tread one of the well-used paths to and from a freshwater river wearing water yokes, more suited to livestock than to men. The yoke lay across a man's shoulders and curved around his neck; on each end was a rope leading down to a bucket waiting to be filled with water. In this way, the water party would slowly, slowly fill their casks, making trip after trip into the tropical forest. It would take hours. Hard work, but still, it was an opportunity to get off the ship.

The salty spray off the longboat's bow blew through Joseph Carlo's sweaty hair. The boys leaned out over the gunwales, watching sea life glide beneath the thin skin of the water. Suchet reached down to trail his fingers in the waves, smiling. He looked up at his cousin and both their grins grew. No words were needed.

A change of scenery is what he needs, Joseph Carlo thought.

As they neared the shore, they heard a whistle and a shout. The men in the longboat turned around and, to their surprise, saw that there were four other longboats following about thirty yards behind.

One of the other *Deptford* sailors, a man named Bartholomew but called Lucky Jack, spoke up. "Must be from the *Anemone* or one of t'other ships I seen come in on the rising tide late last evening. They'll be needing fresh water for sure."

Tomaso had his spyglass to his eye, studying the newcomers. When he lowered it, he turned to look at Joseph Carlo and Suchet with an odd expression.

The bottom of their boat scraped up against the sandy shore. They jumped out to pull her up, beached her, and waited for the other water parties to land. In the bow of the boat in front stood a man in a blue jacket, the gold of his buttons glinting in the sun, an officer's hat planted on his head. He held a spyglass in one hand, and the other gripped the gunwale for balance. As the boat neared, the man lowered the spyglass and doffed his tri-corn hat. Joseph Carlo suddenly understood why Tomaso had given them such an odd look. The breeze ruffled Jameson's red hair as the boat pulled closer and closer to shore, where Joseph Carlo, Suchet, and the crew of the *Deptford* waited to meet him.

When the other longboats had beached themselves and the crews had pulled their boats onto the shore, the group of men totaled around forty, including Tomaso and three other midshipmen, and Jameson, who, as the highest-ranking officer, was making sure no one forgot his authority.

Jameson *had* recognized them, but he didn't show it. He'd stumbled when he saw them but recovered quickly and had been ignoring them ever since, although when he looked their way his eyes glinted with malice. Joseph Carlo wondered if Jameson was going to concoct some terrible retribution for their treatment of him on Madeira but he found he wasn't scared. He saw Jameson for what he really was: a pompous, bitter man, made old before his time by the poison of his own hatred. His hairline was receding and, when not wearing the tri-corn hat, he would swipe at the straggling hairs growing long by his ears, sometimes pulling them across his uncovered head in pathetic stripes. The skin of his skull was freckled by the unforgiving sun and peeling off in flaky patches. He'd grown thinner in his months at sea and his clothes hung on him. Where he wasn't sunburnt, he was sallow. When he spoke, flecks of spittle flew from his lips and gathered in a gummy glue at the corners of his mouth.

The flecks now flew thick as a snowstorm. Jameson was at odds with the midshipmen as he wanted to stay in one of the longboats while the rest of them toiled under the blistering Jamaican sun.

"I'm not well," Jameson sputtered. "I can't get bit by those damnable bugs. Some people think they carry the fever."

"We can't risk our boys either," Tomaso countered. "The fever has carried off almost all the able-bodied seamen on the HMS *Mermaid* in one fell swoop. And with us traveling on to Cuba—"

"Listen carefully, Italian dog," Jameson cut him off. Tomaso's head jerked back at the slur like he'd been popped in the chin. "I am the highest-ranking officer present. Every single man goes for the water. And since all these men are on the edge of mutiny—" several of the sailors hissed at this—"one of the Marines from the *Anemone* will shoot anyone who leaves this beach without finishing his task."

There were gasps of outrage, and Tomaso stepped forward, hands balled into fists, but no one made any other move towards Jameson. They couldn't. He *was* the highest-ranking officer among them and what he said was law, even if it was heinous. Jameson jammed his hat back on so hard that it came halfway down his forehead.

"You!" He pointed at a man twisting his hat into knots.

The man dropped the hat in the sand. "Aye, sir?"

"You and three others will row me out in one of *Anemone*'s longboats, but not so far that I can't see what's happening."

"Yes sir." The man reached down to grab his hat. "Sir, if you don't mind me asking, why?"

"Because it's so deadly hot here!" Jameson retorted. "My constitution can't take it. I'll wait off shore until the task is done, then we'll row back to the ships. Sanders!"

A man in a Marine's plain clothing and a musket across his back stepped forward. He wasn't pleased. His strong-featured face glowered with unspoken condemnation, but he knew not to say a thing against Jameson. None of them could. It crossed Joseph Carlo's mind that Jameson had lost his mind entirely.

Jameson gave the Marine instructions, and the Marine unstrapped the musket from his back with reluctance. Jameson then looked over the group of incredulous men with a mean smile pegged to his face. Joseph Carlo had never felt so much hatred for another human being; bile boiled up the back of his throat and stung his mouth.

"Get to it," Jameson ordered, turning away from the group of men and starting for the longboat.

Under Jameson's instruction, four men pulled a longboat back into the water and held it steady in the rocking waves as Jameson and his two oarsmen clambered aboard. Then the longboat was plowing through the surf while Jameson sat in the bow, facing the men on the beach. He was still smiling.

Tomaso uttered one of the worst Italian curse words Joseph Carlo had ever heard (it actually made him blush a little) and then turned back to the men.

"You heard the lieutenant, boys, let's get this done quick. We'll be back on board before we know it."

It took them an hour to prepare for the long trek into the interior. Sanders in the meantime stood on the white sand looking miserable, the butt of his musket planted between his feet. He hadn't moved since Jameson had given him his orders. The only thing that moved were his eyes as they tracked the men carrying empty buckets and water yokes and the beads of sweat dripping down the sides of his face, darkening the collar of his shirt inch by sticky inch.

When they were ready, Tomaso nodded to the group of hot, sweaty men. "You boys are tough." He pulled out a flask from under his shirt. "Here's to our fool's errand." He raised the flask high. He took a swig and passed to his left. "Have one on me, boys. And then we'll be about it."

The flask was passed around, each man taking a pull. By the time it reached Suchet and Joseph Carlo, the men had mostly drained it, a good thing since Joseph Carlo didn't think that rum would help under the unblinking gaze of the Jamaican sun. He felt dizzy and nauseated as it was, and they hadn't even started into the dense forest.

Then they walked into the trees, a long column of sweating men weighed down by the clumsy water yokes. The buckets that swung from either end banged against their shins and the backs of their knees, making it difficult to keep to the serpentine path. The men angled their shoulders in order for the yokes to pass through the narrow corridor. Joseph Carlo trudged behind Suchet at the end of the line. Before the forest swallowed them, he turned for one last look at the sea. Through the dark green foliage, a slice of ocean shimmered under the line of the horizon. The *Deptford* and the rest of the flotilla seemed to float above the water in a heat haze. In front of them, riding the gentle waves, rocked Jameson's longboat. The lieutenant had his feet up on the rail and his hat over his face. One of the oarsmen was fanning him. Bile jumped back up Joseph Carlo's throat as the forest closed in around them.

Chapter Twenty-Two

SANTO INFERNO, IT WAS HOT. LIKE THE CRUST OF THE EARTH HAD cracked open and the whole lot of them had walked into some anteroom in Hades. It hadn't been this hot on the beach with its diamond-white sand and shadeless expanse, and the air on the ship was positively balmy compared to this. The vegetation created a natural sauna and it felt like an overheated coffin.

As soon as the vegetation closed behind him, Joseph Carlo saw and felt nothing but the swampy heat and unrelenting bugs. The trees' broad waxy leaves were beaded with water from the humidity and when a leaf slapped his face, it left a wet streak as big as his palm. The air vibrated with a hundred thousand insects, many landing and biting before he could get a hand up to swipe.

The buzz and clatter of the insects and the grumbles of men filled the air as the rock trail gave way to mangrove swamp. They waded through ankle- to shin-deep murky water that hid a thousand imaginary horrors. It frightened Joseph Carlo, wading through water where he couldn't see his feet. Every step, his feet sank into decaying leaves and mud as the brackish water swirled around his ankles. He imagined some devilish creature poised between the ropey roots of the swamp trees, waiting for the perfect moment to sink its teeth into an exposed stretch of ankle flesh.

Half an hour in the trail widened and the leaves around them thinned out, dispelling the odd green twilight. The sound of water grew louder and Joseph Carlo heard yokes hitting the earth with thuds and men talking, their voices easy with relief. They'd reached the bank of the river. Joseph Carlo broke through the last stand of brush and thankfully dropped the water yoke from his shoulders. Water cascaded out of a cliff face of gray rock fifteen feet above them. The waterfall sounded like the song of church bells: pure and clean. Some of the men knelt at the pool that gathered at the base of the falls and cupped their hands, lifting water to their mouths. Several stripped down and jumped in, stroking through the water to stand under the waterfall, laughing as it pummeled their heads and shoulders.

Joseph Carlo noticed Suchet standing on the bank with his back to him and soft-footed theatrically up behind him. Before the boy knew it, he planted both hands on Suchet's shoulder blades and pushed. Suchet uttered a surprised *caw* as he stumbled forward, arms reeling in front of him, feet sliding over the slick rocks underneath. He splashed two steps into the water before he went down. He surfaced and spat a mouthful of water at Joseph Carlo.

"What, Gufo? You looked hot."

Suchet flipped a slick of wet hair out of his eyes as a grin broke over his face. "You know what, Brunito? So do you!"

Joseph Carlo furled his eyebrows in confusion when suddenly hands were lifting him up. He shouted in protest as he was carried towards the water and thrown in, suddenly enveloped by the cool water. When he came up, he saw Tomaso and two others on the shore, laughing.

"Better?" Tomaso asked.

In response, Joseph Carlo flipped him a hand gesture that only someone with an intimate knowledge of Italian culture would understand. Tomaso laughed even harder, and the boys joined in. The fresh water felt delicious on their overheated skin and tasted even sweeter. Joseph Carlo and Suchet swam to the waterfalls and clambered onto the moss-slippery rocks, wedging their hands into the cracks between them and pulling themselves up. The cool water thundered on their heads and backs, blocking out the catcalls of the other men. It was, for an instant, paradise.

After they'd filled their buckets and started back to the beach, Joseph Carlo understood why the other men hadn't jumped in after the boys. His wet clothes were at first a welcome balm to the insane heat but they soon became warm and sticky, and afterwards adhered to his skin like a bloody bandage, chafing where the yoke sat on his shoulders. Where the fabric creased, blisters formed and popped. The full buckets were nearly impossible to manage on the yokes, swinging and catching on vines and branches. In the time it took to reach the beach, Joseph Carlo was soaked in sweat and red in the face. He tried to put the yoke down as gently as possible but he'd still sloshed a full quarter of the water out of the buckets on his trip back.

The men poured the water slowly into the casks, savoring the fresh breeze coming off the sea. Apparently the process was too slow to suit Jameson, for after twenty minutes a sharp call came from the longboat. Jameson's face was as red as his hair. The men could barely hear him at this distance, but Sanders's miserable face spoke volumes as the Marine lifted his musket. Lips compressed, he looked like a man going against the fabric of his nature as he leveled the Brown Bess at them.

The sailor beside Joseph Carlo hissed in distaste as he picked up his yoke with the empty buckets swinging.

"Come on, lads," he said as he turned his back on the Marine and the officer in the longboat. "At least in the forest he can't order the poor bloke to shoot us." With that he stalked off down the trail, the rest of the men falling into place behind him. Sanders was left pointing his gun at an empty beach.

They made around six trips to the waterfall and back, but it felt more like fifty. Judging from Suchet's bedraggled appearance, to him it felt more like a hundred. The boy's head was soaked and he stared only at his feet. When he *did* look up, dark red blotches and heat rash tattooed his face. One of his hands bled where it steadied the yoke on his shoulders, probably from a burst blister, and blood soaked the white cloth of his shirt by his shoulder. Joseph Carlo followed behind him, whispering encouragement in both Italian and English.

They were on their final trip back from the waterfalls, slogging silent and miserable through the darkest part of the tropical forest. Their buckets sloshed as woody vines reached out like witches' hands to grab at whatever they could catch. Screams of tropical birds punctuated the cacophonous buzz of insects. Joseph Carlo had his eyes pinned on the trail beneath his feet, trying not to trip over the uneven ground. He kept glancing up to see if he could glimpse blue in the sea of green but saw only the subterranean twilight.

All of a sudden, the buzz of the insects intensified. At first he couldn't understand what was happening. It was as if a thunder cloud had drifted down out of the clear blue sky to surround them. Then it hit him: it was a massive swarm of mosquitos. The men pivoted their torsos back and forth in an attempt to escape them. Some broke into shambling runs to be rid of them, heedless of the hard-won water sloshing out of their buckets, anything to escape the horde of biting bugs. They landed everywhere, the air thick with their teeming bodies.

Joseph Carlo could barely see Suchet although the boy was right in front of him. They covered Suchet like maggots on a corpse; his white shirt was black with them. The boy desperately swatted at them whipping his head back and forth, but the yoke pinned his arms. Before Joseph Carlo could stop him, Suchet dropped the yoke with a high-pitched yell, spilling all the water in the buckets, and broke for the beach in a sprint.

Joseph Carlo trotted in Suchet's wake as best he could, squinting to see through the millions of mosquitos. The other men had made it over the rise and onto the beach when Joseph Carlo burst through the green barrier. Suchet stood close to the shore. He must've been planning to run straight into the water to rid himself of the flying devils. It would've been an apt plan except for the furious officer in the longboat shouting at the Marine who stood directly in front of Suchet with his raised musket. This time there was no doubt how Sanders felt. And who wouldn't despise his lot when ordered to shoot an unarmed boy escaping a cloud of bugs?

Jameson was livid. He stood in the stern of the longboat, hollering orders at Sanders and jabbing a finger at Suchet while a rower held up his hands, trying to calm the officer before he overturned them. Joseph Carlo put down his yoke as carefully as he could and ran to join Suchet. When he reached him, he brushed the final clinging bugs off the back of his cousin's shirt.

Jameson's voice floated over the waves. "You get back in there and get your yoke, boy! You do it *now* or you will be shot! I am an officer of the English Navy! I will not be ignored! This is insubordination!" One more moment and Jameson would be jumping up and down in the longboat, like a toddler refused a sweet.

Suchet studied the sand at his feet. Sanders stood with his back to the sea, the long stock of his musket leveled at the two boys, his face a portrait of misery. He mouthed the words, "I'm sorry," at Joseph Carlo but didn't lower his weapon. He couldn't.

Joseph Carlo turned Suchet around and herded the boy back towards the tropical forest. With his arm slung over his cousin's shoulder, he could feel Suchet's reluctance as the sound of buzzing came from the trees.

"*Non ti preoccupare,*" Joseph Carlo whispered to him. "Don't worry, *cugino*, just walk with me until he can't see you."

Suchet let himself be pulled up and over the rise until they were blocked from view by the sandy knoll. Joseph Carlo sat Suchet down and squatted in front of him.

"I'll be right back. You stay here. *Tutto bene?*"

Suchet looked at his feet, his hands hanging between his knees. Joseph Carlo leaned forward, dipping his head to see into his cousin's face.

"All right?" he asked again.

Suchet finally nodded.

Joseph Carlo took off in a hard trot. When he entered the dark green trees, he pulled his shirt up over his mouth and nose so he wouldn't inhale the insects as he leapt over roots and rocks. The bugs still swarmed in a pestilent cloud. The uncanny light filtering through so many leaves turned the air greenish, as if he were underwater and the insects were a massive school of minnows. If he ran fast enough, they couldn't keep up with him long enough to bite. He came to Suchet's yoke and picked it up without breaking stride, hurtling farther into the forest while dodging vines and leaves until he reached the mangrove swamp. In a few minutes of splashing through the muck, he reached the bank of the waterfall. He ran pell-mell into the water until it was up to his shins and then slammed the buckets down to fill them, not even glancing at the picturesque waterfall above him.

As soon as they were halfway filled, he positioned the yoke on his shoulders and was off again. This time the yoke limited his pace to a fast walk. He was terrified that Jameson had ordered Sanders to go check on the boy and the ill-fated Marine had topped the rise to find Suchet sitting there, hopeless. As he pushed through the steaming streamers and vines, visions of Suchet's blood staining the white sand crowded out the unrelenting bugs, which had ample opportunity to get at him now that he'd slowed his pace.

When Joseph Carlo stumbled out onto the rock and sand trail, he found Suchet sitting where he'd left him, alone. Red welts marked his neck and ran down into the collar of his shirt. His hands no longer hung idle, they were scratching fiercely, all over. Welts covered every inch of the boy's exposed skin. Joseph Carlo saw that he'd only managed to keep about a quarter of the water in the buckets, but he didn't care. He leaned down with effort and worked a hand underneath Suchet's armpit, lifting the boy and tugging him along behind him. The boy's skin was hot to the touch and Joseph Carlo could feel the bumps of bites under Suchet's shirt.

The men had finished pouring the fresh water into the casks and had gotten all of the longboats into the water when the boys reached the beach again. The longboat waiting for them closest to the shore was filled with *Deptford* men, Tomaso in the bow, anxiously watching for them on the beach. Joseph Carlo led Suchet through the small breakers and over the jumbled rocks and coral of the seabed to their boat. When they reached it, many hands reached down to grab the yoke, and then lift first him and then Suchet into the longboat. A call came across the water.

"Midshipman!"

It was Jameson, once again standing in the stern of a longboat and pointing a finger at them. Sanders, sitting next to the officer, was looking pointedly away from the boys' longboat, his musket finally lowered.

"You make sure those boys get the water into the casks. Do you hear me?"

Joseph Carlo could feel Tomaso tense up.

"What a troll—" one man hissed.

"Absolute wanker," another agreed.

"Preying on the boys like that," a final sailor grumbled. "Big man, him."

Tomaso stood up in the longboat, his jaw clenched. "Sir, yes *sir!*" he said with exaggerated formality. "I shall make sure that these boys do their right and true duty by the order of the English Navy, *sir!*" He snapped the man a sharp salute and then turned his back on Jameson before the other man could respond. "Billings," he said through clenched teeth to a man holding a set of oars. "Put your oars in and don't let up until we reach the *Deptford*. I want the last thing that man to see is our arses. Now get to it."

Billings nodded. "Aye, sir. C'mon men, row as hard as you can, if only so the boys no longer have to listen to that blather."

The longboat pulled ahead of the rest of the water party. The last Joseph Carlo saw of Jameson was his blue jacket and grim face staring after them as they rowed hard towards the *Deptford*, widening the distance between their longboat and the others.

Joseph Carlo regarded Suchet's reddened and bite-bumpy face. *Sure*, he thought with frightened sarcasm, a *change of scenery will do him good*.

Suchet caught his cousin's eye and, to Joseph Carlo's astonishment, cocked his head and raised his left eyebrow, gracing his cousin with his most impish expression. "*Stronzo Terzo*," he said decidedly.

Joseph Carlo cackled up to the clouds, out of relief as much as amusement. "Sure enough, *Stronzo Terzo* indeed." He crinkled his nose and chanced a glance behind them. "But I'd take the rooster over him any day of the week."

Suchet's grin dwindled as he reached up to claw at one of his welts.

Chapter Twenty-Three

A FEW DAYS LATER JOSEPH CARLO WAS SITTING ON A BARREL with his back to the mizzen mast when Tomaso found him. He was patching a sail in the late afternoon sun, a stiff sea breeze blowing in off the rail. Joseph Carlo hummed a tune as his needle went in and out of the tough canvas. He didn't know he was humming it until Tomaso put words to the song in a strong baritone. "*Il mugnaio non è venuto . . .*" he boomed out as Joseph Carlo hummed the last of the melody. The final bug bites across the bridge of Tomaso's nose had healed, blending with his freckles.

"Good afternoon, *paisan*," Joseph Carlo said to Tomaso, doffing his hat in deference to the other's status.

Tomaso responded with a tight-lipped smile that did not reach his eyes. "Hello, Joseph Carlo. How are you?" Melancholy tinged Tomaso's words, breaking Joseph Carlo out of his sleepy daze. He squinted at Tomaso.

"I'm fine, sir," Joseph Carlo responded. "But something tells me you're not." He pushed the needle into a fold of the sail, laid it by his feet, and waited.

Tomaso took his time. Joseph Carlo grew more anxious with every passing moment, but he made himself sit and wait.

I've been transferred, he thought in a panic, although he didn't let it surface. *I've been transferred to Jameson's ship. That's what it is.*

Tomaso was still reluctant, his cat's eyes as sad as Joseph Carlo had ever seen them. Joseph Carlo willed himself not to make too much of a fuss when Tomaso told him he'd been transferred off the *Deptford*.

"They're taking Suchet off the ship. Soon. As soon as they can."

Suchet? Off the ship? Why? Joseph Carlo crinkled his nose in his confusion. "Why are they transferring Suchet?"

Joseph Carlo saw with horror that bright tears glinted in the corners of Tomaso's eyes, and when he spoke again, his voice broke on every other word. "No, *ragazzo*, they are not taking him to another ship. They're taking him to the naval hospital in Port Royal."

Joseph Carlo jumped to his feet. "What?! Why? What's wrong with him?"

"You know what's wrong with him, Joseph Carlo. And you know why they have to take him." The world of the ship and the sky and the clouds began to spin. When Tomaso spoke again, it seemed as if it were from far away, as if Joseph Carlo had been put at one end of a telescope and Tomaso at the other. "Bronze John got him."

"Bronze John?" Joseph Carlo gasped.

"That's what the lads call yellow fever."

With that short sentence, Joseph Carlo was transported thousands of miles away and a year in the past, to a dark tunnel in the middle of the night in Italy when a gregarious gypsy had told their fortunes. "Beware a man made of bronze," he'd told Suchet.

"It's just a touch of the croup! A summer flu! It'll pass." Even in Joseph Carlo's own ears, he heard how thin this sounded.

Tomaso looked up at him from his crouched position by the barrel, tears now freely staining his cheeks. "Joseph Carlo," he spoke with all the gentleness of a mother explaining something to a frightened child. "Today Dr. Dover took a look at him. His eyes have gone yellow. It's the fever."

Joseph Carlo felt hot tears bubbling up his throat. He shook his head, as much to negate what Tomaso was saying as to shove the sobs back down his throat.

"Maybe it was the heat," Tomaso reasoned. "Maybe it was the bugs. It certainly wasn't helped by Jameson."

Joseph Carlo shook his head again, and banged his fists against his thighs.

"They have to take him to the hospital. They can't keep him on board. You *know* that. He'll be quarantined . . . until he gets better."

"When?" Joseph Carlo muttered.

"Today. As soon as they can."

Joseph Carlo whipped his head towards the gangplank that led to the pier and finding it empty of men, strode off towards the 'tween deck leaving Tomaso squatting by the mast. The midshipman got up and followed.

"You can't stop them," Tomaso said when he'd caught up. "They have to take him away before he infects us all."

Joseph Carlo whirled on him. "*Scappa!*" Tomaso looked as if he'd been slapped. But when Joseph Carlo started towards the 'tween deck again, Tomaso was still right behind him.

"Please, *paisan*," Tomaso said. "Don't scare him any more than he already is."

Joseph Carlo halted suddenly, and Tomaso skidded to a stop just behind his shoulder. There was movement in the hatch as someone backed out, climbing the narrow ladder backwards. When the sailor exited, it was clear why he'd needed to back out. Holding one end of a stretcher in his hands, he stepped carefully onto the deck with first one boot, then the other, an unseen sailor moving in concert at the bottom end. When the first sailor half-turned to check his footing, Joseph Carlo saw that he'd tied a bandana around his mouth and nose. That got Joseph Carlo moving again.

He was incredibly angry, more so than he'd been at Jameson when he'd called Tomaso an Italian dog. Rage trembled under his skin, threatening to burst forth and spew venom all over anyone it could reach. He marched over to the two sailors bobbling the stretcher up and over the lip of the hatch, fully intending to put a stop to this, to show them that Suchet wasn't sick at all, that the boy merely had a passing touch of something. If they wouldn't listen to reason, then he would have to muscle Suchet out of the stretcher and get out of there. Where? He had no idea. He only knew he had to get Suchet away before they took him away.

A few feet from the stretcher he stopped short, indignation and righteous anger evaporating into a cloud of disbelief. Disbelief and fear. On the stretcher lay Suchet, but a version of Suchet he didn't recognize.

When did he get so bad? Joseph Carlo thought. The sailors carrying the stretcher eyed Joseph Carlo, unsure of his intentions. Joseph Carlo was unsure himself; the idea of getting Suchet out of there faded with one look at his cousin.

Suchet lay with his bent legs canted to one side, knees resting on the edge of the stretcher. Someone had laid a shirt over him. He looked twisted and shrunken. He held his hands in claws over his stomach. But it was his face that'd stopped Joseph Carlo. When Suchet emerged into full sunlight, it became clear why Dr. Dover had diagnosed him with yellow fever: he was yellow. All over. His jaundiced skin had taken on a waxy sheen, making him look as if he'd been carved from an old candle. He squinted in the light as if it hurt his head and moaned. When Suchet looked at him, Joseph Carlo had to physically stop himself from recoiling. Suchet's eyes were yellow, the dark green irises standing out against the urine-colored whites. And they were full of terror. Fear, like ice water, filled Joseph Carlo from his toes to the top of his head.

Time spun out. His mind moved with whiplash speed and yet the automations of the sailors and ship around him wound down, a wind-up toy at the end of its cycle. The sailors shuffled towards the gangplank and the pier, glancing apologetically at Joseph Carlo. One of Suchet's claw-like hands reached out and gripped him.

"Help me, Brunito, please." Suchet's voice was reedy and hoarse, as if he'd been screaming.

Stunned, Joseph Carlo stumbled along next to his cousin, trying to think of something to say. In his mind, he ran frantically over the last few days, the times when Joseph Carlo had seen Suchet on deck or at mess. How could he not have noticed? How could he have been so stupid? He remembered sitting close to him at dinner two nights ago and hearing him cough; just the next day Suchet clutching his stomach while at his tasks on deck. But those seemed so minor, how could they have led to this . . . this waxwork that used to be his cousin?

"Brunito." Suchet's yellowed eyes were a hundred years old. "Please don't let them take me away." His grip tightened. Joseph Carlo felt jagged nails bite into the soft underside of his wrist as he kept pace with the stretcher.

But last night. The realization hit Joseph Carlo like a fist to his stomach, leaving him nauseated. Last night, when they'd lain in their hammocks next to one another, he'd felt Suchet trembling next to him, shaking violently enough to wake Joseph Carlo out of a thin sleep. He'd called over to him, asking Suchet if he was all right, if he needed an extra cover or a jacket or something else to keep him warm. Suchet had replied that he was fine, even though Joseph Carlo could feel the boy's spasms through both hammocks and could even hear his teeth clicking together. Joseph Carlo had started to sit up, concerned, but Suchet had assured him that everything was all right, that he had a touch of something but that the fever was breaking, that was all. Joseph Carlo should go back to sleep. Which is what Joseph Carlo had done, he remembered now with a sharp pang. He'd lain down and gone back to sleep. Probably thinking of nothing but how he would fare in the next day's target practice.

How could this happen? Joseph Carlo asked himself. He wanted desperately to rip his hand away from the other boy, to tear his gaze away from the sunken cheeks, the cavernous eyes, the white paste gumming the corners of Suchet's mouth. But he couldn't, he knew he couldn't.

A hand was laid on his shoulder and Joseph Carlo glanced back. Tomaso's face was filled with such sadness that Joseph Carlo couldn't look at him for long, or he would start to cry.

Joseph Carlo tried to disengage his hand from Suchet's as the stretcher neared the narrow gangplank. Suchet shrieked and floundered violently to the side, gripping Joseph Carlo's hand still harder. The stretcher canted wildly to the right, threatening to dump the sick boy out. The sailors fumbled to correct it, letting Suchet plead with Joseph Carlo one last time.

"*Cugino*, don't let them take me." Suchet's wide eyes bulged with fear. Fear and understanding. Joseph Carlo had to say something to him that would make him feel better, that would fix everything. But there was nothing *to* say. And Suchet could see this too. He started to cry in a shambling way, the sobs barking out of him like an old man coughing as he kneaded Joseph Carlo's hand. "You can't let them! They can't take me! Please, Brunito! Help me!" The last two words ripped out of Suchet with such desperation Joseph Carlo didn't think he could bear it. Tomaso tightened his grip on Joseph Carlo's shoulder, its warmth and strength flowing through him, helping him do what he knew he must.

"Be strong, Gufo," Joseph Carlo said. "You'll get better." This was probably a lie, and both cousins knew it. Two-thirds of yellow fever victims died, and that included strong men with healthy appetites and sturdy constitutions. Suchet's constitution would not be described as sturdy. The sailor at the stretcher's far end tried to mount the gangplank but Suchet's death grip on his cousin's hands wouldn't let them move forwards.

"Don't let them, Brunito!" Suchet's voice was like broken glass grating on Joseph Carlo's heart, drawing blood with each word. "You promised to take care of me!"

Sadness welled up in Joseph Carlo as if coming from the ocean's deep depths. With all the love and tenderness he could muster, Joseph Carlo unlocked his cousin's hands from his own.

"Noooo!" The word turned into a howl, like a wounded animal being driven away from its home. "Please! Brunito!"

The stretcher mounted the gangplank and moved towards the pier.

"I'm sorry, Gufo, I'm so sorry." Tears choked Joseph Carlo's voice. He tried to speak loud enough so Suchet could carry his words with him to what lay ahead. These words might be the last he ever uttered to his cousin. His throat tightened like a noose. "Goodbye, Gufo."

Suchet's desperate cries grew fainter as the men reached the dock and turned left, heading to Port Royal's hospital. Joseph Carlo stayed where he was, his heart shattering into millions of pieces with each of Suchet's fading screams. And, although he would hate himself for it for ever after, he felt relief too.

Joseph Carlo stood on a hillside overlooking the bright blue of the Caribbean Sea. It was nearing day's end and the peaches and tangerines of the sunset spilled over the green forest. The rays filled the air with pastel radiance from the lip of the harbor to where he stood. Each glossy leaf stood out against the painted sky. The evening breeze sighed up the hill, smelling of salt and growing things. To his left stood the ruins of an old church. The roof had caved in years ago and only the whitewashed walls remained, the peaked angle of the roof still delineated in its absence. Vines grew where pews once awaited the faithful. The only faithful that flocked here now were the animals and birds that sheltered in its crumbling walls. The birds greeted the evening with intricate clacks and chirps and songs.

But Joseph Carlo didn't hear them. He didn't see the clouds that frilled like peacock feathers from the horizon. He didn't hear the sea breeze soughing in the palm trees, nor did he feel its caress on his hot skin.

In his mind and heart there was only room for one thing. It lay at his feet, a wound in the earth. It was smaller than most, which made it even worse. It lay there anonymous. The upturned earth that had been black with subterranean moisture was drying brown in the tropical heat. The only thing marking its purpose was a wooden cross at its head. Only a foot high and leaning to the left, it was roughly made and spiky with splinters. A sob escaped Joseph Carlo and he smothered it in rage, gripping the medallion trapped in his fist hard enough to make its edges bite into his palm.

It had all been a huge misunderstanding. That's what the nurses kept trying to tell him at the hospital. Although most of the doctors were white Europeans, the nurses were all from Kingston and the surrounding areas, hence they spoke in deep Jamaican accents that were difficult for Joseph Carlo to understand. The waiting room was comfortable, luckily for him, because Joseph Carlo became intimately acquainted with it in the eighteen hours he was there. If it hadn't been for Tomaso's food deliveries, Joseph Carlo might've passed out from hunger and exhaustion.

The waiting room was large, square, and white with bay windows overlooking the boat yard and the city of ships anchored in Port Royal's harbor. Boats zipped here and there among the larger vessels like oxpecker birds amongst the water buffalo. To Joseph Carlo, the whole room was wrapped in cotton batting. All of it—the frisky gusts of wind, the sound of wood being chopped and sawed in the cooperage, the baritones of men singing at work—filtered through the imaginary bandages that now swaddled him. The only real things were the jagged beating of his heart and the flicker of hope that grew fainter with each passing hour.

He had still held onto hope, though, through that long first night. He tried to convince Tomaso (and in doing so convince himself) that the long wait meant that Suchet was healing, that the medicine needed time to take effect. But when dawn broke on the second day and there was no orderly waiting to take him into Suchet's room, that was when the defiant voice of hope began to whimper. When noon came into the room with clear un-muddied light, his heart filled up with the coarse sand of guilt and despair and regret, dragging it down so he felt like he was drowning as the cheerful daylight stained the floor lemon yellow.

The head nurse had asked him a series of questions in her thick patois, leaving him even more unmoored. The more confused he was by her questions, the louder his inner voice of hope became. Maybe the nurse meant Suchet was on the mend. It was only when she gestured to his hand, indicating that he should hold it open, and then placed the necklace in a gold and pearl puddle in the cup of his palm, that he fully understood. The last time he'd seen this necklace it was around his cousin's neck, and now here it lay, all that was left of him.

On the hill, he gripped the necklace as if it could vanish.

When he was finally told that his cousin was dead, it wasn't a blow. It was more of a dull thump, like getting hit in the head with a piece of wood wrapped in yards of cloth. And now he was up on this hill, on this strange island that grew no trees that Joseph Carlo recognized, bearing fruit he'd never tasted. This was where he would leave Suchet, alone, in the dark, in a place as far away from Villa Franca as the moon. A sob threatened to wrench from his throat; he grabbed his shirt collar and manhandled it back down. Concern emanated from where Tomaso stood a few feet behind. He didn't need to look to see the midshipman there and didn't want to. He didn't want to see Tomaso's sorrow-reddened eyes. It would only make him angrier, not a just repayment for the care Tomaso had shown over the last two days.

Joseph Carlo knew that Tomaso was honestly grief-stricken, but he didn't want to see his friend mourn his cousin. He couldn't bear to see sadness unsatisfactorily mirrored in Tomaso's face. He knew it wasn't Tomaso's fault, it wasn't anyone's fault. He was also angry at the perfect weather: the day was lifted out of an oil painting of Paradise. He was angry at God, but Joseph Carlo didn't want to confront his bleak feelings about God at the moment.

There was only one person to blame—the man who'd ordered them into the Jamaican forest on a death mission, the man who'd been the reason that Suchet was on this God-forsaken ship in the first place: Jameson. Jameson with his sadistic smile who'd ripped Suchet away from the life he was *supposed* to have and given him this one: a life of toil and misery ending in a dirty death.

Tomaso shuffled into his field of vision, and laid a hand on Joseph Carlo's shoulder.

"Joseph Carlo," Tomaso said.

Joseph Carlo sucked in his breath.

"We have to say something for him. You know we do."

Joseph Carlo let this sink in. He knew his friend was right, but he was scraped clean. There was nothing else to say but that he was sorry.

Seconds turned to minutes and Tomaso waited for Joseph Carlo to speak. Instead, Joseph Carlo began to quake, sorrow shaking him to the center. Tomaso stepped up to the grave, and began in a clear voice,

Padre Nostro, che sei nei cieli,
Sia santificato il tuo nome.

The prayer floated through the verdant air like the chime of a bell. Joseph Carlo's knees trembled.

Venga il tuo regno,
Sia fatta la tua volontá,
Come in cielo, così in terra.

Lena's face swam through Joseph Carlo's wavy view of the foreign landscape. It was a dark midwinter night and Joseph Carlo was eight. He was kneeling on the wooden floorboards of the Casa saying his prayers, and Lena was helping him. Suchet was there too, next to him, his small form curled in earnest over his clasped hands.

Dacci oggi il nostro pane quotidiano,
E rimetti a noi i nostri debiti
Come noi li rimettiamo ai nostri debitori.

Then they were aloft on their family's barque, Joseph Carlo's hair flying back in the brisk breeze. Joseph Carlo turned to his cousin as he stood on the yard next to him, and Suchet's smile of exhilaration turned to such sadness. Joseph Carlo's heartstrings broke one by one as if the task of holding his heart together had finally become too much.

E non ci indurre in tentazione,
Ma liberaci dal male. Amen.

"Amen," he whispered, falling to his knees at the side of Suchet's grave. A surge of sorrow took him where it would. He sobbed and wept and screamed into the perfect sunset until he had nothing left. But that wasn't quite true, he had *one* thing left. He opened his hand, letting the necklace fall until it hung from his ring finger. Through tear-blurry eyes, he watched it twirl in the breeze. He knew what he had to do.

Joseph Carlo stood, grave dirt clinging to the knees of his trousers, and walked to where the sad crooked cross stood over Suchet. He laid his hand on the splintery grain of the wood and jerked the cross upright, and then hung the necklace over it, fingering Suchet's medallion for the last time.

Joseph Carlo found his voice for the first time in a long while. "So you never forget who you are."

Tomaso took him by the elbow. They began the long walk away from Suchet, the last one, on the shell-littered road. When Joseph Carlo looked back, he could just see the cross casting its shadow over the newly made grave. Just then, the setting sun hit the medallion, and it flashed, once, twice, three times, as if it was waving goodbye. The next time he looked over his shoulder, the graveyard had disappeared around a curve in the road.

The walk back to the ship might've taken twenty minutes or it might've taken an hour. Joseph Carlo's mind swam in and out of focus. A group of children played with a ball in a dusty side yard, their bare feet raising poofs of dirt at each maneuver and Joseph Carlo could see every stitch on the ball, every shrill of laughter cut him to the quick. Then his mind swam away again, like a fish darting in and out of sight among the coral. Tomaso led him down steep roads, through the outskirts of the naval fort, and then back into the hum and throb of the shipyard. It was amazing to him in his exhausted, distraught state that everyone was going about their business, as if it were a completely normal day, which he supposed it was. A group of men carrying a log destined to become a mast passed in front of Joseph Carlo and Tomaso, and the look of sweaty productiveness on the men's faces bewildered him.

When they reached the gangplank to the *Deptford*, Joseph Carlo paused. Tomaso looked back at him, a question in his eyes. Joseph Carlo could only shake his head and Tomaso moved off. The ship was exactly as it had been when Suchet had been carried away on a stretcher. Men aloft yelled to one another among the swinging ropes; Crickmore banged two pots together outside his cookhouse; Captain Digges stood in his captain's hat on the quarterdeck studying naval charts. All Joseph Carlo wanted was to be delivered to his hammock so he could block out a world that could kill a boy like Suchet and then return to its business in the same breath.

He took the last step down off the gangplank onto the main deck to head to his hammock as quickly and unobtrusively as he could when he heard something. High and reedy like a mermaid singing. He'd heard it before on the night of the storm. Pace was playing his whistle, and he was playing for Suchet.

Tears stung Joseph Carlo's eyes for the hundredth time that day. He found Pace in the crosstrees, leaning against the foremast, his whistle to his lips. The melody was different from the one he'd played on the night of the storm, sadder and quieter somehow. Each note was pitch-perfect despair, as if the instrument itself wept for Suchet. After two refrains, Joseph Carlo recognized it as the Children's Lament, played for those lost too early.

The usual clockwork movement on board ceased. All the men stopped working and were watching Joseph Carlo. He mashed his lips together, trying not to break down in front of the crew, and then the bo'sun's whistle shrieked over Pace's lament. On the quarterdeck Captain Digges had his hat in hand. When Digges saw he'd caught the boy's attention, he nodded to a sailor by the main mast, who untied a halyard and pulled. The Union Jack in its usual place of pride at the top of the mast dipped down the mast in quick jerks. As it descended, each sailor doffed his cap.

"To one of ours who's fallen," intoned Digges. The Union Jack's long length lay halfway down the mast. "He's now captain of his own soul. May he find his way home."

The crew ranged all around muttered "Amen" as Pace's melody took hold again, high and clear like a child's voice. The ship wavered as Joseph Carlo tried to see through the tears. He was grateful for Tomaso's hand once more on his elbow. They stopped at the hatchway and Joseph Carlo climbed down into the smelly depths, Pace's last notes following him. He paused next to his hammock and looked at Suchet's, as if they would once more swing harmoniously together as they slept. He didn't give his own hammock another glance.

He went to the animals' pens among barrels and crates. The quiet quacks of the ducks greeted him as he swung one leg, then the other, over the side of the Duchess's pen. She grunted at him from her hay nest in the corner as he sat down beside her. He had no more tears left in him. He missed Suchet so much. He scratched the Duchess's forehead as she settled down next to him, leaning into his thigh. Her warmth and animal smell enveloped him as her grunts turned into snores. He curled one arm over her, put his cheek against her bristly back, and slept.

Chapter Twenty-Four

THEY PUT THE BLUE MOUNTAINS OF JAMAICA BEHIND THEM ON a blustery May morning. Joseph Carlo could not have cared less, but that was the way he felt about pretty much everything these days. It'd been a little more than a month since he'd buried Suchet. He was relieved to put the whole island behind them. His eyes craved new vistas; maybe a change would help him heal, if that was possible. He'd been sleeping little, eating less. Tomaso badgered him that he'd better get as much food and rest as he could; they were headed into battle where both of those things were scarce.

They left the naval harbor of Port Royal as a flotilla, the *Deptford* one of seven other ships of the line headed out in the gusty morning with their tenders and smaller support vessels trailing behind them. Two layers of clouds amassed behind the indigo hills, wisps of cotton racing across the larger bulbous thunderheads behind. The ships lunged like eager horses, churning the bright blue Caribbean waters beneath their bows, but their captains kept their steeds reined in. They didn't shake out all their canvas, not yet, just let them feel their bits. The jibs pushed them along on the falling tide, and the green, flowery perfume of Jamaica drifted with them until the island was out of sight.

The wake off the stern reflected the bright sun like shattered glass. There was no cajoling or singing this morning, only a heady sense of apprehension. All the crews were glad to be moving. The preparations had been made: gear stowed, cannons cleaned, and cannon shot piled in neat order across the deck. Nonetheless, the men knew what they were heading for and each one was melancholy from thoughts of battle, sickness, hurricanes, or all three. They were like corks bobbing on the edges of a monstrous whirlpool, circling a violent and chaotic end. Teased by their own imaginations, they thought about what would come next. More than one sailor aboard this contingent of the British naval force wondered as he glimpsed his last of peace, who would survive? Who wouldn't? Was it worth it?

No one could answer these questions, of course, so they turned back to the task at hand, waiting for what would come.

Halfway through the midday watch, a shout came from the boy in the foremast top. He was pointing off the port rail and grinning. Joseph Carlo looked up from his lines. Off the port rail swelled another group of sails, all topped with the Union Jack. It was another division of His Majesty's Navy headed for Havana. Both flotillas shook out their larger sails and pointed their bowsprits on a diagonal course that would bring them together to make one large fleet.

In half an hour they were within shouting distance of one another, and shout they did. Men hung off the rail, hollering to the sailors on the other ships, the line of them spread out over a mile. The boys aloft hopped up and down with excitement, waving their caps to one another. The signalmen relayed messages from ship to ship with their flags.

A smile flitted across Joseph Carlo's mouth as he stood at the rail, watching with amazement as their flotilla became a fleet. They were now one hundred strong at least: twenty or more ships-of-the-line, quite a few of them bigger than the *Deptford* and with more guns. There were also frigates, bomb vessels, medical boats, and a cutter, all smaller sloops fighting for space amongst the larger crafts. The transports were the smallest boats, the most numerous, and the quickest. They flitted in between the behemoths of the warships like water bugs.

It was a sight that took Joseph Carlo out of himself. It was impossible to see the broad stretches of white canvas and hear the snap and crackle of hundreds of sails without feeling a surge of pride at being a part of it. The ships lunged as one, riding the waves, their wooden bones creaking with strain. In this moment, every sailor on board felt the beat of battle in his blood and welcomed it. They were not individuals; they were the sailors of the Royal Navy looking ahead to the bloody battleground with eager anticipation. They were many strands braiding together to make one rope: stronger together than apart. Joseph Carlo felt it as well, and for a moment his darkness was gone, a weight lifted.

Evening watch found most off-duty men scribbling away on random scraps of paper with whatever writing utensil they could scrounge while the last of the sun illuminated the unmoving thunderheads piled on the western horizon. The clouds glowed from within like gigantic paper lanterns, and the sun's rays periodically pierced them with great shafts of red and purple. The men sat on barrels, writing awkwardly on their knees or hung from the nests with bits of paper curled around the hard surface of the mast. Those that couldn't write were dictating to someone who could; quite a few of them sat next to one of their mates, murmuring the last words they would send to their families in England, Ireland, or Scotland.

Joseph Carlo wrote a letter to Lena, telling her what had happened to Suchet and asking her forgiveness. He tried it out many times in his head, but there seemed to be no way that he could phrase it without sounding guilty. "It wasn't my fault" seemed to be every other sentence, cementing the fact that it *was* his fault. He should have done better. He could've done something more. In the end, he merely gave her the facts, told her he was sorry, told her he missed Villa Franca, and that he loved her. He didn't tell her they would win the coming battle, and he did not promise that he would come home. He didn't think either one was true.

When he finished, he headed back to the 'tween deck to return the blackened stub of a pencil to Pace, stepping down into the musty dark deck and letting his eyes adjust. He couldn't see Pace's imposing figure anywhere and was about to head back up when a voice called him.

"*Paisan*! Wait!"

When Tomaso reached him, he clapped a hand on Joseph Carlo's shoulder and jerked his head towards the ladder. Both climbed to the main deck where they stood under a purple velvet sky, deepening into black.

Tomaso handed him a piece of thick paper folded many times.

"What's this?" Joseph Carlo asked.

"A letter for my father. In case . . . you know." Tomaso let that sink in. "He lives near Inverness in the Highlands of Scotland. A place called Adverikie Estate in Kinlochlaggan. I wrote it all down at the top of the letter. You can also ask in any pub in the village. They'll know."

Joseph Carlo nodded and then dug into his waistband. "Here," he said, giving Tomaso his own letter. "Casa Mauran in Villa Franca, use my name. Or better yet, use my nickname: Brunito."

Tomaso grinned in the twilight. "Golden, eh? Suits you."

Joseph Carlo smiled back at his friend, thinking how much the nickname Gufo fit Suchet. Little Owl. He didn't mention it to Tomaso. His heart hurt.

"Hopefully, we'll be trading these back on the other side," Tomaso said, putting Joseph Carlo's letter in a leather pouch at his waistband.

"Other side of what?" Joseph Carlo asked taking equal care with Tomaso's letter.

"Where we're headed, of course." Tomaso's grin turned wry and dark. "The other side of Hell."

Traveling as a fleet had several benefits including the free distribution of information between the ships. Transports zipped between the larger warships and, with the supplies and men they swapped back and forth, the sailors also traded stories. Rumors flew between the men-of-war that they were joining an even larger contingent and that their waterborne force would be matched by a land force. Some sailors said that it was the land force that the British were counting on, that the force on the water was merely a distraction. Another story was that the British commanders needed their victory in Havana to be swift as they were worried about the upcoming hurricane season as well as outbreaks of yellow fever and other diseases.

The ships buzzed with disparaging remarks about the Spanish. Joseph Carlo, with his heavily accented English, often had to explain his origins on the *Deptford* to the sailors transferred aboard. A sailor strange to him would furrow his brow and stare hard at the boy before offering a hand and a grudging smile. The crew of the *Deptford* was protective of Joseph Carlo. More than once such an interaction had almost come to blows between a sailor new to the ship and one of the men who'd made the crossing with the boy. The men defensively told the strangers that Joseph Carlo was seasoned.

The first time he'd heard that, he'd needed a translation. "Seasoned" made him think that he was regularly sprinkled with paprika. But no, "seasoned" meant that he was immune to yellow fever, his new archenemy. If a sailor had been exposed to the fever and remained healthy, then he was seasoned. Sailors who'd suffered from the Saffron Scourge and had returned to health were also seasoned, as Suchet would have been if he hadn't died. As much as Joseph Carlo wanted to heal the blackened hole where his heart used to be, or at least dull its jagged edges and toughen it up into a scar, Suchet's shadow was meeting him around every corner, ripping the scabs off his sore heart each time.

Joseph Carlo was removed from reality by Suchet's death. A few weeks had passed and the cotton batting surrounding his mind was tattered and dirty, like an old bandage on a crusty wound. Here he was, barely fourteen years old and heading into his first battle, and yet he felt as if a glass jar had been lowered over him. Everything was blocked out by some invisible barrier, and the worst of it was that he didn't care anymore. About anything, not even himself.

Before, Joseph Carlo had been a sunny boy on the brink of manhood. He did the right thing not because he had to but because it came naturally to him. Now, though, he relished the moments when a black rage eclipsed his vision. It didn't take much—a bump of a hip by accident or a carelessly rigged sail letting go—and the rage would bubble out of the hole where his heart had been. Murderous, he'd clench his fists so he wouldn't leap on the unsuspecting offender and pound his head in. This wasn't even the most frightening part of it. Joseph Carlo *liked* this feeling, enjoyed it immensely, wanted to roll around in it like a pig in mud. Every day, almost every hour, he felt his control slip a little more and he moved one step closer to the abyss. He hoped that they'd reach Castle Morro before he fell in.

Chapter Twenty-Five

THE COMBINED FLEET SIGHTED CUBA AND CASTLE MORRO IN the darkest hour of a blisteringly hot night, halfway through the mid watch. The admiral's plan was to go straight in and begin shelling Castle Morro by first light. Everything was ready for battle: the ship's decks were clear, and the carpenter and his mates had unshipped the wooden bulkheads and made ready their plug shots to stop up any breaches in the hull. The captain's furniture was stowed below and secured; men from each mess had stored the crockery; the topman had stopped the sheets that wouldn't be used during the battle. Around midnight, the fleet had reassembled east of Havana, just off the coast of Matanzas, and were sailing under cover of darkness toward the point on which sat Castle Morro. Once Morro was in range, they were to start firing with all they had.

Joseph Carlo's compatriots had noticed his constantly black mood, although he tried to hide it as best he could. But there was really nothing they could do about it. Preparation took precedence over a serious discussion about Joseph Carlo's state of mind. But then he found himself aloft with Pace the night they sailed into battle.

They were in the main top for a few hours, keeping watch in silence. The Nightjar stood for most of the watch, his back against the mast, whittling. Over the four hours, he slowly turned a chunk of wood into a crude snake. Joseph Carlo watched the patchwork of blacks and grays of the rising and falling waves. The days had been hot, as if they really were approaching Hell, but the nights usually brought a welcome respite. Not tonight. The thick cloud cover created a close ceiling of unbroken clouds, trapping the day's heat. Added to that, a fog hung over the ship like a bad smell. Without wind, the ship jerked back and forth and up and down, a far cry from her usual graceful gait as she raced before a breeze. The halyards banged against the masts and the sails flapped listlessly.

Joseph Carlo could tell that the watch was almost over when the blanket of sky lightened by degrees. First it was pitch black except for the lanterns hung bow and stern, feeble beacons in this weather, and then there was an almost audible *click*, and it was a tiny bit lighter. A few more minutes, a few more *clicks* and then there was enough light to see Pace's hands and the glint of the knife on the wood. In another minute, Joseph Carlo could see the shavings flying from Pace's grip.

Pace looked up, surprised by the dawn. They could almost see the wheeling shapes of the gulls between the ships. The fog around them reflected and diffused the light from the imminent arrival of the sun, making it glow. Pace stretched, his back and knees cracking, and folded his knife in on itself with a *snick*.

"Today's the day," he said.

"Today's what day?" Joseph Carlo asked in a rusty voice.

Pace looked at Joseph Carlo as if he were another piece of wood to shape, like he was looking for what lay underneath. "Today we see battle. You ready for it?"

Joseph Carlo shrugged. Tendrils of rage seeped into him like smoke wafting under a door.

Joseph Carlo felt Pace's intense gaze on him looking for something in Joseph Carlo. Something that, Joseph Carlo was sure, wasn't there anymore.

"Want to know why I play it?" Pace asked, his hand moving to the whistle that hung from his belt. "I'm going to tell you. Listen hard." Pace slid down the mast until he sat in front of the boy.

Joseph Carlo pressed his lips together in annoyance, but he would listen if Pace told him to. It was light enough now for Joseph Carlo to see the line between the older man's eyebrows and how tightly Pace gripped the wood carving. Pace looked down at his strong hands and forced himself to put the piece of wood down.

"We were off the western coast of Africa, but it could've been anywhere. It was so hot there. Hotter than this, hotter than anything I'd ever felt. And I hadn't really felt heat before, I was just a lad from Northumbria. It was my first campaign as a Marine, and I was all puffed up, being just seventeen, only a few years older than yourself." Pace scrubbed his hands together, trying to rid them of an imaginary stain.

"It wasn't my home, it was so strange, and I was terrified all the time. Terrified of the strangeness and terrified of messing up. Of course I did my level best to not show it—first mistake."

The fog was dispelling, revealing wider stretches of water. The sun had not yet raised its head but it would soon.

"My second mistake was to believe that everything my superior officers said was true and should be obeyed to the letter. But I'm getting ahead of myself." He paused again, scanning the sea with eyes that were miles away, off the coast of Africa. "We were assigned to guard an English merchant vessel—an ivory trader—going to Pointe Noire and trading goods for ivory. We were all on the beach except for the cook and the skipper. I was in charge of guarding the goods we were trading, not the ones we were taking back to London. They were heaped in a pile on this beach, which wasn't sand but hard red dirt. I'd never seen a beach like it. Everything seemed to be a shade of red or brown. Even the wide leaves on the trees bled to brown at the edges.

"I remember that there were these funny birds on that beach that made me laugh. They were these little black and gray things with stick legs that would run down as the wave was sucked back and poke their needle beaks into the sand and then scurry back up the dune as the waves came in. They reminded me of a great aunt I had, all skinny legs and determination. We'd had a hard time getting the cargo to shore because there were rocks crowding the shoreline, making it nigh impossible to land the longboat. Laughing at those little birds was a relief.

"I was standing guard near this small mountain of stuff, guarding it and watching the villagers pile their goods a ways down the beach from us. Then we'd meet in the middle to trade, you see? It seemed like the whole village was down there under that hot sun. It didn't seem to bother them the same way it bothered us. Men and women both carried these huge sacks on their heads, moving so gracefully they looked like royalty. And then there were the kids." Pace paused for so long that Joseph Carlo wondered if that was the end of the story. Just when he was about to speak up, Pace raised his head. Joseph Carlo was startled at the sorrow stamped on his face.

"These kids, you know, were just about everywhere. They ran from their camp to ours and back again, kind of like those birds but not so serious. Their voices rang through the air in that funny French patois they speak. Some even tried to investigate us but the first lieutenant of the Marines, my commanding officer, hollered at them and sent them scurrying.

"They were playing a game in the middle of the two piles of goods, all clustered together and darting in and out of the circle. I wasn't really paying attention to what they were doing until I heard the shout from my superior." Pace rubbed the back of his neck. "Seems some of the kids were nicking the goods on *our* side of the beach. At that moment there was this group of three, all about eight or nine years old, right next to the pile and one of them has a lemon from our ship in her hand. Just a lemon, not even ivory. Maybe she was going to eat it, I don't know. She was looking at me with wide dark eyes, and she was smiling, like the whole thing was a big joke. But it was no joke, and I knew it." He stopped again, shaking his head once, as if to clear it. Joseph Carlo realized how hard it was for him to tell this story; he wondered if anyone had ever heard it before now.

"My officer sees the kid, this little girl, and I watch as his eyes move to her hands, to what she's holding. She's still looking at me and she's *still* grinning, like the whole thing is part of the game. He yells at her, walking towards her from the other side of the pile, pointing his finger and his whole face red. Her friends scatter but she looks at him and falters, likes she's not so sure now, but then she looks back at me. Her grin widens, and it's pure joy, nothing malicious in it. She turns and starts to run down the beach, like it's a game of tag, and my superior loses it. He's yelling at her to stop but of course she can't understand him. She's looking over her shoulder, laughing her head off, and that's when the first lieutenant orders me to shoot her."

Joseph Carlo's breath was sucked out of him; he had to physically make himself inhale. When Pace spoke again, it was fast and broken, all coming out in a jumble.

"He screams at me once, then twice to shoot her, that we have to show them who's boss, have to make an example or they'll all steal from the Crown. He says that: 'the Crown,' as if we aren't standing by a pile of ivory on the west coast of Africa but are in Buckingham Palace guarding the majesty's jewels. He's furious with me so I raise my musket, and aim it at her, but I'm not going to shoot her. I can't do that, she's just a kid. Now she's fifty feet away and still running. He's right next to me, screaming in my ear that I'll be court-martialed if I don't obey orders, that I'm a *Marine*! The last thing I think before I pull the trigger is maybe I'll miss, maybe she's far enough away for me to miss. I pull the trigger." He put a fist to his mouth to muffle a dry sob. "But I'm a bloody sharpshooter. I never miss. Through the smoke from the Bess I see her go down like a sack of potatoes thrown on the beach. Her arms fly out and then the shot drills into her, taking her down for good." He paused for the longest time yet but Joseph Carlo knew to wait it out.

"All hell breaks out on the beach but I don't notice. The villagers drop what they're carrying and scatter. The lieutenant is still shouting at me but I'm not listening. I walk up to her. I don't want to, but I can't stop myself. When I stand over her, I see that her eyes are open and she's staring into the oncoming waves. She looks surprised and scared. The blood, the pool of blood underneath her on the sand keeps growing. I stay there as the waves come in, washing over her open eyes and taking some of the blood, staining the water pink. I stay there, standing over her, until the lieutenant yanks my arm. I look up and see four or five villagers running at us, waving clubs and things. He pulls me to the longboat and gets me in, but I keep looking at her, at the woman who flings herself on top of the dead girl as we're rowing away and starts screaming like I've never heard anyone scream before or since. Screaming because of me."

Pace's eyes were far away even though he was looking right at Joseph Carlo. Pace wasn't seeing him at all; he was looking through him to a dark place. The first sliver of sun burst over the horizon, spilling a white-hot path from the horizon across the gray ocean to the *Deptford*. The next time Pace spoke it was so soft that Joseph Carlo almost missed it. "I could've missed. Don't you see? I could have. But I didn't.

"I've never forgotten her. She haunts me. I'll live that day over and over until I die. That's why I play it, the Lament, the one for lost children. I play it to remind myself to listen to my heart, that if I do that I'll never go wrong. Even if it goes against orders, still follow your heart." Joseph Carlo had to look away from the raw pain in Pace's eyes. "Someday you'll be faced with a decision that may be your undoing. Listen to your heart—if you can hear it— and follow it. No matter what."

Joseph Carlo didn't realize it, but he was feeling something different from the raw pain and rage that had been drowning him since Suchet's death. His breath was coming quick, his chest rising and falling. He wanted to reach out and touch Pace but couldn't, so he just sat with him. Pace met Joseph Carlo's eyes with a tortured look. "Promise me you'll listen to your heart, Joseph Carlo."

"I promise," Joseph Carlo said, and he meant it. *As long as it's loud enough.*

Pace nodded, satisfied, and held out the whistle he'd unfastened from his belt.

"This may help remind you," Pace said.

Joseph Carlo stared at it in disbelief. He shook his head. "No, Pace, I . . . I couldn't."

"You can and you will." Pace's face was still carved with the sharp lines of his sadness. "And remember this: I could've made myself miss. But I didn't. And that's who I am now, because of that one decision."

The Nightjar disappeared over the lip of the platform into the morning fog.

Joseph Carlo sat in the growing daylight with his arms wrapped around his knees, staring at the path the rising sun made to their ship. Everything around him was white and gray: the sky a bright white boding a hot day and the sea gray. Wisps of fog flew past him. He knew that the battle would begin as soon as he climbed down from his perch. He'd be ordered to a gun crew and, in the thin light of morning, they'd make their approach. But for now he was content to stay aloft for another moment. He was still sad, but he was sad for Pace, for the little girl lost on the beach. He still felt the rage but in the silver morning light, he held it at bay. He sat high in the crosstrees, waiting for the bell that signaled the turning of the watch, and stared at the sea.

The *Deptford* was at the end of the fleet, trailing the first-rate warships as well as the small boats attending them on the final leg of their journey. Joseph Carlo was up the mast staring off her stern at the boats' wake leaving large stripes across the green-gray ocean. It was almost silent, except for the sounds of the ship coming to life below him: intermittent calls, creaking wood, slapping lines.

As he watched the trail of bubbles and foam the ships left in their wake, he saw a dark shape surface a hundred yards off their stern. Joseph Carlo cocked his head; although it looked small from up here, he knew that the thing was a whale and it was a behemoth.

As he watched, a spout of water spewed from its blowhole and another dark oval—a third of the first one's size—floated up out of the depths like an ink-filled bubble. It stayed close and tucked itself under what Joseph Carlo imagined was the larger whale's flipper. The smaller one had to be the larger's calf. Something about the scene, the fact that he was the only one to witness it, as if it were a secret between him and the whales, brought a smile to his lips, as unexpected as the whales' appearances. As he watched the two whales move away from the fleet of ships, staying close to one another all the while, he relished the secrecy of the whales' appearance and escape. The hush stayed with him as he climbed down to find out to which gun crew he'd been assigned.

It would be the last silent moment he'd have for a long time.

Up until now, Joseph Carlo was Pace's boy, but the sharpshooter wouldn't have many enemies to fire at from the tops as they would mostly be firing at a stone cliff and castle. So Joseph Carlo would be in the rigging, on the longboats scouring the sea for survivors, or basically anywhere an officer wanted him.

For the attack, Joseph Carlo was a powder monkey, busily fetching to and fro for the crew of a large gun named Jumping Billy. Jumping Billy was a mass of heavy-oiled iron with a ferocious-looking muzzle. The cannon sat on a wooden carriage, its rear end bound by thick ropes and pulleys. When fired the gun recoiled in a jolt of crashing iron straining against rope. If a cannon wasn't harnessed properly, it would break free, careening crazily around the gun deck, smashing men to bits, and possibly making a huge hole in the hull. The gun crews fittingly called this a "loose cannon."

The men in the magazines handed out powder bags and cartridges as fast as they could through dampened curtains. One of the other boys, a slight lad with a thick cockney accent, showed Joseph Carlo how to carry the powder.

"Ye carry it underneath your shirt," the boy said, shoving the cylindrical container under his linen shirt. "That-a-ways, as yer runnin' to yer gun, ya won't catch a spark and blow us all to smithereens."

With that, he spat onto the floor and stepped up to receive the powder like it was a precious sacrament. When it was his turn, Joseph Carlo shoved the cylinder of powder under his shirt and ran back to Jumping Billy.

Fresh sand was scattered on the gun deck's painted red floor. Graham, an old tar who sweated profusely as he strewed handful after handful of sand across the floor, told Joseph Carlo that it was for spilled blood: the sand soaked it up and the red painted deck disguised it so the gun crews could maintain control. Or as Graham put it, "So they don't go insane."

From the slice of landscape he could see through the gun port, Joseph Carlo thought Morro looked like a sand castle pulled out of the earth and hardened. Made of white rock, it stood low on a cliff except for one tower spiking to the sky. Bald and scrappy hills rose to the left and behind the castle, which looked impenetrable and haughty up on its perch. Behind it one could see the suggestion of a town: a spire and a few roofs. This was Havana, seat of the Spanish hold in the lucrative West Indies. If the English succeeded here and took the fortress, the city, and the whole island of Cuba, they would knock the Spanish out of the sugar trade and cement the English hold on the West Indies and the Caribbean.

Digges had informed his gathered crew that Admiral Pocock had sent his orders: as soon as they were in shelling distance, the dance would begin. Per usual, the English would configure their men-of-war in a loose arc to optimize an attack on a land-based enemy. The Spanish had already chained the harbor and scuttled three ships at the mouth of it in an effort to keep the enemy out. The British would send their largest ships with the most guns out first. As soon as all the guns had fired, these ships would stand down, replaced by another three. Around and around they would go, shooting at the castle high up on the cliff as they sailed to the forefront, reloading as they sailed around the back. Supplies were ferried by the smaller ships sailing frantically back and forth in the middle of the circle. This crazy carousel would go on until the red tide of English soldiers could infiltrate the castle, lower the Spanish flag in the tower, and raise the Union Jack. That was the plan. But plans rarely go according to their designs.

The *Deptford* bobbed in position at the back of the arc, guns at the ready. Silence gripped the ship. None of the usual shouting or singing accompanied the preparations, only the occasional prayer and that in a hushed whisper. The men of Jumping Billy's gun crew were tight knots of nerves, each of them jockeying for a position near the gun port to see out the porthole's limited aperture. Joseph Carlo was still smaller than most of the men on board, seasoned sailor or not, and so he had to jostle the men in front of him to get a view of what was happening on the stretch of water in front of Castle Morro.

It was a city of masts and sails, hard to discern which sail belonged to which mast to which ship. Not that it mattered: they were all English, that's what mattered. As Joseph Carlo watched, he could see a pattern emerging in the comings and goings of the warships, turquoise sea winking between them.

"There they go," whispered a short fat man next to Joseph Carlo, elbowing him and pointing a stubby figure at three ships detaching themselves from the fleet proper and sailing with full canvas for the cliff topped by the Castle Morro. "They're gonna give 'em the first go around," he intoned, nodding his head with the full gravity of the situation.

And it was true, three ships-of-the-line, all larger than the *Deptford* and thus any boat Joseph Carlo had ever seen, approached the cliff. Before the letters became too small, Joseph Carlo sounded out the names of each ship: HMS *Stirling Castle*, HMS *Marlborough*, and the HMS *Dragon*.

"*Dragon*—now she's a seventy-four gunner, only two years old—good name for the first one to give the Spanish a go, innit?" The portly man smiled at Joseph Carlo, revealing a concerning lack of teeth. "She'll give the Spanish a run. The *Marlborough* is a ninety gunner—she's old but she's quick."

As they watched, the three warships bravely rounded up broadside to the castle. Then he heard it. Faintly, the drums aboard the ships rumbled across the water, signaling an imminent attack. The *Marlborough* ran out her thirty-two-pounders, their black snouts snarling out of the gun ports, belching flame and smoke, and with a ferocious *Blam!*, the cannonballs wailed through the air. As she rolled her guns back in to reload, the *Dragon* rolled hers out to keep up the fierce shelling of the fortress. But the walls held. It was now the *Stirling*'s turn, but before the ship could fire, the fort answered back.

The Spanish unleashed their wrath upon the English vessel. The *Stirling* was suddenly wracked by what looked like an invisible wind filled with needle-sharp razors. Splinters flew and rigging shredded as the Spanish shot slammed into the ship. The sound of sailors' screams and the acrid smell of gunpowder wafted over the ocean to the *Deptford*. The *Stirling* listed to one side, as if an invisible fist had slammed down on her starboard deck.

"She's been hit in the hull! Lord no!" The fat man whispered in panicked tones. "Those poor souls."

The *Stirling* listed even more, her port rail dipping down into the sea. Up on the cliff, men scurried around the armaments of the castle. The crash of cannons was followed by puffs of smoke, and another volley of shot hurtled from the castle. Joseph Carlo heard the faint whistling of cannon shots flying through the air.

Again, the man-of-war in front bore the brunt of the shot, her sails ripped ragged by the scorching pieces of iron. Suddenly there was a *crack* like a tree giving way after an ice storm. The rigging on the front ship let go as if an invisible hand was plucking off each yard and spar. Another groan from the ship and more cracking, louder this time.

"Gorry! Her mast!" his companion shouted.

The ship's mast had a peculiar cant to it, not quite the proud up and down it had once been. With a final crack, the *Stirling*'s main mast arced through the air. Even as the rigging did its best to hold, it slowly crumpled under the strain. The mast slapped the water with a smack and a splash and lay still, tattered sails floating uselessly around it. The *Stirling* had been dismasted. She looked like a wounded elephant sinking to one knee in submission.

It was an awful sight. The mast lay in the water like a sick thing, and the vessel leaned alarmingly to one side. The *Stirling* was done; even he knew it. Most of the seamen had been hurled into the sea by the force of the shot. Others slid off as the ship's rail dipped into the waiting sea, the sailors' arms and legs flailing for foot- and handholds as they fell into the sea. Some jumped into the water from any spot they could reach, escaping the wreckage, the blue of their coats like ink stains on the water. It could have easily been Joseph Carlo in one of those crosstrees.

The bows of the *Marlborough* and the *Dragon* crossed the stern of the wounded ship and made a course to join the fleet once again. No one in Joseph Carlo's gun crew spoke a word. The man next to him clutched his hat to his chest. As they watched, the *Stirling* cut away her rigging and hobbled out of range on just the power of the fore-jibs, leaving her mast behind. The captain was still on the quarterdeck as the *Stirling* listed and limped away. The English's first attack had failed miserably. Then the captain of the *Deptford*'s gun deck shouted for the drums, and she moved to take her place at the head of the line.

Chapter Twenty-Six

JUMPING BILLY'S GUN CREW HAD BEEN RIGHT; THE *STIRLING* WAS doomed from the first. She'd been irreparably wounded during those first strikes and never recovered. She was able to limp just out of range, but the damage had been done. The once fast and powerful *Stirling Castle* would be sunk by the crew to keep what was left of her out of Spanish hands. Late in the afternoon on that first day, Joseph Carlo was deployed on a longboat to find any survivors. They rowed towards the *Stirling* while some of her still showed above water, all the while keeping the large listing ship between them and the Spanish guns.

The Spanish had sharpshooters on the castle walls that could pick off English from a distance without any tell-tale volley of thunder. Death at the hands of a sharpshooter would be preceded by a shrill whine through the air and then the musket ball would bury itself in a soft and vital organ. When he was in the rigging, Joseph Carlo had seen a Spanish sharpshooter pick off one of the men, an officer on the quarterdeck of a neighboring ship. It looked as if a ghost had sucker-punched the man, and then Joseph Carlo saw the blood. The man had sunk to his knees with a surprised expression and keeled face forward onto the deck, and that was that.

In the heat of the battle, no one took the time to sew each sailor up in his hammock before reading him his last rites and sending him into the deep for his final sleep. Not during battle.

In battle, the dead men were simply tossed overboard like rotten provisions to become a meal for the sharks enticed to the battleground by the rich smell of blood in the water.

On the longboat, combing the outer harbor for any survivors of the *Stirling* crew, Joseph Carlo had never been so terrified. Something about being at sea level instead of high above it made it scarier. The waves crashed over the bow and debris slammed against the sides of the longboat with ominous thumps, making him jump. As they approached the sinking *Stirling*, he heard the big ship shrieking and cracking as her seams came apart. She sounded as if she were screaming in pain, matching the voices of the sailors littered in the water below moaning for help if they still could. The survivor boat rowed around her mast, laying like a dismembered limb in the water, ropes and sails floating on the white caps. Three bodies floated amidst the canvas, the men who'd been aloft when the mast had fallen. One of the sailors aboard handed Joseph Carlo a shortened oar as they approached the doomed ship. He looked at the older man quizzically as he took it.

"To check!" the man shouted above another blast of cannon fire.

"Check for what?"

"To see if they're alive!" The sailor made a poking gesture with his hands and Joseph Carlo finally got it. He was to jab any floating sailors with the oar to see if they were living. "To the bow you go, boy. Watch out for sharks. Those beasties go berserk when the blood hits them. They'll pull you right in if you're not careful." With this cheery warning, Joseph Carlo made his way to the bow and scanned the blood-purpled water for any sign of life that wasn't a shark.

Over the course of three hours, the survivor boat fought its way through detritus, the sailors aboard poling through broken bits of boat, slashed sails, and severed lines. It was as if they were attending the burial of some huge behemoth. The air above and around them was filled with the shrieks and screams of battle, shot whizzing overhead and yellow gunpowder smoke drifting through like diseased clouds.

As Joseph Carlo stood unsteadily in the bow, pushing broken things out of the way, he felt as if he were going to jump out of his skin. The shortened oar jittered in his hands as he leaned out to try to make a path for them through the wreckage. So many corpses. Joseph Carlo had only seen two before this day. Now they were everywhere, some of them with purple drowned faces staring up to the sky, some impaled on a spar or mast, hair hanging in their faces. Once, Joseph Carlo looked down into the water to make sure they could get through a particularly clogged area and staring up at him from five feet below the water was another dead man. He looked as if he was staring right at Joseph Carlo, pleading with him to help. Joseph Carlo stared back until their boat floated over the man and he sank out of sight.

Two men were found alive and pulled on board. Only one survived to make it to the *Deptford*. Joseph Carlo counted thirteen sharks.

Battle was chaos all the time. It was difficult to keep track of the hour as clouds of smoke from the cannons obscured the sun and reduced everything to an acrid yellowy haze. And still the attack on the fortress continued. Day and night they fired their shots, rolling out the iron beasts and leveling them to blast at the impenetrable castle walls, then moving off to reload, only to face those walls again.

This went on for days and nights and nights and days. Joseph Carlo lost count as he ran from gun deck to magazine to rigging and back again. The rigging was a devilish place to be, shot flying all around, the smell of sweat and blood and gunpowder stinging his eyes. From up there, Joseph Carlo tried to maintain control of some of the sails and thus the *Deptford*'s ability to maneuver the waters below Morro. The other ships of the fleet looked like islands in the yellow atmosphere, and then the reeking breeze enveloped him in another cloud of smoky death, and the sight of the others disappeared.

It was worse on the gun deck—a dark dank corner of Hell. The air was filled with sailors' shouts, the groan and shriek of hot metal, and the thunder of shots as they exploded out of the mouths of the guns that were then driven back against their harnesses with ferocious speed. Joseph Carlo clambered up and down the ladder from the magazine to the gun deck, avoiding gun crews working their cannons with bare and soot-stained torsos, the black kerchiefs they tied around their ears to protect their hearing blending with the smears of soot and gunpowder on their faces so they resembled demons.

The stink of it was horrific. It stayed with Joseph Carlo everywhere he went. It slid down his throat and stuck there, coating it with a sour taste of gunpowder, war, and death. Then there was the cannon fire. During the first days, he flinched with each thunder roll of the guns, waiting for the shot to raze the deck, the masts, the rigging, sending razor-sharp splinters shooting through his throat, his belly, his back. Every onslaught of shots fired from the fortress, accompanied with lazy puffs of smoke from the castle's gun ports, he was sure he was done. He cringed, waiting for an impact that, as of yet, hadn't come. He felt the guns in his chest, shaking him each and every time. As the days and nights passed, he became so used to the constant shelling he hardly glanced up, even though the thunder still came every few minutes. The bellow of the guns as they rained down their iron death had become his day-to-day reality. Day and night, the cannons fired, but to no avail: the walls still held.

After a couple of weeks of this nightmare, Joseph Carlo considered that perhaps he was insane. He heard the cannons inside of his skull now, bouncing off the bone. He couldn't taste anything but gunpowder; eating was mainly a mechanical necessity: insert, chew, swallow, repeat. Sleeping was worse; his bone-tired body ached from physical activity and the stress of living in a state of constant fright. He wanted so badly to sleep, to escape, but every time he managed to relax, the thunder of the cannons would yank him back. His muscles bunched like marbles under his skin. He was rabbity, jumping at any odd sound. At night he lay in his hammock, as stiff as a corpse, and covered both ears with his hands as tightly as he could, trying to block out the clamor of death.

Pace found him one grim gray evening as he was trying to do just that, stuffed into his hammock, hands mashed over his ears, and eyes squinted shut. The Marine didn't say anything, just stood over the boy's hammock as the battle raged.

Finally he spoke, "Come on, you're coming with me. We're going ashore."

Joseph Carlo got out of his hammock and followed Pace up the ladder.

The castle walls still had not fallen.

The Royal Marines, whose company Joseph Carlo was now officially assigned to, were being sent ashore to protect the land-based contingent of the English attack. The attack was spearheaded by a much-discussed engineer, Patrick MacKellar. A well-seasoned naval engineer forty-seven years of age, he had many campaigns in his repertoire, most recently Quebec and the island of Martinique. His tactical vision was legendary, as was his commitment to his men. He'd been wounded in battle at least four times.

The two admirals in charge—Admiral Pocock and Admiral Albemarle—needed a miracle. Mosquitos were thick as molasses, sailors and foot soldiers were dying of the fever, and hurricane season was upon them. Despite all the shelling, the fort's walls still held. The siege of Havana had to end one way or another, and MacKellar was the man to make that happen. He was their miracle.

MacKellar had devised an attack on Castle Morro that would break the fortress open like an egg. The ships-of-the-line provided a crucial distraction, Pace told him as the longboat made its way to shore under the cover of a white-hot night. It was hard to think of the ships as mere distractions when he could remember the men floating in the water amid circling sharks.

The English engineer, with his miners and sappers, had been tunneling from the flat plains northeast of the castle towards its wall. They'd been steadily burrowing their way to the base of the stone castle despite the constant onslaught of the Spanish on the ramparts, picking the English off when they could, blasting at the shoreside breastworks when they couldn't find a man to aim at. The English had finally made it to the inner wall of the castle. Now all they had to do was pack the tunnels with gunpowder, run out the long fuse, and set a spark to it.

Pace and his newly appointed men, along with a few more companies, would guard the entrance to the tunnels while Mac-Kellar's sappers laid fuse. That was the most crucial part; if they failed to lay it out correctly and it fizzled, all was lost. This was all relayed to the men in a husky whisper as they rowed towards the Cuban coast, muskets laid across their laps.

The bow crunched up onto the beach and Joseph Carlo and the rest of the Marines hopped out, pulling the longboat onto the coarse sand and slinking towards the shot-scarred breastworks where the fuse-layers waited for them. It was dark and hot and Joseph Carlo felt ungainly on land after so long at sea. Pace let his company gather their bearings for a moment on the rocky shore.

The castle cliff rose up to their right, pockmarked from weeks of shelling. Atop it, like the glowing tower in a fairy tale, stood the unbroken Castle Morro. It looked larger from down here, sturdier. Joseph Carlo slung his Brown Bess across his back. Across the dark water, the ships were shadowy shapes until a volley of cannon fire lit them up like fireworks all in a row. A moment later the shots hit the castle cliff, shaking the air. Rivulets of stones showered down. After the air cleared, Pace gave the command to move off, and they crept over the dune and onto the rocky foothill that led to the dramatic rise of the cliff and then the white walls of the castle far above them. Joseph Carlo saw the castle's cannons sticking out like cactus spines.

About forty feet from the base of the walls, men worked around the breastworks and the dark maws of the tunnels. Flickers of lanterns winked on and off, disappearing into the darkness under Castle Morro. A soldier detached himself from a group and approached Pace, who saluted.

"Marine," the man said, looking as dirty, worn, and battle-weary as his counterparts on the ships. He and Pace stepped aside to discuss particulars.

Soon Pace had set them up behind the breastwork that fronted one of the tunnels closest to the ocean. The sound of the waves was muffled by the breastworks they had mounded to chest height with anything the engineers could get their hands on. From this position, they could fire at approaching enemies and then duck down to reload behind the safety of the breastwork. These men had been at it for weeks, tunneling closer to the castle every day, carting out load after load of rock, at times having to rebuild as a tunnel collapsed. The breastworks had held thus far, and they wouldn't have to hold for much longer. The sappers had been packing the tunnels full of gunpowder for hours. If they laid the fuse well, the tunnels would be blown as early as the next day.

This one action would decide the outcome of the battle. If the wall crumbled, the castle was breached and Morro would be theirs. If it didn't, all was lost.

To hear the engineers speak of him, MacKellar was as esteemed as beloved Captain Digges was by his sailors. A no-nonsense Scot, he wasn't scared to blister his hands on the working end of a shovel. Among the men handling their explosives and fuses like newborn babes behind the breastworks, MacKellar was a downright saint. The scrappy, hard-working engineers were inspired by Crown and

Country to achieve their end, but they really worked for Mac-Kellar. They wanted to make him proud. Joseph Carlo tried to remember a time he'd felt as if he were part of something good and honorable. But he couldn't. Suchet was dead, and the English Navy and Jameson were to blame. Their golden Mauran future was gone.

The engineers worked more quickly with the Marines guarding their backs as they didn't have to set watches or use up precious manpower to guard the mouths of the tunnels. Besides Pace's men, ten more companies hunkered down behind the mounds of rock and rubble, keeping watch. The stretch of rocky land in front of them led to a shadowy forest, illuminated by the far-off cannons and the heat lightning that spiked down from the overheated sky every few minutes. The smell of ozone mixed with the stench of burnt gunpowder. The Marines stood, staring in the darkness as behind them, the English engineers packed the tunnels with their last-ditch attempt at victory.

Chapter Twenty-Seven

THE ONLY THINGS THAT WERE CLEAR TO JOSEPH CARLO THAT night were the mounded rubble of the breastwork, the stretch of barren land, and the men-of-war revolving across the sea like ladies dancing until their shoes were scraps. Afterward, the men marveled at how fast it had all happened. First there was nothing, then there was something. The Marines were highly trained. There was no excuse. The Spanish shouldn't have been able to creep up on them like they did.

The Spanish had launched darkened schooners full of soldiers from the far side of the castle in an attempt to abort the assault on the castle walls. The schooners had sailed close to the shore and unloaded their deadly cargo unnoticed by the sharpshooters in front of the tunnels. One moment there was the empty plain in front of the breastworks lit up by heat lightning. The next stroke of lightning showed forty Spanish soldiers, muskets in hand, creeping across the rock towards them.

A cry of alarm was followed by the sound of men running, and then the first volley of Spanish iron slammed into the breastworks. But they were trained for this. Terror tightened in an icy coil around Joseph Carlo's heart, freezing him, and then he went on automatic. His hands knew what to do with the gun in his hands and he fired it, the jolt of the long heavy musket bruising his shoulder.

Bits of broken rock flew off the breastwork from the Spanish assault, stinging Joseph Carlo's face and arms. A man next to him got hit and went down. It was not a quick death, and the man screamed and cried in agony for hours. Unlike the clockwork-like cannon fire of the ships, the Spanish fired when they could, and the blasts from the muzzles ranged terrifyingly across the whole battlefield. There was no telling how many were out there. But the Marines would hold the Spanish off for as long as it took for the engineers to lay their fuses.

All around him, the air stank of gunpowder and the white-fire blasts were disorienting, making it hard to mark the Spaniards in the darkness. Again Joseph Carlo felt like at any second a shot would find him, but instead of terrifying him, this time his blood became as hot as the iron in his hands. The tremor of the gunshots shook his bones, whetting the honed edge of his anger as he used it to slice down his enemies. If he had a chance to reflect, he would've been horrified at his murderous side. As it was, he acted on pure instinct. Although it was his first time in battle, the darkness hid any casualties his gunshots caused.

He squatted down with his back to the breastwork, holding the strap of his gunpowder pouch in his teeth as he primed and reloaded his weapon. There was a pause in the fighting. Except for the groans of the dying and the sound of approaching feet at a dead run, for the moment there was no deafening gunfire.

From the next breastwork came a yell: "Come at me then, you Spanish dogs!"

That familiar voice punctured the grime of gunpowder and lightning straight through him. As Joseph Carlo stood, newly loaded musket in his hand, he had a disorienting sense of déjà vu. Heedless of the musket balls flying pell-mell around him or the enemy soldiers sprinting at him across an ever-shortening distance, he stared at the breastwork to his right. He saw the long shapes of muskets laid over the top of it and men's hunched bodies behind.

Where is he?

Joseph Carlo knew who was over there. He'd known as soon as he'd heard the yell. He erased the noise and dust and danger, trying to find that voice. Then, as if from a dream, it came again, and there was no mistaking who it was, even if most of it was drowned out by the bellow of the guns.

"I am a naval officer," the voice threatened, imperious as ever. "I will not be ignored!"

With that, Joseph Carlo found him. Among the hulking bodies behind the breastwork, light glinted off the gold epaulets, golden buttons, and bronze hair. Jameson stood tall amongst the shadows of his fellow soldiers, fist in the air, cursing the Spanish as musket balls flew.

There was the man who'd taken Suchet away from Lena and the family and sent Suchet into the bug-infested forest. He was *right over there.* Joseph Carlo prayed one of the Spaniard's shots would cut him down. And on the tail end of this thought, Joseph Carlo's world changed. His musket was locked into his shoulder before he knew what he was doing, his finger poised over the trigger. Jameson was less than twenty feet away from him and Joseph Carlo was now a trained sharpshooter.

It came to him suddenly and then it was there, as if it had always been a part of him, like some sort of malignant tumor hidden from sight. His feet pivoted to the right. The thought overtook his mind. The tip of his musket moved from the Spanish soldiers in front of him to the English soldiers to the right until he had Jameson's head locked in his sights.

No one will know it was me, they'll think it was the Spanish, Joseph Carlo thought as he glanced around. There were two other soldiers using this breastwork as cover but they were so intent on the oncoming Spanish soldiers that they paid the boy no mind. Joseph Carlo looked at Jameson's profile through the sight of his musket and his finger grew tighter on the trigger. Jameson, oblivious, kept shaking his fist at the Spanish, spewing blasphemies.

The misery that man has caused, the despair, Joseph Carlo thought. *All because Suchet humiliated him by mistake.* Outside his head, the world was a maelstrom of smoke and the scream of guns; inside, it was as quiet as a church on a weekday. The only thing Joseph Carlo saw was the man in his gun's sights. Nothing else mattered.

I can stop him, Joseph Carlo thought. His thoughts were not scattered or incoherent. He'd never thought more clearly. *He'll never ruin anyone's life again.*

The finger on the trigger tightened. In the corner of his eye, Joseph Carlo saw the flint hover above the frizzen, that much closer to igniting the gunpowder that would hurl the musket ball through the air to embed in Jameson's rotten skull, silencing him forever. A rush of blood flooded Joseph Carlo's face. His vision tunneled until there was only darkness and Jameson in his sights.

This is for Suchet.

With that his mind cleared like a guillotine whisking down and he put pressure on the slim piece of metal that would end Jameson's life.

Jameson, unaware that his life pivoted above the abyss by a string which was snapping one strand at a time, screamed again, spit flying from his lips. "You will not defy me!"

Fitting last words. Joseph Carlo tightened the finger on the trigger.

Then, in the bone cathedral of his mind, an airy melody circled down like a leaf falling to dimple the surface of a motionless pool of water. He blinked. The song was familiar, like a lullaby from his childhood. It was as if his very soul was singing to him. And then he recognized it, the Children's Lament. But it was more than that, it was Suchet, it was the Mauran medallion, it was the golden part of him that would always do the right thing, no matter how difficult. His trigger finger loosened. It was the lament of his own heart, and it was singing loudly enough. He could hear it.

Joseph Carlo lowered his musket.

Chapter Twenty-Eight

WHEN MACKELLAR LIT THE FUSE, JOSEPH CARLO HAD A FRONT-row seat. The Spaniards' nighttime attack had been squashed and the sharpshooters had moved back into the forest's scanty shade for the end game. The fuse was now strung along the long tunnel, ending in a wall of firepower, or so the English hoped.

MacKellar was there for the event, emerging from a group of engineers with his jacket off, hat doffed, and sleeves rolled to his elbows. The sharpshooters were tasked with picking off any Spanish soldier they had a clear shot at up on the ramparts, child's play compared to the night before. Gunfire was sparse as the Spanish knew they risked their lives if they showed head or hide above the stone wall of their castle.

Joseph Carlo lay on his stomach in the brush, elbow to elbow with his cohorts, half-heartedly scanning for Spanish targets but really watching MacKellar and his crew light the fuse. Since his close call with Jameson, Joseph Carlo was not in the mood to murder any Spaniards, regardless of what the English Crown told him to do. He wasn't English. *Dios*, as an Italian, he was closer to the Spanish than their English neighbors.

Joseph Carlo was no longer interested in what the English Navy required of him. He only wanted to escape this battle with his life, and get out of the Navy altogether. He also knew he didn't want to go back to Villa Franca. He was a different person than the boy who'd left his home harbor long ago, and he didn't want to live where he'd be constantly held up to the light for inspection. He didn't want to be blamed for Suchet's death, didn't want to be hated for not bringing him home as he'd promised. He wanted to go to a place where no one knew him, where he could start anew with no worldly goods except what was in his sea bag.

A cry from the barren plain broke him from his reverie. One of MacKellar's men had a spyglass trained on the ships, and another waved a code flag as he faced the fleet. MacKellar waved over the sapper holding the slow burn. Once lit, it would take ten minutes or more for the spark to reach its destination, a nail-biting, white-knuckled ten minutes while thousands of men wondered if the fuse had fizzled out and lay dead and useless somewhere under the earth. If this failed, the English would sail away from Havana with their tails between their legs. With rampant disease carrying off men every day and hurricanes gathering force to pummel the West Indies, without MacKellar's miracle, the entire battle would be for naught.

In the center of the plain, the man of the hour cracked his knuckles and took the slow burn in his hands. MacKellar threw his sizable chest forward with confidence. This was a man who would not be denied.

"You've done a right trig job, men, and you all should be proud of yourselves." His hawk's eyes scanned his men, who returned his measured gaze. "This is for all those who've come before and lost their lives. This is for the Union Jack!"

A roar came from the men as MacKellar leaned down and touched the slow burn to the end of the fuse. There was a sizzle, and a trickle of smoke disappeared into the tunnel. MacKellar handed the slow burn back and hunkered down on his haunches to watch his handiwork.

It felt like a lot longer than ten minutes; the men in the forest around Joseph Carlo had begun to grumble, standing up and stretching their backs. But not Joseph Carlo. He had his eye on MacKellar, who'd barely moved from his squatting position. Suddenly MacKellar raised his right fist above his shoulders, silencing the soldiers. Joseph Carlo cocked his head, and then he heard it too. A distant rumbling like strong surf still a dune away. It was a giant's drums, boulders rolling their way, a herd of mastodons running at them. Suddenly the white wall of the castle looked as if it were trembling and a large boom shook the foundation as smoke issued from the base in a black cloud.

Part of the wall came down with a sound like waves on a rocky shore pulling thousands of pebbles back into the ocean with its salty arm. Starting at the top, the wall crumpled as if made of paper. They'd spent more than a month firing shot after shot at those walls to no avail. As the smoke went up, the wall came down with ferocious swiftness. One moment it stood, as impenetrable as always, and the next, in a smoky shower of thunder and rock, it lay in shattered stones at the base and they could look *into* the castle. Joseph Carlo even saw the surprised and terrified looks on Spaniards' faces. When they began to run, he knew they had them. A wave of foot soldiers wearing the red coats of the English militia surged over the breached wall, scrambling over the pile of rocks, and into the castle.

Men everywhere erupted in hoots and hollers; MacKellar himself held both arms out, like he wanted to embrace them all. His grin was irrepressible and contagious. Men threw their muskets down and their caps in the air, knowing that breaking Morro spelled Spain's demise. The red tide surged over the rocky remnants of the Spanish stronghold and just like that, the English took Havana.

Of course, it wasn't just like that; it took many days of hand-to-hand combat, relegating these men here and those men there, transporting prisoners of war, and writing tracts, but eventually Havana became the new jewel in the English crown. MacKellar had delivered on his miracle and for that, England was grateful. For Joseph Carlo, it was a miracle of another sort: it meant that they'd be leaving Havana, their job done.

On the third day after the wall fell, Joseph Carlo, Pace, and the others were transported back to the *Deptford* to receive new assignments and orders. Since his moment on the front line, Joseph Carlo hadn't given Jameson another thought, and he imagined he never would again. Jameson would go on, spreading his poison throughout the world, but he hadn't infected Joseph Carlo. That was the important part.

The atmosphere on the *Deptford* was jubilant. Digges came around and shook every man's hand, congratulating them on a job well done. Joseph Carlo was assigned to a transport ship traveling with a contingent of sick and wounded soldiers to the Colonies. They were taking them to the closest medical facilities but, even so, most of them would not survive the journey.

The rest of the crew, including Digges, Tomaso, and Pace, would set sail for England. Joseph Carlo was the only one of the *Deptford* crew staying west other than the wounded or the dead. He didn't mind. He'd requested it. He had a plan to start fresh. It was sad to bid goodbye to his friends, but Joseph Carlo wanted new opportunities beyond the Royal Navy.

He was walking to the port gangway when he heard a call from behind him.

"*Paisan! Aspetta!*" Tomaso ran up to him with a grin, a piece of paper held in his hand.

Joseph Carlo waited for his friend to catch up.

"What's that?" he asked Tomaso.

"It's your letter. To your family. You gave it to me, before the battle, in case . . . you know." Tomaso handed him the oft-folded slip of paper.

Joseph Carlo shook his head. "You keep it, *paisan*. Deliver it if you can. I'd like them to know that I'm all right and that Suchet . . ."

Joseph Carlo trailed off as they both looked at the letter in Tomaso's hand.

"Not planning on returning home anytime soon?" Tomaso asked, tucking the letter away again.

Joseph Carlo thought of what Lena might say to him once she found out that he hadn't been able to keep Suchet alive. "No, I'm not. Not for a while. I'll take my chances in the Colonies."

Tomaso nodded with a half-smile. "Can't say that I blame you. But I'll miss you. It's been a pleasure serving with you. You're a true friend."

"I'll never forget you. Thank you. For all that you did for me, for Suchet." Joseph Carlo held out his hand to Tomaso, who grabbed it and pulled Joseph Carlo into an embrace.

"Hey, we're countrymen." Tomaso's voice was muffled against Joseph Carlo's shoulder. He pulled back. "We stick together."

Tears stung Joseph Carlo's eyes and he shouldered his sea bag before they could spill over. "*Dio Velocita, il mio amico.*"

Tomaso shoved his hands in his pockets. "You too, *paisan,* you too."

Joseph Carlo was halfway down the ladder to the small boat that would take him away from the *Deptford* for the last time when he heard a whistle. He looked up. Pace stood in the foremast crosstrees and when he saw he had Joseph Carlo's attention, he raised his fist to his forehead. Joseph Carlo's breath hitched once in his chest as he raised his own fist in return. Pace smiled sadly, his dimples showing. Joseph Carlo glanced once more at the ship that had been his prison, his classroom, and briefly, his home. Then he turned away from the *Deptford.*

Chapter Twenty-Nine

Although a seasoned sailor at fourteen with two years on an English man-of-war under his belt, nothing had prepared Joseph Carlo for his time on the *Deliverance*. She was a small transport taking four hundred sick and wounded soldiers to the Colonies. Half the men that started the journey would die by the time they reached their destination.

The first thing that struck Joseph Carlo as he clambered aboard was the stench of vomit, blood, and death. The smell of the gangrened, dying soldiers was putrid—cloying and sweet, like rotting barbecue. After only a few hours on board, Joseph Carlo and the other sailors had handkerchiefs tied around their noses and mouths to dispel the worst of the odors. They looked like a boat chock full of bandits.

The sounds were also fearsome. Luckily, Joseph Carlo's ears hadn't recovered yet from his time on the gun deck. Although many tars assured him his hearing would return, the ringing drowned out the groaning, moaning, and screaming coming from every available bunk and square foot of cabin. Additionally, bodily fluids covered the decks except for the moments after a strong rainstorm or swabbing. The sailors slid around the slick deck in the muck. Few would live to talk about it, for most of the men on board wouldn't see the sun rise in the new land, let alone a hospital bed.

When the men did die, which they did by the scores, there was no preparation, no formal rites, just a quick prayer. They were tossed overboard just as the ship's cook tossed scraps for the flock of scavenging seagulls that trailed them from the shore.

It was Hell on earth, but even this Hell held one glimmer of light: this Hell was taking him out of Havana and away from the English Navy. Sure, the English officers on board were still the ringleaders of this show, but this was a ship from the colonies returning to her home harbor. Another step away from the iron grip of England.

The *Deliverance* weighed anchor and left Havana harbor for good five days after MacKellar blew the wall. The day was brilliant and promising to be hot, the sky a rain-washed blue and the clouds like dandelion fluff over the island. Joseph Carlo was on deck, swabbing, which was fine by him as it kept him away from the sickest of his compatriots. He'd just scattered sand across the deck and was filling his buckets with seawater when he saw them.

Adjacent to Castle Morro was a convent, its white-washed walls as pockmarked with English shells as Morro's. As the *Deliverance* sailed out of the harbor with her doomed cargo, Joseph Carlo hauled his buckets from the sea. He maneuvered his bucket up and over the rail, trying to slosh as little as possible back into the ocean when a flicker of turquoise caught his eye. He looked up and there they were.

The nuns were on the roof of the convent, perhaps as a show of solidarity against the English or merely to take in the brilliant morning. Their cloister wore habits of Virgin Mary blue, a robin's egg blue that spoke of promise, and hope, and forgiveness. Thirty to forty of them in head-to-toe blue looked out to sea, an ethereal vision after the smoke and thunder of the cannons. Joseph Carlo stared slack-jawed at this apparition as they sailed by. He put the bucket by his feet and, before the vessel tacked and put the convent to their stern, he waved at the nuns, hoping one might make a move that she'd seen him. None did. They turned their faces to the bright morning light, like sunflowers in a field. For the first time in a long time, Joseph Carlo hoped for his future.

Joseph Carlo's *immediate* future was pretty disgusting. If the English Navy could have tempted a strong young sailor to stay among its ranks, living on a death-ship amongst the slimy filth, puke, and excrement of hundreds of dying soldiers wasn't the way to do it. The worst sound was the *ker-splash* of a body hitting the water, and it happened far too often. They were all expendable, every one of them, regardless of the effort and time they'd spent in service. Just one more casualty waiting to happen. He was particularly affected by the officers' disdain and dismissal of the sick and dying men on board. If Joseph Carlo had his choice of a death, he'd pick a quick one in the heat of battle, not the long, drawn-out agony of disease and dehydration.

It would be a few weeks with their puking, dying cargo. A short trip to be sure, thanks to the swift currents of the Gulf Stream and the fact that the *Deliverance* was a quick ship with an able skipper. Her northeast course maximized the Gulf Stream currents and the prevailing winds. Joseph Carlo spent as much time on deck as he could, even sleeping up there rather than going below. Anything to stay out of the stink of death.

The warm Gulf Stream buoyed their ship northeast for most of their trip. When they changed course to make landfall, they crossed yet another line in the ocean. Joseph Carlo was at the bow and saw it coming, so much like the border of the Mediterranean and the Atlantic by Gibraltar that he did a double take. The Gulf Stream was as turquoise as the sea he'd grown up with and just as warm. As they altered course, they left the Gulf Stream and plunged into the deep jade waters of the Atlantic.

This time it did not feel to Joseph Carlo as if he were leaving his home but as if he were returning to it after a long while. Somewhere between Villa Franca and here, he'd become an Atlantic sailor. He mused on this, turning back to his task at hand, when a familiar smell hit him. It wasn't the salty tang of sea that he'd lived with for so long, nor the sweet, sickly smell of disease. Whatever it was smelled warm and brown, and reminded him of Conchetta's bread, freshly baked and cooling in the mid-morning sun. He raised his head and inhaled deeply, a slight smile turning up his mouth.

"That's Block Island you smell," said the salt next to him.

Joseph Carlo looked at him.

"What yer smellin', it's land."

The slight smile on Joseph Carlo's face turned into a grin.

The *Deliverance* rode into New London's bustling harbor on a hard-running tide. They swished into their berth and began to off-load the dead and dying. The sun-warmed bread smell had taken on the tang of wood-fires, sawdust, and burning leaves. Joseph Carlo was struck by the deep red of the maples and the golden green of the oaks. Beyond the clapboard houses spitting smoke into the September air, yellow beech and red chestnut painted the woods. He'd never seen anything like it.

As he stepped onto the pier, Joseph Carlo couldn't tear his eyes away from the gorgeous colors swirling through the air as the leaves chased one another on the breeze. He and five other sailors towed an empty cart over the cobblestones to the coffin-makers to procure some coffins (the dead sailors may have been thrown overboard but the dead officers needed coffins).

The sailors manning the cart with him were strangers; he hadn't spent enough time on the *Deliverance* to get to know them as he knew the crew of the *Deptford*. And the *Deptford* was long gone by now, on its way to being de-commissioned just as Captain Dudley Digges would be retiring his tri-corn hat for good. No, these men were strangers and he planned to keep it that way. What was the use of making friends with men he'd never see again?

As they turned the last corner to the coffin-makers down a lonely alley on the edge of town, Joseph Carlo heard something strange. It sounded like the softest thunder, a cross between a whisk and a thump. He looked around him in surprise, trying to find the source. Where the buildings petered out at the end of Coffin Alley was, fittingly, a graveyard, and beyond that a gentle hill and the swell of farmland. There were figures working the fields, blue shirts solid against a flickering gold and white stand of beeches. The swaddled, thudding sound continued to swell and, as he watched, a thousand dark shadows lifted as one from the marshland beyond the field as the sounds of their flapping wings filled the air. He stopped pulling his weight to stare in astonishment. The other men stood by as the line of birds approached them.

"Geese," one of the men told him as the birds winged their way in a gigantic V above him. The geese started to call to one another as they flew over town, honking back and forth in the muffled cacophony of their wings. To Joseph Carlo it was the loneliest sound he'd ever heard. It made him realize how alone he was. The other sailors were looking at him expectantly, as was the lieutenant in his blue coat, tapping his toe on the cobblestones. The birds' plaintive calls and the feathery thwacks of their wings filled the narrow street. He looked down at his work-hardened hands and then at the cart which soon would be stacked with empty coffins, waiting to be filled with the *Deliverance*'s morbid cargo.

That was it. Joseph Carlo had finally had enough. He was done.

Joseph Carlo started away from the cart and he didn't look back. He didn't even walk that quickly at first, just strolled over the uneven cobblestones, his eyes on the sky.

"Oy, you there!" One of the men called from behind him.

Joseph Carlo didn't turn around. He kept striding across the cobblestones towards the fields beyond the graveyard. He pulled the red kerchief from around his neck in one movement, letting it flutter to the gray street. Then he began to run.

"Stop! In the name of the Crown!" called the lieutenant.

Despite the rising volume and anger in the lieutenant's voice, Joseph Carlo smiled. He hadn't felt so free in a long time. Two years to be exact. His soul lifted to the dark line of birds on the horizon and the flame-like leaves swirling in the wind. He was done with the English Navy.

"He's deserting!" the lieutenant hollered. "After him!"

As Joseph Carlo leapt over a wrought iron fence onto the soft grass of the graveyard, he chanced a look back at his pursuers and some of his buoyancy was replaced with urgency. The sailors had abandoned the cart and taken up the chase, their blue coats vivid warnings as they barreled after him. What was he doing? What had he done? He vaulted over gravestones and leapt over the rounded mounds of the buried dead.

A shard of panic pierced his heart and Joseph Carlo ran faster, arms pumping. As he approached the far side of the cemetery, he glanced back again as the four men pushed the iron gate open and came streaming across the grass. The officer, face red, brought up the rear.

"Men! Shoot him!"

At the order, the sailors pulled their pistols without breaking stride. Joseph Carlo began to feel as if he'd made a very stupid decision.

Adrenaline pushed him up the rise and across the ridged rows of the field, stumbling on clods of mud. The farmer in front had on a pair of worn pants and an equally worn shirt, a straw hat cocked on his head and a hoe in his hand; behind him, ranged across the rows, were five other men, similarly dressed and working the soil. As Joseph Carlo approached in a final burst of speed, the farmer looked up at this most unusual sight: a young man sprinting towards him with four English sailors and an officer on his tail, pistols drawn. The farmer looked puzzled yet calm.

Joseph Carlo skidded to a halt, breathing hard, not knowing what else to do or where to go. The English were forty yards away and closing the gap. The eyes of the sailor in front were narrowed in determination above his pistol. He looked like a furious weasel. Joseph Carlo hated weasels.

"They're coming," Joseph Carlo wheezed at the stranger. "They're going to . . . going to . . ." He couldn't finish, he had no breath. The farmer hadn't said a word; he stood leaning on his hoe, his gaze switching from Joseph Carlo to the men approaching. Joseph Carlo snatched a glance over his shoulder. Now they were only twenty yards away, and they *all* looked like furious weasels.

"They're English sail—" he stopped to cough, and then tried again. "They're English sailors, and they think I'm deserting."

The other men working the fields formed a silent semicircle behind the first. The English pulled up and, one by one, leveled their pistols at Joseph Carlo.

"Are you?" The farmer looked thoughtful beneath his straw hat. "Deserting?"

"Yes, sir. Yes, I am," he said. "They pressed me into service when I was thirteen. I didn't want to go. They stole me from my home. And now they're going to shoot me." With that, he turned to face the irate lieutenant.

"Not if I have anything to say about it," the farmer said from beside him.

The furious officer pointed at Joseph Carlo. "Return to your assigned vessel this instant!"

Despite himself, Joseph Carlo cringed. The farmer stepped up and shifted his hoe so it fell in front of Joseph Carlo. "Officer, you're mistaken. This is my land."

Startled, the officer looked at the farmer for the first time. "I'm an officer of his Majesty's Navy," he sputtered, "and this is

English land. That sailor is deserting. A heinous crime. Deserters are shot on sight." The pistols pointing at Joseph Carlo trembled with anticipation.

"This may be English territory, but you're a long ways from England and, as I've already pointed out, this is *my* land." The farmer's voice was quiet but stern, as if used to giving orders that were obeyed without question.

The officer's face turned another degree redder. "Why this is—this is mutiny!"

"No," the farmer said, still using the same measured tone. "This isn't mutiny, this is the Colonies."

The officer's mouth opened and closed, open and closed, like a goldfish. A ray of sunshine burned through the mist, illuminating the earthy loam between the farmers and the group of pistol-toting sailors.

"Why don't we ask him." The farmer turned to Joseph Carlo. "Do you want to go with them?"

"No," Joseph Carlo said without hesitation.

A smile lifted the farmer's mouth, only to disappear a split-second later as he turned back to the officer. "It's settled. He's not going with you."

"This is ridiculous!" The officer challenged. "I'm acting on behalf of the Crown of England!"

A ripple went through the farmers. Joseph Carlo wondered if the sailors would shoot them all now, farmers included. Could a farmer be guilty of mutiny?

The farmer took a step forward. "This is my land," his voice cold, "and on my land, a man makes his own decisions. He doesn't want to go with you. He stays."

Behind him, the other farmers closed rank, each of them with a tool that was now held as a weapon.

The officer's face turned a furious shade of purple.

"Take your men and go back the way you came." The farmer's voice tinged with steel. "Now."

The officer stood his ground, mouth twisting. His gaze burned into Joseph Carlo but this time, Joseph Carlo didn't cringe. He stared right back.

"Fine!" The officer said. "Keep him!" He turned on his muddy boot-heel and strode away. "The English Navy doesn't want deserters in its rank," he spat over his shoulder.

The other sailors followed, looking at Joseph Carlo in disbelief.

"You see a deserter, I see a man who knows his own mind," the farmer said to no one in particular, watching the sailors retreat.

When the blue coats of the lieutenant and the rest of the sailors disappeared over the hill, the farmer turned to Joseph Carlo. "Do you have a home? Somewhere you can go?"

Joseph Carlo answered as honestly as he could. "No, I don't. Not anymore."

"We can do something about that. Would you like to come with us?"

"Yes," said Joseph Carlo. "I'd like that."

Afterword

JOSEPH CARLO STAYED IN NEW ENGLAND FOR THE REST OF HIS life. He was the master of the rowing galley *Spitfire* in the Revolutionary War, sailing Narragansett Bay looking for enemy British ships. He then captained the privateer *Weasel*, bringing home many prizes to Newport.

Joseph Carlo married Olive Bicknell in 1772 and they had ten children. All of the sons took to sea and two established the Mauran Shipping Company. Their ninth child was a boy they named Suchet. Like his namesake, he became an exceptional navigator.

Joseph Carlo Mauran died on May 1, 1813, and his beloved Olive followed him six months later. They are buried side by side in Providence, Rhode Island.

About the Authors

Marshall Highet is a professor and writer. Her YA sci-fi novel *Spare Parts* was published in 2014. She lives in Pittsburgh with her family and two rescue dogs.

Bird Stasz Jones is professor emerita at Elon University with over thirty years working with teachers and young people in the United States and abroad. This is her family story and is based in historical fact (with fiction filling in the gaps). She lives in Vermont and Rhode Island.